The Earl's Brazen Bargain

IMPROPER LORDS
BOOK THREE

BY MAGGI ANDERSEN

ARE YOU SIGNED UP FOR DRAGONBLADE'S BLOG?

You'll get the latest news and information on exclusive giveaways, exclusive excerpts, coming releases, sales, free books, cover reveals and more.

Check out our complete list of authors, too!

No spam, no junk. That's a promise!

Sign Up Here

www.dragonbladepublishing.com

Dearest Reader;

Thank you for your support of a small press. At Dragonblade Publishing, we strive to bring you the highest quality Historical Romance from some of the best authors in the business. Without your support, there is no 'us', so we sincerely hope you adore these stories and find some new favorite authors along the way.

Happy Reading!

CEO, Dragonblade Publishing

Additional Dragonblade Books by Author Maggi Andersen

Improper Lords Series
The Duke's Masquerade (Book 1)
The Marquess Takes a Misstep (Book 2)
The Earl's Brazen Bargain (Book 3)

The Never Series
Never Doubt a Duke (Book 1)
Never Dance with a Marquess (Book 2)
Never Trust an Earl (Book 3)
Never Keep a Secret at Christmas (Novella)
Bella's Christmas Wish (Novella)
The Duke's Brown-Eyed Lady (Novella)

Dangerous Lords Series
The Baron's Betrothal (Book 1)
Seducing the Earl (Book 2)
The Viscount's Widowed Lady (Book 3)
Governess to the Duke's Heir (Book 4)
Eleanor Fitzherbert's Christmas Miracle (Novella)

Once a Wallflower Series
Presenting Miss Letitia (Book 1)
Introducing Miss Joanna (Book 2)
Announcing Miss Theodosia (Book 3)

The Lyon's Den Series
The Scandalous Lyon

Pirates of Britannia Series
Seduced by the Pirate

The fountains mingle with the river
And the rivers with the ocean,
The winds of heaven mix for ever
With a sweet emotion;
Nothing in the world is single;
All things by a law divine
In one spirit meet and mingle.
Why not I with thine?—

See the mountains kiss high heaven
And the waves clasp one another;
No sister-flower would be forgiven
If it disdained its brother;
And the sunlight clasps the earth
And the moonbeams kiss the sea:
What is all this sweet work worth
If thou kiss not me?

"Love's Philosophy," Percy Bysshe Shelley

Prologue

The Grosvenors' ball, Mayfair, March 1819.

B Y ELEVEN O'CLOCK, Miss Laura Peyton had danced every dance. She'd promised to take supper with Lord Wadsworth and danced once with the Earl of Debnam. Now she was in Debnam's arms again for the waltz. As they turned during the dance steps, she glimpsed the disapproving looks from the dowagers. With no mother to advise her, and only her brother Robert, who spent most of the evening in the games room, to accompany her, she'd believed herself safe from censure when she'd accepted the earl as her partner. Now, doubts crept in, especially when she recalled the gossip about him. But surely, at her age, she could dance with anyone? It had surprised her when he'd asked her. There were so many pretty young debutantes in need of a partner.

Whispers seemed to follow them around the room as they danced. Curious, she raised her chin and studied the enigmatic earl at close quarters. A few golden sun-streaks dared to lighten his wavy, brown hair, and his lightly tanned skin confirmed her opinion that he liked to be outdoors. His straight nose looked as imperious as a Roman general's, and the cynical cast to his mouth completed the picture of someone it would not be wise to cross. His smoky-gray eyes gave away little and added to the air of mystery which seemed to follow him, and the reason the *ton* called him "the Phantom Earl."

A sensual gleam lit the gray-blue depths of his eyes and an amused smile tugged at his lips. "Have you had your fill of me yet, Miss Peyton?"

"I suppose you stir my curiosity, my lord." Laura bent her head and studied his white, embroidered silk waistcoat stretching across his wide chest.

"Do I? In what way?" he asked.

"You are very much talked about. Do they not call you 'the Phantom Earl'?"

He lifted an eyebrow. "I've heard it said." His gaze roamed over her face. "Are you aware your beauty eclipses that of every other lady here tonight, Miss Peyton?"

It was a ridiculously overblown compliment. Her simply styled blue gown, made for economy's sake, and her dainty, gold jewelry in no way rivaled the loveliness of the other ladies present. Perhaps he intended to lead the conversation onto safer ground. "That is prettily put, my lord." Laura knew her worth, but youth was valued at the marriage mart. She was familiar with the way society worked. Marriages carefully arranged between families for financial reasons, or the addition of a title. Seldom for love. She had learned that lesson cruelly when their neighbor, Edward Ryland, who had been her beau since she'd emerged from the schoolroom, had bowed to family pressure and married a wealthy debutante. It had hurt for a long time and left her wary. She trusted few men. And she certainly didn't trust the Earl of Debnam.

"Although not the most biddable, I suspect," he added as he guided her smoothly over the floor.

Aware she'd been frowning, she laughed. "Perhaps you are right."

"And something of a puzzle."

She widened her eyes. "Am I? I was thinking the same of you, sir."

"Why haven't you married?" he continued in his distractingly deep, sensual voice, which caused a brief shiver to ripple through her. "Is there a story behind it? Some love lost on the battlefields of the Iberian Peninsula?"

"Nothing quite so dramatic. I am sorry to disappoint you."

"You would have caused quite a stir when you first came out."

Which was some years ago. The earl had been absent from ballrooms and card parties when she'd first come to London. She would have remembered him. Which perhaps explained the *nom de guerre* the *ton* had given him. "I've yet to meet a gentleman I wish to marry," she said, disconcerted by the course his questioning took. She would never tell him the whole. What she was prepared to offer failed to cover the real reasons she found herself here again at almost twenty-six.

"Then you are most particular," he surmised.

"We should be, shouldn't we? You must spend your life with that person."

"Not necessarily. The *ton* has its own rules."

"I daresay." She held her tongue on observing how loose the morals of some members of London society were. She would sound horribly prim, and she was sure he would laugh at her.

"You keep frowning, Miss Peyton. May I know why?"

"Must you be privy to all my thoughts, sir?"

His hand at her waist tightened. "It's my wish to discover more about you."

"I cannot imagine what it is you find of interest. I am just as you see. There is no mystery."

"And yet you are defying the dowagers by dancing with the Phantom Earl." He shook his head. "Perhaps you are not the best judge of how interesting you are."

"It is poor etiquette to refuse an invitation."

She doubted the sincerity of Lord Debnam's supposed interest in her. It was likely he was this way with every woman. It was part of a rake's charm to make a woman feel special. But, gallingly, his words had the power to penetrate her defenses. Her other dance partners' empty flattery, which failed to impress her, in no way resembled Lord Debnam's smooth talk, which, for some reason, she found to have a serious undertone. Outrageous as he was, he touched something within her and made her pulse leap. Something she had carefully shut away deep inside. And for that reason, if none other, she should be wary of him. He could have the power to hurt her.

She leveled a glance at him, refusing to encourage him. "One thing I will admit to. A love of the waltz. And to be blessed with such a skilled partner."

"You flatter me. Or is it because you wish me to stop asking troublesome questions?"

Laura smiled. She didn't really want to silence him. She could listen to his voice forever, while gazing into his handsome countenance. But it was true she loved to dance, and being in his arms. As he took her at her word and silently guided her masterfully through the steps, she gave herself up to the pleasure of the waltz. The music rose to a crescendo, as did her rapture. And the evening turned from tedium to something infinitely special, the moment as delicate as a cobweb. The other dancers in their finery swirled past in a rainbow of colors as the earl, holding her firmly, turned her and twirled her over the floor, until her breath came in gasps. His gaze dropped brazenly to her bosom, which gave her emotions away, rising and falling rapidly above the scoop neckline of her pale-blue silk gown. He excited her, and he knew it.

So this was a rake. Known to flout society's rules. She had never encountered one at close quarters. There was a reason these men were so successful with women. Not all were handsome, although Lord Debnam undoubtedly was. Like Casanova, they could charm a woman into giving up everything for them. Even face ruin. She had seen him only twice during the busy London Season. Perhaps he wasn't often in Town. But she didn't doubt a man such as he would have bedded many women.

Had he left some of them desperate and heartbroken? She could only guess. But it was not just rakes who behaved without honor. She knew that only too well.

Despite her critical assessment of him, she felt some regret that the dance had ended. There had been so little during this Season that had given her pleasure. With her hand resting lightly on his forearm, they left the dance floor among the other couples.

"It has grown hot and smoky in here. Shall we seek the cooler air on the terrace?" he asked.

What was his intention? To whisk her away into the gardens and seduce her? She had heard horrible stories of debutantes being ravished by ruthless men. But she was not a foolish, young girl. She had a good head on her shoulders. And yet… What was wrong with her? She should say *no*. "I wonder if we should. People might talk." *Much that he would care*, she thought. He seemed impervious to criticism, but a man could afford to be.

"Let them, Miss Peyton. You have braved the dance floor with me more than once. Tongues already wag. It is what the *ton* like to do. Before the night is out and some other more interesting indiscretion occurs, we will be forgotten."

His deep voice made her tingle all over, while his eyes invited her to misbehave. He flirted, but he did so with such elan. Bored silly with London manners and polite conversation, she wasn't ready for this to end. It was a small rebellion, and harmless. So, why not? Even if he tried, the earl could not convince her to leave the terrace for the shadowy gardens. And as he'd pointed out so adroitly, at her age, she must be of little interest to the gossips. As they approached, a glance out through the glass told her several guests had escaped the intolerably hot ballroom and stood along the terrace rail.

Safety in company. "Why not?"

"Why not indeed." He led her in that direction as Laura searched the guests for signs of disapproval, but it appeared she and the earl were no longer of interest, and right now, she didn't care.

Her chin raised high, she walked with him through the French doors a footman opened for them. "I trust you will remain within the bounds of propriety, Lord Debnam," she said with a slight smile as they crossed the terrace. He could hardly behave otherwise, for even more guests came up the steps from the lantern-lit gardens.

He chuckled, evidently appreciating her humor, but also reminding her of how he thumbed his nose at society's rules. It was intoxicating. A sensation deep inside shook her, followed hastily by a warning she must heed. He might act as he wished, but she could not. She must never allow him to lead her into controversy.

Above them, the sky was a midnight-dark blanket, the glittering stars strewn across the heavens, like diamonds on velvet in a jeweler's display cabinet. She took a deep breath of the perfumed air from the flowering shrubs. Taking her arm, he drew her away from the other guests and managed to find an unoccupied corner.

When Laura went to move away, he shook his head. He leaned forward and ran a finger ever so lightly beneath her bottom lip. "Moonlight becomes you, Miss Peyton."

He made her tremble with sexual awareness. What he offered gave a glimpse of how sublime it could be between them while it threatened to wreak havoc on her life. Did he feel the same? It would be just a game for him. But oh-so-devilishly attractive and hard to resist. She'd thought herself too mature and sensible for this.

She stepped back, seeking a safer distance while unnerved by the impulse to stay close. To want more. Could she not rely on her good sense when with this man? "Was I wrong to trust you, my lord?" Of course she had been.

His gaze rested on her mouth then lifted to search her eyes. "Did I ask you to trust me, Miss Peyton? I'm sorry I gave you that impression. Where you're concerned, I am very untrustworthy, indeed."

She swallowed and forced a laugh. "Then I am fortunate to

be surrounded by people."

He smiled, teeth white in the shadowy light. "Or unfortunate. It depends on how you look at it. We would be very good together."

Excited, then appalled at how he affected her, she shook her head. So much more at ease than she, he threatened to draw her into something which would be a calamity for her.

She struggled to regain her calm demeanor, which had served her so well in the past. "Is this tantamount to a proposal, Lord Debnam?" she asked in a brisk tone. It wasn't, but she wished to shock him. To give herself time to recover from his sensual assault.

If she'd expected to fluster him, she failed. He frowned and shook his head. "I shall never marry."

"Never?" Laura sensed she had at least startled him. "Why so adamant? An earl must marry to safeguard his lineage, must he not?"

Lord Debnam shrugged, having gained his composure. "It is something I decided some years ago. I've had no reason since to change my mind."

"That is not an answer." She was being rudely inquisitive, but she really wanted to know.

He smiled. "It is all I'm prepared to give you."

"But you seek knowledge of me, which hardly seems fair."

He grinned. "Just being with you tells me much about you."

"Surely not." Was she that easy to read? But it was true her life had been unremarkable to date, and with no opportunity for improvement.

Annoyed, although she wasn't sure why, she glanced around at the terrace and discovered with surprise that most of the guests had gone inside. Only one couple remained engaged in a heated discussion. Along the empty garden paths, the braziers flickered in the brisk breeze. "The night turns cool. Everyone has gone in. We should join them."

"If only we could become lovers, Laura." His mouth was

close enough to her ear to stir a ringlet, his hand on her arm, holding her back.

She drew in a sharp breath at the thought of him holding her, kissing her. He was outrageous. Were women of her age there for the taking? "And should the *ton* learn of it, what would happen to me when it ends?" She was too shocked to make her attempt at flippancy sound convincing. And she was angry and unsettled by the leap of excitement his words provoked.

"A gentleman takes care of such matters."

"Yes. A bracelet or some pretty bauble when you replace me with another?"

He lifted his dark eyebrows. "Where have you heard of these things?" It was a question, not a condemnation.

She had seen the jeweler's bills her brother, Robert, received in the post. "I find this conversation distasteful."

"Then I apologize," he said without a trace of humility.

"I wish to return to the ballroom."

"Of course. Should you change your mind, you have only to let me know. We are certain to meet again."

She smiled sweetly. "It would be unwise to be so sure of it."

He laughed and offered her his arm. "Ah, Laura, then I should regret it."

Laura placed her gloved hand on his sleeve, disturbed by the strength of the man beneath the silk. What would he regret? Did he mean this extraordinary invitation? Or was he merely enjoying himself at her expense? She didn't find it amusing. A wealthy earl of thirty or so would hardly choose a dowerless bride of twenty-six. But why did he shun marriage entirely? And so forcefully? There must have been a story behind it. There was more to this man. Why did they call him "the Phantom Earl"? Did he have a dark past? Although aware he was a dangerous rakehell, she couldn't help being a little intrigued. Might a lover have broken his heart? Robert would laugh should she tell him, but apparently, she was still susceptible to a romantic tale.

Lord Debnam led Laura to her seat, where her friend, Emma

Burton, in her white muslin, stood hovering, watching them, her green eyes wide, waving her fan before her flushed face.

"It has been a pleasure, Miss Peyton." With a graceful bow, Lord Debnam left her.

"Was it wise to dance twice with the earl?" Emma took the seat next to Laura and glanced around at the groups of ladies near them. She fluffed up the feathers of her headdress on her dark hair, looking like a startled owl.

Laura wondered at the force of Emma's objection. "I don't see why not."

"They call him 'the Phantom Earl,'" Emma said in a conspiratorial whisper.

"He told me."

Emma looked flummoxed. "He did?"

"Do you know why?"

"Not really. I've heard some talk; you always do when you spend time in the ladies' withdrawing room. It must be because he is seldom seen in London. And yet he has danced with you before, hasn't he? But the waltz! Many women here will be pea green with envy."

"What nonsense. He is just a man like any other." Laura couldn't really bring herself to believe that, however.

"It's said he had an affair with the Duchess of Holcombe while the ailing duke was still living. She gave birth to a son not long afterward. And some say he had an affair with a member of royalty, although I haven't discovered anything more. The royals close ranks on their own."

"I'm sure that is merely scandalous gossip, Emma." Surely, it couldn't have been true? Although thinking of Lord Debnam, some of it did seem possible.

Emma patted Laura's arm to gain her attention. "You should be careful of him, Laura. You could damage your standing in society."

He had said they should become lovers. Her heart pounded at the very thought of them together, that way. She shrugged, feigning indifference. "Nothing much can happen during a dance."

Lord Debnam had certainly enlivened her evening and stirred her in ways she didn't intend to think about until within the seclusion of her bedchamber. She waved her fan before her hot face and sought to change the subject. "Tell me, did you enjoy dancing with Mr. Lang?"

Emma raised her eyebrows. "I did. He is so big and brash, and his Scottish accent was fascinating. I wanted to ask him if he wore anything under that kilt."

"*Emma!*" Laura laughed.

"Maybe I'll get the chance to find out someday," Emma said, looking about for the gentleman. Emma was another who lacked a proper chaperone, her grandmother seldom at her side. But at twenty, a girl needed supervision.

Laura admired her friend's honesty. Emma knew what she wanted, and Laura hoped life would be good to her. "You wish to marry him?"

Emma grinned. "I can't imagine any other way of discovering the answer, can you? Unless I become a trollop."

"And we know what sad lives courtesans live," Laura said, thinking unaccountably of Lord Debnam. If she had invited him to pursue her, that would have been what she would have become.

"Not all," Emma said. "Remember Lavinia Fenton? She became the Duchess of Bolton."

"A rare occurrence, I should think. Many fall into poverty when they grow older."

Laura's dreams might not have turned out as she'd hoped, but she would never agree to become a man's mistress. She pushed the outrageous earl's suggestion from her thoughts as the orchestra tuned their instruments and her and Emma's partners for the gavotte approached them.

Despite everything, the hope remained that she'd meet a suitable gentleman. She might have given up on love, but not her wish to marry. She wanted children.

THIS EVENING'S ENTERTAINMENT took a surprising turn. Brendan Cowper, Earl of Debnam, had not expected to find Miss Laura Peyton so irresistible. There was something about her lack of pretense and clear blue eyes, like the sun shining on the lake waters at Beechley Park, that set her apart from the sophisticated women with whom he usually associated, ladies who often said one thing and meant another. It wasn't a lie that he wanted her, although his intention had been to tease her. He wondered about her past. Like a sleeping beauty, she wasted her life in the pretentious marriage mart. He wasn't blind to the way she responded to him, how her eyes darkened with desire. Had there been a man in her life once? He would like to have been that man, but as a baron's daughter, she wasn't available to him for a liaison.

More mature than the debutantes who came to London with the sole purpose of marrying a lord, Laura was different. She had character, humor, and wit. A pretty woman with creamy skin and a body to match. One he would give a lot to see naked in his bed. He couldn't fathom why she hadn't been snapped up. Brendan had heard Netterfield's estate was in trouble, but surely, not every man looked for a handsome dowry. He sighed. But it was impossible. She looked for a husband and he merely wished to amuse himself, with no intention of making a commitment to any lady. The earldom was damned. He'd never wanted it. Let the title die out with him.

Chapter One

Longworth, Surrey, June 1819

LAURA SAT IN the parlor by the fire, Tibby, the family's black cat, on her knee. She sighed as she stroked the soft fur, feeling the deep, appreciative rumble as Tibby purred. Almost two years had passed since she and her brother, Robert, had lost their parents to illness, and having cast off her mourning clothes, she'd returned to the London Season in March, with Robert as chaperone. But in April, disaster had struck again, forcing them to give up the lease of their townhouse—the family's London house having been sold after their father had died—and depart London for Longworth, Robert's country estate.

Robert entered the room, his face etched with guilt. "We must use the last of our money to finance your return to London before the Season ends." He threw himself onto the sofa. "Once you marry well, our problems will be solved."

Tibby jumped from Laura's lap with a mew of protest. "Why can't *you* marry?" she asked. "It is your fault we are in this predicament."

Robert raked his hands through his blond hair. "Certainly. Tell me which lady with a wealthy papa will have me?"

Laura studied her tall, handsome brother. He resembled their father, but for the signs of dissipation, which had crept around his mouth. His blue eyes were bloodshot. He was, however, Baron Netterfield, even if he didn't have two pennies to rub together. "You might marry an heiress in search of a title."

"Ha!" There was no sign of amusement in his eyes. "They are thin on the ground this year, and my title rates near the bottom, barely above hereditary knights. Most heiresses look for a marquess or even a duke, not a baron with a drafty mansion and rundown estate. The creditors bombard me with threatening letters. If we lose Longworth, I'll have nothing to offer."

Laura suspected it was the pretty heiresses, not the title-seeking ones, who were absent this Season, but she felt too tired of arguing to mention it.

"Lord Wadsworth revealed a considerable interest in you back in March, Laura. It's a shame we were forced to give up our accommodation and come home."

She gazed at him, exasperated. It was because of his disastrous night playing dice at some gaming hell that their already struggling finances had worsened. If they failed to pay their debts, they would lose Longworth and end up in debtors' prison with no chance of a reprieve. The news of their misfortune would already have spread among the tradesmen wishing to be paid. Laura would rather die than return to the Season under the scrutiny of the *ton*. She wasn't sure what she would hate worst, sympathy, or when those who had embraced her friendship now lost interest in her.

"Perhaps I could find a position as companion to a well-to-do lady."

Robert stared at her. "Don't be absurd."

"No more absurd than me finding a wealthy husband in search of a bride to fill his nursery."

"Men find you attractive, Laura. I've often witnessed it. Only the other day, Lord Fulton told me he desired to marry you, but you rejected him."

She almost shuddered recalling the widower Fulton's mean eyes and receding chin. "He looks for a mother for his children."

Was it too much to hope the father of her children would want her for herself? And if she did not love him, at least could she not be repulsed by him?

"There must be others. If you would only smile at them, make them think you might be interested."

"They do not want to marry me. And I doubt what they do want would be of any help to you."

"Don't be cynical. It doesn't become you. You never used to be this way."

"Not when I was a girl filled with hope for the future. It started after waiting years for Edward Ryland to ask me to marry him, and finding my affection misplaced. Then caring for Mama and Papa after they fell ill, followed by the year of mourning. I turn twenty-six next month, Robert. Hardly a debutante. Close to being left on the shelf. Few gentlemen looking for a wife would consider someone my age. And by the way, my friend Emma Burton wrote to tell me Wadsworth has since become betrothed to Mary Greyburn. She is eighteen and has a handsome dowry."

Robert dragged his fingers through his hair again. It grew too long on his neck and needed cutting. "But you are better bred and a darn sight more attractive than plain Mary Greyburn." He eyed her carefully. "What about the Earl of Debnam? He danced with you at least once at the last two balls we attended. And twice at one, as I recall. The fellow never concerns himself with convention. Even so, that is out of character for him. He is rarely seen at balls, let alone dancing with the same woman more than once. So it shows he has a particular interest in you."

A tingle of happiness at Lord Debnam's desire for her quickly faded when she realized how impossible it was. "I wasn't aware you emerged from the gaming room long enough to watch the dancing. It's common knowledge the earl has no wish to marry."

"You can't be sure of that. He is obviously smitten."

"He is a flirtatious rake. That means little."

Laura rubbed the goosebumps on her arms, recalling how he'd made her aware of her own heartbeat when she'd gazed into the earl's gray eyes as they'd danced. How wonderful it had felt to be in his arms. He'd made no bones about wanting her, assuring her he was happy to wait for her to change her mind and become his mistress. He'd drawn her to him with little effort on his part. It was extraordinary, the effect he'd had on her body with just one look, before she'd managed to gather herself together, smile sweetly, and tell him she would never agree. It had not deterred him, she'd realized immediately. Was that what she had become? A woman men might consider for their mistress but not their wife?

Laura watched her brother retrieve a letter from his coat pocket with a shaking hand. She grew intrigued when she sighted an earl's crest. "What have you there?"

Robert looked flushed. "Laura, as it appears you don't wish to marry any of the gentlemen you've met, Debnam might be the very answer. I've received a letter from him. He makes a proposal of a different sort." He cleared his throat as he waved the letter about. "It's like a miracle! He offers to pay all our debts. To make Longworth secure." Robert gazed at her pleadingly. "We can both marry, given time, and the Longworth corridors would be filled with the sound of our children."

"You paint a lovely picture, Robert." Laura wondered what the earl might want, but it was sure to involve her. She arched her eyebrows. "What sort of proposal?"

Robert paled, his gaze swinging away from hers. "Debnam invites you to spend a month with him at his country estate. Just a month, Laura. He promises to be discreet. He will not reveal your time together to anyone. And he assures me no harm will come to you." As she shook her head, alarmed, he hurried on. "He is a handsome man, is he not? It couldn't be so very bad? I've heard many women say they would like to have him in their beds."

Laura glared at him, and for a moment, was speechless. "They would not be ladies," she said, finally finding her voice. "You don't associate with them, do you, Robert?"

He flushed. "Yes, ladies, Laura. Not tavern wenches."

"Tavern wenches have probably already bedded him." Laura swallowed hot tears.

"All right! You won't agree. I shall write to him and refuse. Then the only thing I can do is put a gun to my head." He jumped up and banged out of the room.

Laura was on her feet in an instant. She followed him into the corridor, her anxious gasps choking on the smell of dust. She hurried into the library. "Robert, you wouldn't do such a thing?"

Robert sat behind his desk. He snatched up a pile of bills and released them to scatter over the leather desktop. "If I were dead, you might have a better chance of finding a husband."

Laura put her hands on her hips. "You are fooling yourself. I would be completely alone and out on the street. Or pleading sanctuary with Aunt Gertrude, who would make me her lady's maid and tell me endlessly how right she'd been to warn us. Although what I could do to change anything, I don't know. And, Robert, for heaven's sake! I would miss you terribly."

"Would you?" He looked doubtful, then shook his head. "You will be better off without me," he said bitterly. He selected a letter and pushed it across the desk with a finger.

Laura, her heart pounding, picked it up. It was a threatening letter from their banker. They would foreclose on Longworth at the end of the month should no payment be received. She uttered a moan and sank down on a chair, staring disbelievingly at her distraught brother. "You have mortgaged Longworth?"

He seemed to shrink before her, all his bravado gone. "Of course. What did you expect?"

She could see no way out of it. She had considered returning to London to find a husband, if not to love, hopefully to like. Who would care for her? But with time now so short, it was a moot question. This letter made that clear. It was useless to remain angry at Robert's inability to make the estate financially viable. They had been over that many times. And she feared he meant what he'd said. She had seen the pistol in his desk drawer.

But becoming Debnam's temporary mistress terrified her. She feared for the loss of her self-respect. Even her soul. She would become a fallen woman, like those she and Emma discussed at the ball.

"I hate to see you living an unfilled life here at Longworth. The earl might fall in love with you and want to marry you. When he realizes how special you are."

"Nonsense." She refused to fall for his attempts to legitimize it. Really, they might be discussing a house party for all the levity he brought to the topic.

Robert fell silent. His defeated expression worried her.

An unmarried sister was a burden. Why wasn't it possible for women in her position to find ways to support themselves without relying on men? Might she be a governess? They lived such dreary lives caught between the family and the servants, never quite fitting in anywhere. And should she become one, it would not solve Robert's financial problems. "All right," she said, her voice a bare whisper. "Write to the earl and accept his offer. But he must supply you with a signed letter stating he'll pay your creditors before we meet. And you must promise me you will do nothing foolish once I'm gone. You will not consider ending your life."

Robert's mouth sagged, his eyes registering his shame as they dropped to his hands clasped together on the desktop. "I promise, Lolly."

He'd used her childhood name, and it tore her heart in two. Where was the brother who had always been there for her?

He nodded enthusiastically. "I promise to change my ways. This is a second chance for me. I'll involve myself in the estate. Make it pay again."

"That is good news, Robert." While she offered encouragement, she struggled to believe him. She would not put in plain words what he was about to do to her. To prostitute her for monetary gain. It would destroy him. As there was no other alternative open to them, let him fool himself into believing this was best for both of them. At least it would give Robert room to breathe and think clearly, and not be tempted to do anything reckless.

So Lord Debnam was about to get his wish. He had been so sure of himself. He was nothing but a spoiled rake used to crooking his finger and getting any woman he wanted. She doubted a woman had ever refused him before her. He might be surprised to find she would not be so easy. Would he keep his promise to protect her from gossip? She didn't believe him. In her experience, men, apart from honorable gentlemen like her father, did not keep their promises.

Beechley Park, West Sussex

SEATED BEFORE THE fire, Brendan Cowper, Earl of Debnam, nudged the lazy hound sleeping at his feet. Hunter merely stretched and rolled over onto his back. Brendan reread the letter in his hand, then looked up at the portrait of his father on the opposite wall. He should take it down. Shove it in the attic, where it belonged. But somehow, there it remained. A daily reminder that he must stay the course and never be tempted to marry.

A log rolled in the grate, and he rose to push it back with the poker. That he was unable to marry did not bar him from enjoying life. There were always comely women to discover. Miss Laura Peyton, for instance. She'd offered no explanation as to the reason she hadn't married years before. He could only guess at a love affair gone wrong. He'd found a potent mix of expressions in her dazzling, sky-blue eyes. While he'd expected her to be innocent, he'd begun to doubt it. He'd caught his breath at the smoldering spark of arousal before she'd turned away. Intrigued, he wished to discover more about her. There would be little harm in a brief affair, he told himself. It was common knowledge her brother was in financial straits. He could help with that. They could conduct their liaison in secrecy at his country estate to avoid gossip. Then, when they tired of each other, Laura would return to the security of her home, with no one the wiser. She could then find a suitable husband who would be lucky to have her.

"Come on, boy. Let's take that walk." Brendan polished off the last of the brandy in his glass and stood. His dog, Hunter, rose and shook himself, impatient to have one last chance to catch the squirrel who had been taunting him, before bed.

"You should give up, Hunter. You make a mockery of your name." It had grown late. The moon shone down from the long windows above the dark hulk of yew trees, the gardens bathed in silvery light. He was tired but would not sleep well, for the nights haunted him. Even a woman sharing his bed failed to give him that longed-for contentment. But it'd be fun to try to forget with the lovely Miss Peyton.

Chapter Two

IN THE AFTERNOON, Laura's reluctant steps took her to the great hall, where her luggage waited. She glanced around at the high-beamed ceiling, the carved, oak staircase winding to the upper floors, the dusty tapestries and faded paintings on the oak-paneled walls. She'd been born here. Her father had taught her to ride a pony and then a horse in the paddocks behind the stables, while her mother had presided over the house, which had always smelled of flowers and polish and the aromas of delicious meals. Laura rubbed at the tightness in her chest and eyed a cobweb near the door. How changed the house now was. And how changed she and Robert were. Was it even possible for her to return here and find peace, after… She bit her lip. It was nonsense to suggest she could marry. A gentleman expected to marry a virgin or a respectable widow. And she refused to live a lie.

The rattle of coach wheels and jiggle of harnesses sounded on the carriage drive. Moments later, the bell clanged at the door. Robert hurried from the library.

On the porch, a footman in Lord Debnam's livery awaited them. Robert directed him to the luggage and walked out with Laura to where the coach waited with a groom at the head of four fine thoroughbreds. Her brother avoided meeting her eyes as they said their farewells, pecking her cheek and wishing her happiness, as if she were going to her wedding. His voice was gruff with emotion, but to her, his words had a hollow ring.

Laura glanced once more at the dark, brick walls covered with ivy, the aged trees of the park, and the rim of woodland as Lord Debnam stepped down from the coach. How serious he looked as Robert greeted him. Laura felt as if they were embarking on a runaway marriage. *Far from the truth*, she thought bitterly, aware the curious servants observed them from behind the curtains. Cook had looked worried when Laura had told her she would be away for a month.

His tall beaver in his hand, Lord Debnam's eyes met hers. He bowed. "Miss Peyton."

"My lord." Laura caught her breath. In his tight-fitting, light-colored trousers, pale-green waistcoat, and dark-green tailcoat, he looked so big and so commanding, her courage almost deserted her. And then he smiled.

Lord Debnam gave every appearance of being a gentleman, and she would expect him to continue to act like one. She tried not to think ahead to when they would be alone. And what he would expect of her. But the question kept returning to her thoughts and unsettled her further.

"Shall we?" He gestured to the coach, a glossy, dark-blue vehicle with the earl's crest on the door. The magnificent chestnuts stamped their hooves, as impatient to be gone as he appeared to be.

She realized she'd been hesitating. A glance at his face astonished her. She'd expected to find the rakish gentleman she'd met at the ball, not this serious man who took her arm to help her inside the coach.

Sitting opposite him, she busied herself ordering the skirts of her lavender carriage gown around her like a fortification, reassured by the more-than-a-dozen toggle fastenings down the front.

"I'm pleased you came." He reached over, took her nervous gloved fingers, and raised them to his lips.

She withdrew them. "You must have expected it, surely. You

arranged this with my brother."

He frowned. "Your brother's letter of agreement implied you were quite willing. That you were both delighted to have your financial difficulties at an end. It's not too late. I can take you back…"

Back to Robert? When he might kill himself? She forced a smile. "Do not concern yourself, my lord. Robert was correct."

"Not 'my lord.' 'Debnam' will suffice." His eyes searched hers. "It's my hope you'll enjoy our time together." His eyes darkened to slate, making her wonder if anything she did or said could upset him. While she was angry with him, and more so with Robert, she didn't want to hurt him. It would be of no purpose to reveal the truth of her situation when he clearly was mistaken. And it would make for a very unpleasant journey. He might still order the coach to turn around and take her home. Back to what? Demanding his money returned, which would cause uncertainty and heartache. What lay ahead could hardly be worse. But even while she forced a smile on her lips, she thought of ways she might delay matters. At least until he became less of a stranger to her. She wondered if that was even possible.

Lord Debnam's smile revealed even white teeth. Undeniably attractive. Confident. A practiced rake who had bedded many willing women. The thought brought the blood rushing up her neck. Laura put a hand to the high collar and took a deep breath to calm herself.

"We have a lengthy drive ahead." The earl removed a rug from beneath the seat and spread it over her knees. He sat back and looked at her. "Perhaps you could tell me more about yourself."

She shrugged. "There is little to tell. Robert and I were born at Longworth. My father and mother died there." How different it would have been if they'd lived. What would Father have made of this? Appalled, she pushed the thought away.

The earl raised dark eyebrows at her brief reply. She looked into his changeable gray eyes, which seemed to reflect his mood.

In a ballroom they had been a warm, blue gray, teasing and full of humor, but now they took on the color and impenetrability of a deep lake on a cloudy day. She suspected he was a complex man, for why else would he have made this unconventional arrangement? And why her? Because she had refused him when no other woman would? He could have his pick of eager women. Beautiful women, younger than she. Or was he bored with his mistresses and wanted something different? She kept returning to this and really must stop. It made her shiver. She tucked the rug around her knees.

"You're still cold?" Lord Debnam produced a flask from his pocket. "A little brandy to warm you?"

She never drank spirits but could certainly do with some Dutch courage. "Thank you." She reached out for it and took a deep sip. The rush of strong liquor ran down the back of her throat, setting a fire as it went. Laura gasped and coughed. She handed it back, not trusting her voice.

"Unused to brandy?" he asked, raising his eyebrows.

She nodded, suspecting he found it amusing.

He tucked the flask in his pocket and crossed his long legs. "Shall I tell you something of my estate?"

"Yes, please." It seemed a safe topic.

"Beechley Park is renowned for its beauty. The house is quite ancient. My family built the first dwelling on the land in the thirteenth century, and a wing of the original mansion remains. The fifth earl rebuilt it in the late seventeenth century. Do you ride, Miss Peyton?" He frowned. "Laura?"

It shocked her to hear her Christian name on his lips; Laura fought a nervous giggle when an image popped into her mind of him calling her Miss Peyton while they were naked. She swallowed, fearing she might be on the verge of hysteria. She pressed her lips together. Well, she had agreed to this.

"There are some splendid bridle paths through the woods."

His deep voice made her feel foolish.

"I enjoy riding and reading. I imagine you would have a good library?

"An excellent one," he said, a glimmer of a smile in his eyes.

It appeared she amused him. Did courtesans not read? This was exhausting. If they were to spend the hours in conversation, she feared she would give away her distrust of him and her dislike for this arrangement. What might she talk about to fill in the time with a man she barely knew? Her cat? The latest in the gossip sheets about the Prince of Wales? Laura could write her knowledge of royalty on the head of a pin. She might discuss her latest book, *Frankenstein*, and the earlier work by whom she suspected to be the same author, titled *A Vindication of the Rights of Woman*, and they could debate the need for women's emancipation, but it hardly seemed fitting. And she would bore him to death! She put a hand to her mouth to feign a yawn, while in truth, she was indeed exceedingly tired. "I slept little last night. Forgive me, but I should like to rest."

Lord Debnam's lip quirked. "Of course, please do."

He didn't believe her. He had probably already decided he'd made a poor bargain. Right now, she couldn't summon up enough energy to care. She closed her eyes but found it impossible to blot out his presence; his musky cologne lingered in the small interior, as did the vision of his elegantly clad body which took up so much space on the seat opposite. At least he hadn't made a grab for her. He would behave like a gentleman, she trusted, not a brute. Having somehow convinced herself he would deal gently with her eased her concerns a little, and she settled back against the squab. In truth, she was exhausted. Had been since Robert had first explained this extraordinary agreement to her.

Laura failed to sleep but kept her eyes closed, aware of him opposite as the superbly sprung coach raced toward her inevitable fate.

Sometime later, Laura came to her senses, roughly jostled as the coach jerked to a stop. Her eyes flew open, her heart banging in her chest. But if she wanted an explanation, she wasn't about to get it. For, without a word, Lord Debnam flung the door open and leaped to the ground.

Laura leaned forward and peered out the open door to watch the scene unfold before her. The coachman had pulled the horses up beside a bridge. Below, the river rushed past in a flurry, in danger of breaking its banks after recent rains. Lord Debnam stood on the road conversing with his footman. "What has happened?" Laura called out.

He turned to her. At the flicker of amusement in his eyes, she realized she hadn't fooled him. He knew she hadn't slept. But he hadn't disturbed her, and for that, she was grateful. The footman put down the steps and offered her his arm.

"A carriage accident," Lord Debnam said when she'd joined him. "It's gone into the river." He was pulling off his coat. Surely, he wasn't going into that violent, surging water?

"Are the people still inside?" It was difficult to see. She prayed they were now somewhere on dry land; otherwise, they would be in great danger.

"We are about to find out," he said. "The driver of the stricken carriage is nowhere to be seen. He's uncoupled the horses, and we trust has gone for help."

There were deep track marks in the mud where the carriage had entered the water. It rested a few yards from the shore, listing dangerously in the tide's surge.

The earl handed his coat to her. In his shirtsleeves, exposing his muscled arms, he joined his footman on the bank. They both waded into the water, which rose fast and was almost to their waists before they'd gone a few yards. Both were vigorous men, but they still struggled to open the door against the fast-moving current. It appeared for several terrifying minutes that the river would sweep away the carriage, taking those inside and the men with it.

Alarmed, Laura clutched his coat to her, aware of his scent. She cried out with relief when they wrestled the door open. Inside was a woman and a child.

Lord Debnam carried the woman across to the bank while the footman brought a young girl.

Moments later, with a loud groan, the carriage turned on its side with a loud spray. Luggage floated out. A heavy trunk rolled off the coach into the water and sank beneath the surface. Two footmen waded out, located the trunk somehow, and dragged it to shore.

Laura climbed into Lord Debnam's coach for the rug. She hurried down the bank. The victims were both soaked and shivering. The woman's face was deathly pale. She looked to be about to faint. Laura placed the rug over her shoulders. She handed the earl his coat. He took it with a nod of thanks.

"Come inside the coach." Lord Debnam took the woman's arm to assist her. "It's warmer. You can rest there and then tell me what happened."

Laura smiled at the young girl and held her small hand, which trembled in hers. "What is your name, dear?"

"Mary," the girl whispered.

"We shall have you warm and dry in no time, Mary."

Once settled inside the luxurious coach with Laura and the earl, the woman expressed her relief amid shuddering gasps.

Lord Debnam spread his coat over the young girl and ordered the coachman to drive on. The coach rocked as the footman packed the trunk they'd retrieved onto the coach, then jumped aboard. The horses drew them away down the road.

"Are you hurt?" Laura asked them.

"No, thank the Lord." The woman sank back against the squab.

"My mother has been sick," the young girl said, snuggling into the earl's coat. She looked to be not much above ten years old. Her pelisse had a large patch on the sleeve and her boots were worn. Mary pushed her fair braids back over her thin shoulders, her hazel eyes anxious as she watched her mother.

"I am indebted to you, my lord." The woman, who was also shabbily dressed, passed a hand over her brow as if her head hurt.

"I am Mrs. Anne Joyce, and Mary is my daughter. We were on our way to stay with my aunt in Horsham."

"That is a fair distance from here," Lord Debnam said. "There's an inn a few miles on. You can recover from your ordeal there. Your coachman must have gone to the village seeking help."

"He is not my coachman," she said faintly. "I hired the carriage, but it was a terrifying journey. I feared something like this would happen. He cracked the whip over those poor horses going too fast. After we crashed, I couldn't open the door! Mr. Frisk didn't help us. He took off with the horses." She put a hand to her mouth, her eyes wide. "I feared we would drown."

"I'll have a word with him," Lord Debnam said, a tick beginning in his jaw. "Find out what happened. And arrange new transport for when you are ready to continue on to your aunt."

The woman still shivered with cold and shock. "You and your footmen were brave, sir, and so very kind. I cannot thank you enough."

Laura tucked the rug more snuggly around the woman. "Rest until we reach the village."

With a murmur of thanks, she closed her eyes.

"You will be all right, Mama. This nice man will take care of us." Mary patted her mother's arm. "You'll feel better after a hot drink."

The girl seemed wise beyond her years.

Laura glanced at Lord Debnam. He would be cold and uncomfortable in his shirtsleeves and waistcoat, his trousers and his highly polished boots soaked, but he seemed not to notice them. His brave rescue impressed her. But she would not change her mind about him. Would the earl care? She didn't know, but she would never forgive Robert.

To keep his promise to her brother, Brendan had told the innkeeper Laura was a relative. If he'd hoped to leave the inn the following day, he was doomed to disappointment. Mrs. Joyce's condition worsened, and she developed a high fever. He sent for the village doctor to treat her. From what he was told by the innkeeper, Dr. Williams was a capable man. That should have been enough, in Brendan's view, but not Laura's. She tirelessly nursed the ill woman and insisted on remaining to take care of Mary until the woman rallied. She'd be ill herself if this went on too long. He would have to hurry things along.

Leaving Laura to deal with what occurred upstairs, Brendan sought the owner of the ruined carriage and found the fellow in the taproom, deep in his cups. He took him by the shoulders and shook him, but the man's eyes rolled, and he slumped over the table senseless. Leaving the innkeeper to deal with him, Brendan went to the village stables to arrange for a carriage to take Mrs. Joyce and her daughter the rest of their journey.

He dealt with some correspondence in his private parlor during the day, while impatient to get on. In the afternoon, he read the two-day-old newspapers and talked to the innkeeper. They discussed racehorses after the man had discovered Brendan had raced two thoroughbreds, one of which had won at New-market.

When Laura joined him for dinner, her conversation centered on the two people she cared for. Frustrated, he could but enjoy looking at her. In a lacy dinner gown of primrose, her dark-blonde hair swept into a careless updo, she was undeniably lovely. He admired her slender arms and dainty hands. Her lissome body, he tried not to think too much about. After dinner, she returned to the sick room, and he saw no more of her until breakfast. He was down in the breakfast room the next morning, although it wasn't his habit to eat until close to midday. But the maid told him Laura had eaten her breakfast in her bedchamber.

At first, he suspected Laura merely hoped to avoid him, but he came to realize she really cared about the woman and her child. On the next evening at dinner, she seemed more relaxed and talkative. He tried to draw her out, but she avoided any reference to what lay ahead for them. Nor did she flirt with him. That was a novel experience but unsettling. Had he made a mistake in inviting her? He still didn't know why he'd taken such a chance with a woman he barely knew. It had been purely selfish on his part. Laura's brother might have found other means to pay his debts, although they were substantial.

Longworth was a fine estate, yet obviously rundown. Peyton was a gambler, Brendan had learned. And he had no patience with such men. Especially considering how his actions had affected his sister's life. Laura had more mettle than that selfish weakling. She showed more compassion for the two upstairs than her brother would have been capable of.

"Anne Joyce was widowed last year," Laura said. "It is very sad. She has nowhere to live and must make a home with her aunt. I have feared that I might face a similar fate."

"Why?" he asked, outraged for her.

She shrugged her slim shoulders. "When we faced financial ruin, I considered casting myself upon my Aunt Gertrude's good graces." She smiled, but it failed to reach her eyes. "Aunt Gertrude isn't an easy person."

She pushed her meat around the plate with her fork, not attempting to eat it. "Mary is a bright child. She deserves better."

"Sad, indeed," he agreed. "That animal on your plate is dead, Laura. There's no need to kill it again."

Her blue eyes met his filled with laughter, then he watched them grow shadowed. She ducked her head. Brendan cursed, but he grew hopeful that in time, they might laugh together. Especially as she had opened up to him tonight about herself. It had maddened him to hear it. Her brother needed a good thrashing.

If only they could leave this inferior inn and reach his estate, then this infernally polite wall between them would disappear. Beechley Park was a place made for romance, although it had seen little of it. "Is Mrs. Joyce rallying?"

"Her fever abates."

"Excellent. We can leave tomorrow."

Laura's frown condemned him for such a rash statement.

"We cannot leave them yet. Not until Mrs. Joyce is out of bed and able to take care of her daughter. We cannot leave a young girl alone in an inn. Anything could happen."

Brendan poured her a glass of wine. "And does the doctor know when that might be?"

Laura twisted a curl in her fingers. "He says it's too early to say."

Was she being deliberately evasive? "I hope it is soon. In any event, we are to leave on Friday."

Her fair brows knitted. "So soon?"

He sighed. "Yes. I have urgent matters that cannot wait."

She chewed her full bottom lip. "Very well. If we must."

He wished she wouldn't do that. It was distracting. "I'm glad you agree," he said solemnly.

Laura took a hasty sip of wine, then put down the glass. "I'll go up and see if Mrs. Joyce has managed some of the soup. I had the cook prepare it and a coddled egg, especially for her."

Brendan watched her graceful form cross the dining room. He had been rebuffed, but at least he had won a round. They would depart early on Friday and reach his home by the late afternoon.

The innkeeper brought the bottle of port. He poured Brendan a glass. Brendan took a sip of the smooth, mellow liquid. It was a surprise Laura proved to be so caring. For a moment, having her fussing over him seemed eminently desirable, but only for a moment. He would hate to be seen as a poor thing in need of care. Ridiculous when he'd been caring for himself since a boy, and had needed no one, even when the headaches had begun. He sharply drew his thoughts away from anything which threatened to dredge up the past. The past was buried. Let it remain so.

Chapter Three

LAURA SAT OPPOSITE Lord Debnam in the breakfast room. His attractive face and good manners had become familiar to her, and she was more comfortable in his company. Growing in confidence, she felt able to stand up for herself. This morning, he wore a blue coat. It made his gray eyes softer and somehow less intimidating. His square jaw closely shaven, she breathed in the scent of his musky soap. How did he manage without a valet? Robert would go nowhere without one and had grumbled when he could no longer afford to pay him. For a foolish moment, she thought she and the earl might become friends. Until his next words reminded her she was there to obey him.

"I am informed they moved Mary into your chamber."

She concentrated on buttering her toast. "Yes. The child has developed a cough, and I thought it unwise for her to remain with her mother. She needs her sleep."

He frowned. "So now the child disturbs you?"

Lord Debnam appeared suspicious. Did he suspect another motive behind the move? Perhaps it suited her to have Mary sleep in her bedchamber, even though the earl had not tried to force himself on her in the dead of night. "No. Mary doesn't disturb me." She stifled a yawn before it made a lie of her words. "When I was younger, my father accused me of being difficult to rouse in the mornings. He said I would not wake if the house were on fire."

"Are you still?" He raised an eyebrow. "Difficult to rouse?"

She felt her cheeks burn. Why had she said that? It invited an intimacy she tried to avoid. But the cat was out of the bag now. He studied her speculatively, making her pulse race. She took a bite of her toast and chewed. "Not that it ever happened, thank goodness," she said airily. "Although Cook did set fire to the roast turkey once on Christmas day, which caused such an uproar in the kitchen. We ate ham sandwiches for supper."

Debnam sliced into his bacon and the awkward moment passed. "As it is Friday tomorrow, we shall depart from this dreary place. Please order a maid to pack your bag."

"Oh, is it dreary? I have quite enjoyed meeting new people."

"I am pleased for you," he said dryly.

"But it must be tedious for you. I am sorry."

His eyes met hers as if questioning her sincerity, which made her nervous because he was right. "I have no need of a maid," she hastened to say. "I will pack myself." Laura picked up her teacup and drank the last drops, eager to leave the table. She supposed there was no way of putting off their departure? No, he looked determined. Truth to tell, she wanted to see Beechley Park. It might help her understand the man seated opposite. And she realized she *wanted* to understand him. *Needed* to. She refused to allow an absolute stranger into her bed and must delay as long as she could.

"How fortunate that you are so…independent," he said wryly. He picked up the napkin and wiped his mouth.

"One becomes so when one must," she said, not allowing him to get the better of her.

A slight smile lightened his features.

Might she hope he wasn't the callous rake she feared? After all, he had gone out of his way to help Mrs. Joyce and Mary, engaging rooms for them and ordering a doctor. But on the other hand, he seemed happy enough to leave them and go on. There were moments when she would have liked to let down her guard and ask him all the questions which buzzed around in her head. But this morning, when she sensed his rising impatience, was not one of them.

She excused herself and stood. "I'll pack."

"We shall leave not long after dawn."

"That early? Before breakfast?"

"I will not allow you to starve, Laura."

She stared at him, caught by the sound of her name on his lips, then hurried from the room.

In her chamber, Mrs. Joyce ate her breakfast with Mary. "You look much better," Laura said warmly.

"I feel much better today. Thanks to your cousin and you, Miss Peyton. I've even had my hair washed." She patted her brown locks. "I shall get up after breakfast."

"Don't rush." Laura flushed, uncomfortable with the lie. "You may stay here as long as you need to. Lord Debnam is a very generous man." And he was, Laura thought. He'd become difficult to hate. But she imagined before long she would find a good reason for it. "You must write to me at Longworth, Mary," she said. "I should like to hear how you get on. You have my address. I will return there in a month."

"I will write," Mary promised, as her large brown eyes filled with tears.

Laura went to hug her. "Oh, please do. I should like that very much."

When she returned to Longworth, would she be her same ebullient self? Or would she become too low in spirits to even enjoy a letter from Mary?

She would not allow Lord Debnam to overwhelm her. If he wanted her, he would have to prove himself worthy. Although, how she managed to keep him from overwhelming her, she was yet to decide.

ON FRIDAY, BRENDAN ushered Laura into the coach after her lengthy goodbye to Mrs. Joyce and her daughter, along with promises that one day Laura would visit them. He found it fascinating how a friendship could develop so fast. Men were more cautious regarding whom they befriended.

"I told them I was a relative of yours," she said.

Laura's composed manner made him glance at her. "They had little reason to doubt it," he said wryly. After all, she had slumbered undisturbed during the last few nights with Mary ensconced in her bedchamber. They'd lost days when they might have gotten to know each other better. Not that he relished bedding a lady for the first time at an inn.

He admired her sympathy for the woman and her child, when most well-born ladies would consider it beneath them to notice, let alone nurse, such people, but it also irked him. While he had no intention of falling in love with her, he couldn't deny she was a good-hearted person.

He had her to himself now. His gaze roamed over her, still puzzled why he had ventured into this arrangement, while still not sorry for it. He had never brought a mistress to Beechley Park, his time with them always spent in London among friends, where he could escape to his Mayfair home when he felt the need to be alone. What was it about Laura that made him prepared to spend weeks alone with her in the country? Such a gamble when a lengthy time with a woman could quickly lose its appeal. Few of his mistresses lasted longer than that, even with the entertainments offered in London. It was true, Laura's mouth would make a saint's knees tremble. As delicate a form as a fragile Dresden shepherdess, but he had discovered there was nothing fragile about this flesh-and-blood woman whom he suspected sought to hold him at bay. To continue this affair on her terms. To be wooed, perhaps.

While it surprised him, he wasn't disappointed. He hid his impatience and looked forward to a battle of words with the hope she would soon warm to him. To come to desire him as he did her. That fascinating dimple on her cheek when she smiled beguiled him. It had been absent since he'd danced with her at the ball, and he wanted very much to see her smile again. It would mean she was more at ease in his company. That she might even like him a little.

"How long before we arrive at your estate?" Her soft voice drew him out of his thoughts.

"We'll be there within a few hours. Are you eager to see it?"

She sighed. "I am eager to end this tedious journey."

Brendan frowned and crossed his arms. No, no sign of her frosty demeanor beginning to thaw. He had never encountered a woman so remote and disinterested in him. When her brother had written to him, assuring him that Laura was more than happy with the arrangement, that she wasn't an innocent and knew what was what because of some fellow in her past, he'd been a fool to take the man at his word. But he still didn't want to end it. If within a week, matters didn't improve, well, then, he would send her home and write off the money he'd given her brother as pure folly. But there was always the chance a gently handled seduction could improve matters. He wasn't a man to give up easily.

Two hours passed in almost complete silence, then Laura turned from the window where she'd been watching the landscape pass by. "Why do I smell salt on the breeze?"

"My estate lies close to Chichester Harbor."

In the bright light, there were hints of gold in her eyes and at the tip of her fair lashes. "I should like to see it."

"And so you shall," Brendan said, pleased to have found something to break the ice between them. "We can walk along the beach if you'd care to."

She smiled. "I would like that."

At last, a smile, and that dimple. The pleasure it caused him gave him pause. Disastrous to get too fond of her when they could not marry. He was skating on thin ice and was the worst kind of fool. He steeled himself against it. Laura was a brief interlude in his life, and nothing more.

The coach passed beneath the gatehouse archway and followed the long, curving, oak-lined drive emerging into the sunshine.

"Your park is wonderful," Laura said, turning from the window.

"Some oaks are more than five hundred years old."

The Elizabethan, three-story stone-and-brick building came into view on the next turn. The coach followed the sweep of raked gravel drive to the house, where the coachman pulled up the horses.

"Don't wander too far from the house. It's best if you take a maid with you," he said as the footman opened the door and put down the steps. Leaving the coach, he reached up to take her hand and help her down.

The heavy paneled door stood open. His butler, Redfern, was in the doorway, dressed in his usual garb of sober black, still refusing to adopt the new fashions. Brendan's dog, Hunter, rushed out from behind him and darted down the steps to leap up at Brendan with an excited bark. After the dog had received a welcome pat, he ran over to greet Laura.

"Hunter wouldn't hurt a fly," Brendan said as the dog launched himself into Laura's waiting arms.

"Of course you wouldn't," Laura said soothingly as she patted him. "What a cruel jest to call you 'Hunter.'"

Hunter apparently agreed as he licked her face, forcing her to fend him off with a laugh.

"Down, boy!" Brendan demanded.

For once, Hunter obeyed. He left them to chase a bird over the grass without a chance of catching it. Brendan offered Laura his arm, and they climbed the steps.

"My lord." Redfern bowed, adopting his usual gravitas. He was quite an age now and should consider retirement, but it wasn't something they discussed.

"Redfern, this is my guest, Miss Peyton."

The butler bowed again. "Miss Peyton."

"How do you do, Mr. Redfern." Laura's smile was wide and inclusive. "It is a glorious day, isn't it?"

"It is indeed, Miss Peyton." Redfern's face underwent a change. Was that a smile? Brendan hadn't seen his butler smile since… Well, never. In the great hall, Redfern ordered a maid to show Laura to her suite. "Afternoon tea will be served in the blue salon, Miss Peyton."

"I hope I don't get lost," Laura said with an appealing grin.

"Never fear, Miss Peyton. The footmen are here to attend you, and Penny will show you the way." Redfern rose on his toes. "Mrs. Brandt, the housekeeper, is at your service. You have only to ring the bell."

Amused, Brendan thought it remarkably effusive for old Redfern, when a scant few words usually served to get his message across. As he turned to go to the library, Brendan watched Laura ascend the staircase with Penny. She asked the young, redheaded maid a question, which caused her to stifle a giggle behind her hand.

Brendan wondered what she'd said. The household seemed in danger of succumbing to Laura's charm. Charm she so far withheld from him. He entered the library, where, despite the warm day, a small fire burned in the grate to take the chill off the lofty room. Hunter had been chewing something nasty on the rug. The remains of a large bone. His French chef, Arnaud, had erred again. All the staff indulged the dog, despite his order not to. The dog in question scampered in before Brendan could close the door.

Bending, he ruffled the dog's fur. "Well, Hunter, what do you think of Miss Peyton?"

Hunter gave an approving bark and returned to finish whatever it was he'd demolished before the fire. Brendan could imagine the housekeeper's face when she saw the valuable rug, which was treated with great care, slathered in doggy spittle.

He sat at his desk and sifted through his mail. Nothing worthy of his immediate attention. His excellent secretary and his steward handled the most pressing problems. Pushing the letters aside, he turned to view the gardens, hazy beneath the summer sun. Despite the violent memories from his boyhood, he preferred to live here most of the year, although lately, the silence of the empty mansion seemed to draw in upon him, sending him back to London, while leaving his efficient staff to run Beechley Park in his absence. He had plenty to distract him in the city. Politics, Prinny's latest exploits, a few good friends, and attractive women. But none of it held his interest for long. He feared he would never find a cure for his low spirits.

He might have brought his former mistress to Beechley Park. Or invited half the *ton* for a house party where laughter and frivolity would fill the quiet reception rooms and empty corridors. Why had he never done so? It would have surprised them into accepting. He had one or two loyal friends and no interest in making more. Society was curious about him. Why else call him that ridiculous name, "the Phantom Earl"? He supposed he was stuck with it. He wasn't about to change.

And why, even though this liaison with Laura had not begun well, did he remain hopeful? Brendan wondered why that was important to him. Was it the challenge? He rarely had to think about his relationships with women. They developed naturally and remained until he ended them. He pushed himself away from the desk and left the library to go upstairs and change his clothes. Did Laura ride? On horseback, things might improve between them. They hadn't broached the subject, but then, they had talked very little. Was she only here because she'd given in to pressure from her brother? He supposed he would find out soon enough.

Chapter Four

W ELL, SHE WAS here and had arrived unscathed. To Laura's great relief, her fear that Lord Debnam would force himself on her in the carriage had proven wrong. He was so big and had such long legs, it had been impossible to ignore him in that confined space. Toward the end of the journey, dark bristles had painted his jaw. They'd rasped when he'd run a hand over them.

Were they prickly or soft? Laura's fingers had curled into her palms with the desire to touch them.

Laura followed the maid along the corridors. In such a vast estate, did it really matter who saw her wandering about? The staff would know about her, and she disliked being hemmed in. She loved to walk, and dragging an unwilling maid along would spoil her pleasure.

As they climbed the stairs, she realized the house was built in the *E* design of Elizabethan times, with the wings on either side linked by a long gallery.

The guest bedchamber was the same as the other rooms Laura peeked into, luxuriously appointed and readied for her occupation. While she took off her bonnet, two well-built footmen carried in her trunk.

She turned to survey the bedchamber which would be hers for a month. A retreat, perhaps, if she needed one. A flowery scent filled the air from several vases, the walls papered in a rich gold printed with white flowers and exotic birds. The soft-pink swag of curtains were edged in spring green. Penny, the small, red-haired maid who seemed inclined to chatter, assisted Laura out of her travel clothes and into a fresh, if slightly crumpled muslin.

"It's my dream to become a lady's maid one day, Miss Peyton. I've been told I'm good at needlework." She did up the buttons on Laura's pale-lemon crepe. "This is so pretty. The stitching is very fine, if I may say so."

It should be. A modiste in London who charged the Earth had made it. Her life had changed considerably since she'd had to part with her lady's maid, for economy's sake, after her parents had died. It had hurt her deeply. She and Sarah had formed a friendship over the years. But an excellent position had been found for her in a neighboring house. "If you like, I can teach you a few skills a lady's maid requires while I'm here."

Penny's brown eyes widened, and her freckled face broke into a grin. "I would be ever so grateful, Miss Peyton."

"Milady."

"Yes, mis…milady."

Perhaps she shouldn't have rushed to help the girl. Laura worried she might have given the maid false hope. It was unlikely she could reach such an exalted position within the household without the ability to read and pen a neat letter. Laura could school her in how to apply a hare's foot and rouge, create the complicated hairstyles popular today, and also take care of her mistress's clothing, jewelry, and shoes. While Penny might excel at mending and altering garments, and she could draw the bath and bring her mistress breakfast, but was a country girl like Penny able to read and write? It would be required of a lady's maid. Laura didn't like to ask her. After she left Beechley Park, would it leave the little maid unhappy and dissatisfied? Lord Debnam seemed determined never to marry, so there would be no countess.

She wondered again why the earl was so strongly committed to remaining single. She would like to discover the reason. But he would not welcome her prying into his affairs, and she was careful not to incur his wrath. Not because she considered him a violent man, but because he appeared unwilling to open a door to his past. She was curious by nature. What made him a selfish rake who thought he could have whatever he wanted? She still knew little about him, but to call him that no longer seemed to fit. After all, he had rescued Mrs. Royce and Mary with no concern for his own safety and had treated Laura with respect, so far at least.

Laura went downstairs for afternoon tea. Smiling at a footman who opened the door for her, she entered the blue salon. It was almost disturbingly perfect. The Delft-blue-paneled walls of the lofty-ceilinged salon were framed in gold. Vases of perfect delphiniums sat on tables and complemented the walls. How unlike Longworth it was, even when Mama had been alive, where ancient, threadbare damask covered the chairs and sofa, needlework and books perched on tables, and vases of flowers gathered in a bright bunch, adding cheeriness and color. Laura hesitated to sit on the dainty satin sofa and chose instead a wide armchair covered in cream damask with a golden fringe. She brushed down her skirts and carefully sat as the door opened.

Lord Debnam strolled in. He had changed into riding clothes, snug breeches clinging to powerful thighs and narrow hips. His shoulders were impossibly broad in the Carmelite-brown, double-buttoned tailcoat. *No need of padding*, Laura thought, unsettled but impressed all the same. Fearing he had noticed her appraisal, she quickly raised her eyes to his in a welcoming smile.

He strode across the exquisite carpet of pastel hues. "Do you approve of my home?"

"It's magnificent. This room..." She waved her arm to encompass the carved marble fireplace, the enormous mirrors and artworks and the festoons of silk at the windows. Fat cherubs danced with ribbons across the painted ceiling. "It simply takes one's breath away."

Debnam sprawled in a wing chair beside the fireplace. "I have little fondness for it. I seldom use it."

She frowned. "Even when you have guests?"

"I don't care to entertain."

She knew he was reclusive, but why? Had he always been this way or might it have been something in his past? "It seems a waste when you have such a gracious home. Surely, you are proud of it."

He looked at her quizzically. "Why should I be? I inherited this estate, Laura. I am uninterested in the shallow indulgences of society. Half the year is spent in London with the company of those who think there's no more to me than this." He propped one large, booted foot on his knee, making her even more aware of his size and maleness. "It is my hope you might come to understand me better than that."

Why care what she thought? Did he really believe they could become close in a matter of weeks, and after such an inauspicious beginning? After which she would leave and probably never see him again. But there was much he hid behind his relaxed pose. Troubled, she traced the pattern on the arm of her chair with a nervous finger. "I see you plan to ride this afternoon." Would he leave her to her own devices? He puzzled her. The pull of magnetism he seemed to exude without effort made it difficult for her to think. Would she have to guard herself against being hurt again?

"Would you care to join me?" he asked. "We can ride to the river."

"I should like to, thank you," she murmured, forgetting her intention to avoid him. The footman carried in the tea tray and set it down on a table before them.

"Shall I pour?" Laura asked.

"Please." Debnam sat back and crossed his arms.

While she fussed over the hot water and the teapot, she was conscious of being alone with him in this quiet room—his sensual, gray eyes watching her, his large hand making the teacup look small and fragile when he took it from her, his handsome mouth when he raised the cup to his lips. She drank a little and put her cup down before her hand shook. She would feel safer outdoors, although the reason for that eluded her. Perhaps the fresh air would bring clarity to her rampaging thoughts.

An hour later, she emerged from her bedchamber, having changed into her olive-green habit, which she considered quite stylish with gold braid and frog fastenings on the snugly fitted spencer jacket. It had been made especially for riding in Rotten Row during her brief London Season. She had never worn it because Robert had run out of money, and they'd returned to Longworth. And she'd had no reason to wear it since. Tying the strings of her black riding hat with its curving, audacious feather, she picked up her crop and went to join Lord Debnam, who waited for her on the porch.

When he raised his eyebrows and smiled approvingly, Laura couldn't help feeling pleased.

They walked to the stables through the formal gardens with low hedges bordering the flower beds planted with brightly colored snapdragons and geraniums, the hum of bees hovering around them. The yews were clipped into pyramids and rounded shapes.

The stables proved almost as grand in style as the house. A dozen thoroughbreds thrust their heads over the doors of their stalls to observe them. Laura tucked the crop under her arm and smoothed her leather riding gloves over her fingers. "You stable quite a few horses. Why? You cannot ride them all."

"Breeding thoroughbreds is a hobby." He strode over to a small bay. "This mare should suit you."

"She will. What is her name?"

He lifted his eyebrows. "I haven't named her. They pass through my hands quickly. This one will attract a buyer at Tattersalls auction. At present, her name is Bay Mare."

Laura had crossed the cobbles to stroke the horse's nose. She swung around to the earl. "You can't mean to call her that."

He looked amused. "I do."

"But… But." She pointed to Hunter, who had joyfully accompanied them, but whose interest was caught by something in the grass. "You named your dog."

"Yes, but my dog lives with me. I don't intend to sell him."

She folded her arms. "Well, I shall name her."

His mouth quirked up. "If you wish."

Laura turned to study the horse. The mare had a striking, white marking on her forehead in the shape of a flower. "I'll call her 'Honeysuckle.' 'Honey' for short."

Lord Debnam chuckled. "Is that an improvement? Will she approve of such a frivolous name?"

"Surely, you must agree it is better than *Bay Mare?*"

He addressed his waiting groom. "Saddle…*Honey* for the lady, Keagan. And bring my horse. I'll saddle him myself."

The groom led out a tall, dark-brown gelding whose ears twitched. He snorted and shook his head. "He's keen for a gallop, milord," Keagan said.

"Then I'll oblige him." Lord Debnam stroked the horse's glossy flank.

Keagan disappeared inside. He reemerged with a saddle and bridle. The sight of the earl's quick, competent hands as he saddled the horse drew her eye. She imagined those on her body, which caused a rush of heat to her face. Turning away, she was glad of the distraction when the groom brought out her saddled mare.

"I'll assist you, milady."

Laura climbed on the block while the horse sidled nervously. "Thank you, Keagan. She has been exercised?"

"It is not always possible. She's spent time in the paddock. Be wary of her, miss; she'll be frisky."

Laura took the groom's hand and put her foot in the stirrup. She swung up onto the sidesaddle, then hooked her leg over the pommel and arranged her skirts. Honey danced about until she settled her.

In one smooth movement, Lord Debnam mounted his horse and Honey followed the earl's mount out of the stable block onto the drive. As the horses ambled along, Laura inhaled the sweet fragrance of honeysuckle from the creamy, trumpet-shaped flowers growing on the vine over a wall.

Lord Debnam turned in the saddle. "The wildflowers are flowering in the meadows over the river."

"How wonderful. I am eager to see them."

They cantered along the drive and turned onto the bridle path, entering the well-kept woods. Unlike Longworth, where bracken grew wild, with dead trees and leaves and branches left where they fell. Only to be cleared away when they blocked the path. The scents of moss and earth rose as the horses churned up clods of damp soil. Birds chirped in the tree canopy above them. The earl did not attempt conversation, so Laura followed suit. But when they emerged from the trees, she gasped and couldn't keep silent. "It's glorious!"

The river flowed by in a noisy rush, churning all in its path. On the far bank, the meadows and hedgerows were a riot of wildflowers: blue harebells; the white flowers of wild garlic; yellow lady's mantle; purple Jacob's ladder; and others she had not seen before.

"I thought you might enjoy it," Lord Debnam said with a smile. "Care to dismount?"

"I will." Caught by the surrounding beauty, she acted impulsively. Then she wondered what he might have in mind. But Lord Debnam had already jumped down. He walked over to assist her. Conscious of him, so large and purposeful, she leaned into his waiting arms. His hands on her waist, he lowered her slowly to the ground. Slower than she considered necessary, her body brushing against his. She inhaled his manly scent, disrupting the peace of a moment ago. The warm imprint of his hands remained as if he'd touched her skin. "Thank you." She stepped away and turned toward the view.

He looped the horses' reins over a bush. "Shall we walk?"

"Oh, yes. Let's," she said, relieved. They strolled along the path by the riverbank. He made no oafish grab for her, and the pounding of her heart eased. She allowed the beauty of nature to envelop her senses, the air heavy with the scents of foliage, reeds, and the rushing river. A wide arc of an azure sky with barely a cloud stretched across the heavens. Laura had forgotten how wonderful it was to ride on a summer's day. It had been such a disastrous year that she and Robert seldom took the horses out. A few yards away, a fawn emerged from the woods, its tail flicking nervously, causing her to sigh anew. It turned and disappeared into the trees.

She glanced up at the earl's profile, feeling a little like the fawn herself. What was he thinking? He was a difficult man to understand. "You must come here often."

"No, riding for me isn't just an enjoyable exercise. I visit the tenant farmers with my steward, or I take the gun out with the gamekeeper to keep the game bird population at a sustainable level."

"That certainly seems devoid of pleasure."

His smoky-gray eyes gazed into hers. "Pleasure is always available. Should I wish to find it."

An innocuous statement, and yet a ripple of sensation rushed through her. A warning of his intent? She wasn't sure if she wanted to stay and see what he would do, or hurry back to the house. She wanted to discover more about this enigmatic man. But she didn't know where to begin. Her mind was mush when he spoke in that deep voice. He might recite the Commons Parliamentary Hansard and hold her in sway.

Laura feared she could lose control, beguiled by him amid this beautiful place he had brought her to. She urged herself to be careful. This was not a chance meeting in Hyde Park. She was here for his pleasure but was determined that whatever happened between them would be on her terms.

A glance from his smoldering, gray eyes sent a pleasurable shiver down her spine. He watched her like a panther might watch his prey. When would he pounce?

She must not allow her imagination to run away with her. After all, he was a gentleman. They would likely dine this evening, enjoy wine and conversation, and then perhaps he might invite her to… She flushed, unable to pursue the thought to its conclusion.

She had increased her pace when Lord Debnam halted her with a hand on her arm. "No need to hurry. We have all afternoon."

His hands on her waist anchored her in place as he slowly drew her to him. She stilled, breathless, as he framed her face in his gloved palms and lowered his mouth to hers.

Laura let the crop drop to the ground at the rush of sensation, her senses alive, her heart thudding. She gasped when he claimed her mouth in a masterful, experienced kiss. When his tongue touched hers, electricity spiraled through her body. So unlike anything she had experienced, she lost herself, her hand at his nape, her fingers sliding into his silky hair. The kiss in no way resembled Edward's brief press of lips. Aroused, she gasped when he broke the kiss, and she feared she would fall when he let her go. But he kept hold of her, his hands roaming her back, a smile in his eyes. "You are uncommonly pretty, Laura." As she went to push him away, he released her.

Was this a prelude to something infinitely more? She pulled herself up sharply. She had come to terms with the fact that they would become lovers, but she refused to be taken on the grass like a common trollop. Like one of those courtesans she and Emma had talked about. She'd thought herself safe then from ever falling this low. A rush of confusion and humiliation washed over her. "Shall we walk on? There's a bridge ahead, around the bend in the river." He spoke as if the kiss hadn't happened. "If you wish, we can cross it for a better look at the wildflowers."

Bending to pick up her crop, Laura felt deflated, so ready to fight him, and now… It was as if the wind had left her sails. She couldn't make sense of his behavior. He left her totally baffled, and she suspected he had intended to do just that. Her pulse still raced, and she struggled not to trace her lips with her tongue over where his mouth had touched hers.

He took a firm grasp of her hand, and they followed the river, walking along the rocky path. If he chose not to refer to the kiss, neither would she. But she would be foolish to believe kisses would be enough for a man such as him. And naïve indeed not to believe that was why he'd brought her here. It was the first step in a seduction, she surmised. And she couldn't deny it had been, as he'd phrased it, pleasurable.

IN THE MEADOW, Brendan stood and watched Laura sitting on the ground with a very appealing lack of concern for her habit while she filled her lap with wildflowers, some the color of her eyes. What a delightful picture she made. She did not appear, as her brother had led him to believe, very experienced. Having realized it with a shock, he'd intended to break the kiss, thinking it best to take things slowly, but the touch of her soft lips, her scent and sweet breath, and he'd deepened the kiss, wanting to taste her.

Beneath his hands, her slim body had revealed enticing curves. Her full breasts had pressed against his chest. She was enchanting, with an unassuming charm, and possibly very inexperienced in the ways of love. The thought pulled him up. He had not expected such a possibility and didn't welcome it. He kept to his intention to proceed slowly, although somewhat regretfully. Laura deserved better than a roll in the grass. Although they might at some stage… She'd enjoyed the kiss, after all. At the ball, he hadn't been wrong about what he'd seen in her as they'd talked on the terrace. Laura was a passionate woman. But he was discovering more about her than he'd expected.

He smiled and walked over to her, and it was all he could do not to join her there on the ground and further their acquaintance. "You remind me of the Greek goddess Flora, in your flowery bower."

"I do?" She glanced up and her smiling, blue eyes caused an odd throb in his chest. Surely, not in the region of his heart?

"Isn't that enough flowers?"

She pursed her lips. "I have picked rather a lot. They are so pretty, I couldn't resist."

And so are you, he thought. Far too lovely and hard to resist. This was not how he'd envisaged their brief interlude to go. A more predictable affair, like all his others. With both understanding the terms. One he could control. And it surprised him that already, he struggled to keep his head around Laura. It unsettled him. He could always rely on his ability to keep his emotions in check.

Laura climbed to her feet. She shook out the skirts of her habit and surveyed the pile of wildflowers. "We shan't be able to carry them on horseback. How shall we get them home?"

"When we return to the house, I'll send a servant to collect them."

"I hope they don't wilt," she said with a regretful glance at the colorful bunch. She stooped and picked two flowers, a red poppy and a yellow daisy, and tucked the yellow into the bodice of her habit.

He smiled, very aware of the enticing curve of her breasts, as she approached him.

"And this is for you." She tucked the red flower into his buttonhole.

Her laughing eyes, her scent, enveloped him. It was all he could do not to draw her into his arms, as his body burned with wanting her. Waiting for her might drive him mad. The word "mad" made him scowl and brought him back to Earth. To reality. He studied the bank of clouds advancing on the horizon. "The weather changes," he said, his voice sounding bitter to his ears. "There's a good chance we'll get rain soon. Best we hurry."

Laura glanced up at him with a wary arch of her brow, as if

she'd noticed the change in his voice. She didn't comment as they walked back to the bridge. One thing he'd noticed about her, she was sensitive to people's feelings.

When they reached the horses, he assisted her onto Honey, then mounted his gelding.

"You must have a name for *your* horse," she said, riding her mare up close beside him. He noted her mischievous smile. Apparently, she would not spare him. "Or is he called 'Dark Brown Gelding'?"

"Bruno." He fought a grin as he gathered up the reins. "Shall we go on?"

They rode single file along the narrow path into the woods. "'Bruno' is the Italian word for 'brown,' is it not?" she called. "Not a very inspiring name for such a fine horse, but I suppose Bruno is glad of any name. Considering he may be the only such horse afforded the honor."

Brendan's mouth twitched. "He hasn't complained." He turned in the saddle to look at her. "But haven't I allowed you to name the mare I intend to sell? And how suitable a name it is, bearing in mind the rider."

Her laugh was lighthearted. Brendan couldn't help admiring her spirit. Despite everything that had happened to her—and the previous few years must have been difficult and sad with the loss of her parents, as well as a possible failed romance—Laura found humor and delight in the simplest things. "I fear what any child of yours might be called," she added as the horses emerged onto the drive.

She was clearly curious about his avowal never to marry. He glanced back and found her expression one of innocent inquiry. "Not a problem I intend to have." His tone made it clear he did not wish to continue the discussion. It would be dangerous if she broke through his defenses.

When she fell silent, he wondered if he had said enough to dissuade her, but apparently not.

"I haven't forgotten your declaration that you would not

marry," she said as they approached the stables. "I don't wish to pry, but it sounds so utterly final from a man still in his prime."

He laughed. "In my prime, am I?"

He turned and saw her flushed cheeks.

"I meant you are still young," she said.

Of course she wanted to know why. Women always did after he made it plain early in a flirtation. But he would not tell her the reason. Not now. And most probably never. To see the horror or pity on her face would undo him. "I imagine it is unusual," he said lightly. "But I realized some years ago I am unsuited to marriage."

"I see."

She didn't, of course. Although she seemed to genuinely want to understand him. But it would be impossible for anyone to understand. He fell silent, refusing to oblige her, as their horses entered the stable courtyard.

Chapter Five

ONCE SHE AND Lord Debnam had reached the house, Laura became uneasy. Now he had kissed her, surely a seduction would follow? Or would he wait until dark? Not having any experience in such matters, she felt out of her depth. A few rushed kisses at a house party or behind the stables with Edward seemed so innocent now. But she'd thought she'd been in love at the time, and if Edward had done more, would she have stopped him? While she didn't need to love Lord Debnam, and it was probably better that she *didn't* fall in love with him, she wanted to feel more than an attraction for him when they became lovers. She wanted to respect him as a person and enjoy his company. But how could she delay the inevitable?

"You've become very quiet," he observed as they entered the hall. "Has picking all those flowers tired you?"

She laughed. "I am made of sterner stuff. But you will send someone to fetch them, won't you?"

"Redfern will arrange it."

"I'll go upstairs and change."

Redfern entered the hall. "The steward awaits you in the library, milord."

Lord Debnam turned to her. "Please forgive me for being a poor host. There are matters I must attend to in the library. A footman will come to your bedchamber and escort you to the dining room when dinner is served."

Laura viewed his tall, athletic body as he walked down the corridor. He paused and turned back to her. "You are welcome to come and choose a book to read. You'll find a variety of reading matter on the library shelves."

"I will, later, thank you," she said. He didn't appear eager to seduce her. Shouldn't she have been glad? She really couldn't understand herself. "As the day is still warm, I prefer to walk in the gardens."

"Capability Brown designed the gardens in the last century, and little has changed since." He paused, a hand on the door latch. "Enjoy your walk, but stay close to the house."

"Thank you." She'd taken a few steps but turned back and called after him before he entered the library. "Shall I arrange the flowers?"

"Mrs. Brandt will deal with them."

She would like to have something to do, but it was just as well. Her flower arrangements lacked the studied elegance of the housekeeper's. But then Laura disliked stiff, formal arrangements. The library door closed behind him, and she mounted the staircase, her mind full of questions.

Had the kiss disappointed him? Had he decided she was not what he wanted? Would they continue in this vein until it was time for her to go home? She wished they could talk more, but it seemed as if he'd drawn a line which Laura couldn't cross. He had secrets—well, most people did, even her, but his seemed to be deeply ingrained in his soul. *Perhaps he didn't enjoy the kiss*, she thought, returning to her first and most unsatisfactory postulation. She paused on the stairs. And he didn't wish to proceed. Surely, a blow to her vanity wasn't as important as her chastity. She became as much of a mystery to herself as he was.

She decided not to venture into the garden like a polite houseguest. Instead, she would visit the portrait gallery she'd glimpsed in passing and study the family portraits. It seemed unlikely she would find a clue to tell her more about him, but she could think of no other way.

In her bedchamber, she rang for the maid. By the time Penny had hurried into the dressing room, Laura was half-undressed, the muslin gown embroidered with lilies waiting on a chair.

"Milady, you should have waited for me." The maid was close to scolding her as she picked up the gown.

Laura smiled at the young girl's unaffected manner, wishing she could take her home with her. But of course, that was impossible. And although it would have been nice to have a lady's maid again, she didn't need one. It wasn't as though she would marry into society, and she'd grown used to caring for her clothes and dressing herself during the last year. She made her gowns with front fastening to make it easier in dressing. And she'd become quite skilled at arranging her thick, fine hair, which frequently escaped the hairpins.

As Penny fussed around the bedchamber, restoring order to Laura's clothes, it occurred to her that the maid might have heard something of the family's history from the servants. In her experience, servants loved nothing more than to gossip about their employers.

She would ask her, but first, she would view the portrait gallery.

Emerging from her room, she made her way to the gallery, initially designed for the family to exercise indoors during inclement weather. Furnished with gilt chairs, sofas, marble tables, shrubbery, and statues, the gallery's long windows overlooked a walled garden with a fountain at its center. Over the top of the trees, the roof of some hexagonal structure could be seen. A gazebo. Beechley Park was such a beautiful estate. Yet it did not appear to make Lord Debnam happy.

She turned to roam along the walls where portraits of the family hung, stretching back over the years. As if it made what he had done more acceptable, Robert had informed her Henry IV had gifted the Debnam family the title and lands for some act of bravery.

Laura came to the most recent portrait, judging by the fashions of the day, and stopped before a fair-haired man who bore a resemblance to the earl, with the same straight nose and square jaw. The former earl, Lord Debnam's father. He had an engaging smile, which might have been like his son's if the latter ever allowed himself to smile that broadly. The earl looked pleased with life as he leaned against a tree with a loyal spaniel at his feet. The portrait hanging beside him must have been the countess. Lord Debnam's mother had a strong face that was, if not precisely beautiful, arresting, her dark hair dressed in the elaborate style of the late eighteenth century. Her eyes appeared to be the same gray as Lord Debnam's. A dark-haired, solemn boy of about six or seven years stood beside her. The current earl. Laura moved closer. The countess, Lady Debnam, rested her hand at the boy's waist, her smile friendly and indulgent. Laura foolishly smiled back, as if they'd just met. The countess looked to be of a similar age to Laura in this painting, and the former earl around thirty. Where were the portraits of them in their later years? When had they died? And how? Laura checked along the walls but found none in the gallery. Deciding she might have missed those hanging in the great hall, she started down the staircase.

As the lofty hall was deserted, she could inspect every painting hanging there. None featured the late earl and his countess. Among the tapestries, the crossed swords, and ancient relics, the few portraits were dated centuries ago. Deciding to take that walk, she smiled at the footman seated in the foyer and slipped out into the gardens.

Finding some warmth in the sun, she pushed her bonnet back onto her shoulders to enjoy the summer afternoon. Her mother would have been cross with her and warned her about freckles, but dear Mama wasn't here. During summer's long twilight, Laura judged she could walk to the lake, see the gazebo, and be back in time to change for dinner. She wondered if Lord Debnam looked for her. If he missed her. Should she have told him where she was headed? But then he would have insisted she take a maid, and she enjoyed her own company.

Wishing she wore her half-boots and not thin-soled shoes, she set off on a path leading through the trees in the general direction of the lake.

A woof made her spin around. Hunter, tongue lolling, ran to join her.

She bent down to pat his soft fur. Then she gave him a gentle push. "Go back, Hunter. If you bark, his lordship will know I'm alone." She pointed to the house. Once she'd continued on, Hunter followed at her heels. "Very well. We shall walk together, but don't run off and get lost." She could imagine Lord Debnam's steely expression if the dog should disappear. But Hunter stuck by her. He appeared to know his way around the estate and would be better at finding his way home than she was.

Familiar woodland smells greeted her as she ventured deeper into the trees. Hunter darted off in pursuit of some small animal. Alarmed, she called to him, and when he didn't return, she made her way through the bushes. A squirrel he'd been chasing had run up a tree and sat looking down at the dog as he scratched at the bark and whined. "Never mind, come along," Laura ordered him, and thankfully, the dog obeyed her as they returned to the path.

Her tight shoulders eased. Away from the tension she felt at the house, she enjoyed the quiet and being alone. But as she trudged on, the worry that the lake was farther away than she'd first thought began to alarm her. It would now take her much longer than she'd estimated to return to the house. Laura didn't want to cause any anxiety among the servants, or, heaven help her, the earl. She should start back. But the dog rushed ahead, and she followed.

Laura walked out from the trees. Before her, the magnificent, wide lake sparkled in the sunlight and illuminated the small temple overlooking the water from a small rise. She simply couldn't go back until she'd entered it. The marble-columned building would offer a splendid view of the lake and the distant shore, where tall, flowering trees grew.

Laura followed the path bordered by rhododendrons and flowering shrubs to the elegant structure. Climbing the steps, she leaned against a cool, hard column, Hunter panting beside her. A pair of elegant, snow-white swans serenely crossed the lake in front of her, the water rippling in their wake. "Heavenly," she murmured.

"A pleasant scene, is it not?" a man said behind her.

Startled, Laura swung around.

"And who might you be, little miss?" he asked.

The man was likely in his mid-forties, his fair hair threaded with gray. He stood at the bottom of the steps with a shotgun resting on his broad shoulder. His stance, with legs a little apart, suggested power and self-confidence, and although his manner was avuncular, his eyes roaming over her said otherwise.

She swallowed, suddenly vulnerable. "How do you do? I'm Miss Peyton. A guest of the earl."

His autocratic features pulled into a smile, but a calculating one. "Don't believe I have met your parents, Miss Peyton."

"No, you would not have, sir." If he fished for information, he would not hear it from her.

He rested a booted foot on the step. "I can't recall Brendan ever having guests. He's a lone wolf."

"He is a gracious host," Laura said crisply to dissuade him from further discussion about Lord Debnam. "Might you be the gamekeeper?" Surely, it would be audacious for the gamekeeper to call the earl by his Christian name. But who else would wander the estate with a gun?

He chuckled and offered a belated half-bow, which seemed to mock her. "Ralph Mather, Viscount Gaylord. Debnam's neighbor. Well, whatever my relative gets up to is of no interest to me."

"Then I shall go on my way, sir." It was unlike her to take an instant dislike to anyone, and yet she had. He was a lord, but there was something unrestrained about him which put her on edge. She had the absurd desire to flee. He had insinuated himself into her thoughts and spoiled her enjoyable contemplation of the lake. She began down the steps to where he stood, blocking her. When he did not try to move, she frowned and dropped any pretense of politeness. "You stand in my way, sir."

Beside her, the fur rose on Hunter's neck, and the dog growled.

He hastily stepped aside. "That blasted animal scares the birds away. Totally useless on a shoot."

Laura eyed his shotgun, fearing for the dog. Surely, he wouldn't shoot Lord Debnam's dog? But she didn't trust him. "Hunter is most obedient. Hunter, come." Hoping the dog would obey her, she edged past the man. She had only taken a step when she felt a light touch from his gloved hand on her nape.

"You should wear your bonnet. You'll ruin your lovely skin."

She recoiled in alarm but didn't acknowledge him, walking on, her hat bouncing on her shoulders, held by its ribbons. Fortunately, Hunter followed. Laura retraced her steps to the wood while putting on her bonnet and firmly tying a bow at the side of her chin.

"Charmed to meet you, Miss Peyton," he called after her. "I trust we'll cross paths again." He chuckled. Laura's heart thudded in her chest, and she fought the urge to break into a run, not willing to give him the satisfaction. How curious. He was Lord Debnam's relative, and he roamed this estate as if it were his own, yet his manner toward the earl had been rude and dismissive. There was something about Lord Gaylord she didn't trust. What did Lord Debnam think of him?

When Laura reached the trees on the rim of woodland, she allowed herself a quick glance back over her shoulder and was relieved to see Gaylord had not followed. He stood holding his gun, watching her. Something about his stillness, like a man stalking an animal, struck her. Chilled, she called the dog to her side.

While telling herself she'd reacted hastily, she still broke into a half-run, the delighted dog bounding along ahead of her.

Gaylord was probably just an arrogant, bad-mannered lord. But if he wished to frighten her, to put her off-balance, he had certainly succeeded. When her breath shortened to gasps, she stopped. Gazing around, she tried to get her bearings. It grew late. The last rays of sunlight struggled to penetrate the leaf canopy. The trees seemed to crowd around her. Nothing seemed familiar, but then, she hadn't thought to mark her way when she'd come, keen to discover the lake and the Grecian temple. She remembered admiring clumps of dainty rock orchids which grew over the mossy rocks. But were they the same plants? Could she have taken a wrong turn? She'd been so preoccupied with getting herself and Hunter away safely, she'd scarcely noticed.

Somewhere close, footsteps approached. Muffled by the soft, leaf-strewn ground, she was unsure from which direction they came. Was it Gaylord? She spun around and dithered, searching for a place to hide. There was nowhere among the tall trunks and low scrub. Her throat dried as Hunter abandoned her, racing ahead. She called after him, her voice thready, but he didn't come back. Head down to watch for potholes, she ran after the dog.

Laura banged up against a hard chest and shrieked.

"I told you not to wander around on your own." Big, firm hands on her shoulders steadied her. "Why were you running?"

She gasped and gazed into the earl's annoyed, gray eyes. "I...didn't know it was you. I thought..."

Lord Debnam dropped his hands. "Then who might it be?"

"I met your neighbor at the lake." She gasped between breaths. "He carried a shotgun." She suddenly felt foolish. "I found him rather intimidating."

"Gaylord seems to have forgotten his manners." Lord Debnam looked furious. He swiveled and began walking back toward the house.

"He said he was a relative of yours," she said, trying to keep up.

"My uncle. My mother's younger brother. Her elder brother, Simon, died some years ago."

She struggled to catch her breath. "Why was he roaming about your land with a gun?"

The earl stopped and turned to observe her. He reached up and straightened her bonnet, which had slid down almost over one eye. "Scaring young women, by the looks of it."

She searched his eyes, needing him to tell her more.

Lord Debnam sighed, obviously reluctant to indulge her. "Gaylord's estate adjoins mine on the eastern boundary. He takes it upon himself to shoot some of my birds."

"Why don't you order him not to?"

"As it serves both of us, I permit it. But I don't seek his company."

"I didn't like him."

He stared at her, something unfathomable in his eyes. Anger, frustration? "Did he behave in an ungentlemanly manner?"

"No," she said hastily. Although he *had* touched her. "I expect I surprised him. Finding me there alone." She wasn't about to tell him how cheap the man made her feel, or be the cause of trouble between them.

"Viscount Gaylord has an unfortunate manner. He does not try to get on with people. My father was often irritated with him, according to Redfern."

Lord Debnam's butler, Redfern, was in his sixties and would have worked here back when the earl's father had been alive. This was the first bit of information about his family Lord Debnam had divulged. In need of more, Laura considered probing him further, but while keeping pace with his long legs, she stumbled over a rock hidden beneath a pile of leaves. "Ouch!" She hopped about as pain from her ankle spiraled up her calf.

He came back to her. "What have you done?"

He looked impatient, and aware she was a nuisance, she shrugged. "It's nothing." She put her weight on her foot to test it, then bit her lip at the pain.

"For God's sake, Laura. Let me see."

Lord Debnam crouched and lifted her skirt. "Mm. A slight

strain by the look of it." Holding her stockinged leg, he probed her ankle with gentle fingers. His touch brought him sharply into focus. She no longer thought him an uncaring rake, but a gentleman capable of concern for others.

Laura fought an impulse to touch his thick, wavy, brown hair, which grew in a whorl at the crown, and instead held his strong shoulder to keep herself upright. How extraordinary! She had never wanted to touch a man's hair before, not even Edward's.

She disliked being seen as a fragile woman. "It's nothing, really, my lor—*Debnam*."

With her weak ankle, she should have taken more care. Annoyed with herself, she felt foolish, hating to be dependent when she wanted to be determined and strong, in control of her own fate. A match for this man, although every aspect of their relationship seemed to favor him. And it appeared to have annoyed him to have to come to find her.

He straightened with a relieved sigh, and she realized he'd been genuinely concerned. She had been about to apologize for roaming about unescorted, even though she thought it nonsense to drag Penny everywhere. But she gave up any such notion at his obvious disapproval. Besides, the fact that he was walking too fast made her stumble. "Why go traipsing about the woods in those slippers?"

"They are not slippers. I hadn't intended to walk this far." This was untrue, but he was being mean. Admittedly, her shoes weren't sturdy boots, but neither were they flimsy slippers. Further objections died in her throat when Lord Debnam hoisted her into his arms.

"What are you doing?"

"I'm taking you back to the house, unless you'd like to remain here and contemplate nature."

"You can't carry me all that way."

"Can't I?"

He pulled her closer, as if to silence her. It was effective. She shut her lips tightly on another useless demand, nestling into his arms. He smelled wonderful—manly, and clean.

Lord Debnam called to Hunter, who raised his head from rooting about in a pile of leaves, and without further comment, strode with them along the path.

She began to feel foolish. "I am too heavy." She wriggled.

"Light as a feather," he said, though his voice was strained. "What is that scent you use?"

"Lily of the valley," Laura said, unnerved. She gripped his coat. He meant to distract her. And she was. Very distracted. It was really very pleasant to be in his arms. She fought to resist laying her head back against his shoulder.

They emerged from the trees, and he crossed the drive to the lawn and walked through the gardens. Gardeners at work in the flowerbeds raised their heads to watch them. Her gown had ridden up and revealed too much of her legs. She was sure her face was scarlet. "You can put me down now."

"And make a poor decision a worse one?"

Laura considered that comment unkind and unnecessary, but her objections would have to wait until she was back on her feet. She took advantage of her position to study him at close quarters. He was hatless and without his neckcloth. Had he raced from the house, fearing something had happened to her? She liked to think so. His shirt, open at the neck, revealed the strong column of his throat and a glimpse of dark chest hair. Overcome by a powerful emotion new to her, she listened to his heartbeat. "Heavens, I *can* walk." Her voice sounded shaky, and she pushed at him half-heartedly, while her anguished breath drew in the slightly salty, musky scent of his skin.

"Be still or I'll drop you on your bottom."

That shook her into silence. How had he made it sound so erotic?

"What drew you into the woods?" he asked as he strode along. At least he wasn't panting with strain.

"I caught sight of the temple roof from the window, and

naturally, wished to see it." Laura shifted in his arms, fearing she tired him. "Would you like to rest?"

"No." As he strode on, she studied the hard line of his jaw painted with the slight shadow of a heavy beard.

"Why were you there?"

"Mm? Why was I where?"

He seemed to be having difficulty focusing. She was too heavy. "Walking in the woods," she said patiently.

"I wasn't *walking in the woods*, as you put it. Naturally, when I was informed you had disappeared and been gone for some time, I came to find you."

"I'm sorry. I should have told Redfern," she said, feeling guilty.

"Yes, you should have. I can't have guests wandering about the estate willy-nilly. They can come to grief."

Willy-nilly? She clamped her lips together at the temptation for a smart rejoinder. She supposed he had a point. There was nothing she could offer in her defense. She frowned. There was no getting the better of this man.

The house came into view. He rearranged her in his arms, his hold on her firmer. Such an intimate gesture that Laura screwed up her eyes, overwhelmed and embarrassed. His big hand gripped her thigh. He wore no gloves, and his warmth penetrated her clothing. A man had never put his bare hands on her before, even to help her. It wasn't entirely unpleasant.

"I'll have ice brought from the icehouse. It will prevent any swelling."

She sighed. Her ankle wasn't worth all this fuss. She had twisted it once before and knew how to treat it. "Surely, that isn't necessary. I can raise my foot on a cushion. I'm sure it will be perfectly all right after a night's rest." Her injured ankle might keep him from her bedchamber tonight, and that was a reprieve, she supposed. What sort of lover would he make? Practiced, was the answer. And she, the antithesis of skilled, and nothing like the women he would have known in a carnal sense. She tensed. Must she add boredom in the bedchamber to her list of embarrassing failures? Horrified at the thought, she struggled. "Really, my— *Debnam*, why won't you put me down?"

"You like to argue, Laura," Lord Debnam said, making no attempt to do so.

She sagged against his chest, the amused rumble of his voice taking the sting out of his words. "I don't believe I do," she said, her objection milder than she'd intended. She was at a great disadvantage in this position. "My request was perfectly reasonable. It is you who are being stubborn."

"There, you see? Still arguing."

Carrying her up onto the porch, he entered through the open front door. The footman struggled to hide his surprise. As embarrassed as she was at her predicament, Laura stifled a giggle.

"Redfern!"

At Lord Debnam's call, the butler miraculously appeared through a doorway.

"Miss Peyton has injured her ankle. Inform the housekeeper," the earl said. "Mrs. Brandt can find her in her bedchamber."

"Certainly, milord." Redfern gazed at her, concerned. "I hope it's nothing serious."

Laura shook her head, but Lord Debnam answered for her.

"A slight injury caused by wandering about the woodland wearing unsuitable footwear. Send for ice."

Annoyed, Laura frowned up at him, wanting to protest. But she remembered his accusation, that she was argumentative, and she was hardly in a position to make a scene. A pity she would like very much to poke him on his hard chest. She sighed and gave in to the indignity of being carried like an invalid up the stairs. She couldn't despise him, although she tried hard to. And she no longer feared him. He wasn't the charming gentleman she had danced with at a ball. He was gruff and often silent and a complete mystery. Yet, for some unfathomable reason, he reminded her of a bird with a broken wing she had cared for until it could fly away. She found that disturbing and pondered on it.

She had been a mystery to herself too, since she'd come here, and she was no longer sure what she wanted.

He carried her effortlessly, taking two steps at a time and not at all puffed when he reached her bedchamber. He opened the door and carried her inside, walked to the bed, and laid her down. Taking hold of her foot, he slipped off the shoe, then turned to the other one. Laura tensed. Was he about to disrobe her? Her heart fluttered. He stood over her, his gaze roaming her face and down over her body, making her aware of her legs bared above the knee. Desire darkened his eyes. She trembled. "Shall I remove your stocking?" he asked gruffly.

Did he plan to seduce her? She shook her head, unable to trust her voice. Surely not now, when she was hurt. But the heady moment passed, and he straightened up.

"Thank you for your help, milord," she said briskly as she arranged her skirts to cover her limbs.

Lord Debnam's lip quirked up. "It's unnecessary to thank me. I enjoyed having you in my arms." He moved away from the bed. "And the glimpse of your pretty legs."

He thought her legs pretty? Momentarily distracted by his compliment, she sighed with relief. He didn't intend to behave like a callous rake and take her when she was at her most vulnerable, which would have profoundly disappointed her. Lightheaded, Laura grinned, grabbed a small pillow, and threw it at him. Lord Debnam caught it neatly, tossed it onto the pink, velvet chaise lounge at the foot of the bed, and, with a chuckle, left the room.

Laura stared at the closed door. What had just happened? Were they now friends?

The door opened and Penny came in, wiping the foolish grin from Laura's face. She lay back on the pillow in total confusion about him and herself. If only their meeting could have been under different circumstances. That he could be the one. The hero she wanted so desperately to return her love. But Lord Debnam was not that man. And never could be.

BRENDAN THOUGHT OF Laura lying provocatively on the bed. Her delightful laugh warming him. He wanted to turn around and go back, join her there. It had been a torturous journey carrying her from the woods. He'd been in a constant state of arousal from the moment he'd picked her up. Her soft, curvaceous warmth had rubbed against him the whole way to the house.

It was bad enough that visions of kissing his way up those long, shapely legs, and other more intimate places, disrupted his sleep. He had decided to wait for Laura to show she wanted him. But the longer this went on, with him dancing around her, and her natural, unaffected nature making him doubt the wisdom of bringing her here, the more he felt this was torment. He sensed she wanted to be wooed, and he'd been happy to oblige, but now, fairly certain she'd never lain with a man, he found himself hamstrung.

Laura wasn't so naïve as to believe she'd come here for a passionless holiday, he reasoned. She would know what the arrangement entailed, but he liked and respected her as a person. And that was the most damning of all. It complicated everything. He felt like a villain. Smarter by far to have chosen a woman with some experience, not an innocent, but without thought, he'd sought the one woman he would like to marry. A big mistake. Brendan should call himself fortune's fool and send her home. He would have done so before this, but the stark thought of the empty months ahead, before returning to a different kind of loneliness in London, had stayed him. He was a rational man and disliked how out of sorts he was. A few delightful weeks with Laura might make him feel better for a time. But when it was over? What then? Would his low mood deepen?

And now Gaylord had seen Laura. His uncle would be interested in finding out why she was here. He must not learn she was without parents or chaperone. Brendan didn't trust him to keep silent.

He groaned. There was no option but to send for her brother to come take her home. He would tell her in the morning before he could change his mind. And in case he weakened in his resolve to take her to bed, he would do as he promised and take her to see the beach. If Laura's ankle was better, they could have a picnic near the water. But they'd have to take the maid, damn it.

In a few days, Laura would have gone. At the thought, the dark shadows which plagued him when his mood was low seemed to gather around him. Would he never know true contentment?

Chapter Six

MRS. BRANDT, THE housekeeper, was a polite and efficient woman. If she disapproved of Laura staying here unaccompanied, she didn't reveal it. Upper-ranking servants were inclined to be prudish. She left Laura to Penny's ministrations, which were enthusiastic rather than gentle. But the ice helped to prevent any swelling and Laura could put her weight on her foot with only a twinge. "A storm in a teacup," she said crossly to the maid, who prepared her bath. She felt as if she had an itch she couldn't scratch. Lord Debnam made her heart race. She had wanted him to kiss her, not leave her as if he couldn't stand to stay with her another minute. Had he changed his mind about her? She was not what he wanted? That hurt more than her ankle.

"His lordship carried you all the way from the wood, milady? How romantic."

"It wasn't, Penny. My ankle throbbed. But it was kind of him." Laura wondered what the downstairs staff said about her. She supposed her ears should burn, but the sting of gossip didn't hurt so much now. She'd gone through the misery of how it would be ever since she'd agreed to come here.

Penny sighed as she laid out the soap and towels. "It wouldn't have bothered him, carrying you like he did. His lordship is big and strong. Handsome too, isn't he, milady?"

"I suppose he is, Penny. Have you ever heard any gossip

about his lordship's parents? I'm curious, but I don't like to ask him."

Penny turned from pouring fragrant bath oil into the water. She nodded gravely. "It's said his father went mad," she said in a dramatic whisper while she helped remove Laura's robe. "And he suffered strange spells—saw visions, too, they say."

Startled, Laura nearly slipped as she climbed into the hip bath, the tenderness in her ankle reminding her to be careful. "The former earl saw visions?"

"So it's said. But that's not the worst of it. He shot and killed the countess, Lady Debnam, and then shot himself in the head. His lordship was only a child when orphaned."

Shocked, Laura's knees trembled as she sank into the warm water. How dreadful for Lord Debnam. But it made his attitude to marriage perfectly understandable. Might he fear he too would suffer his father's sickness? After viewing the calm, clever face of the former earl in the portrait, she struggled to believe him to be the madman Penny had described.

But what else would cause Lord Debnam's father to become so violent? Surely, he cared about his son?

She smoothed the washcloth over her shoulders. "Did they discover the reason he did such a terrible thing?" she asked the maid.

"That's the trouble, milady. A happy couple, those who remember say of them, and her ladyship was pregnant."

Deeply moved, Laura drew her knees to her chest and wrapped her arms around them. Tears blurred her vision and sympathy for the scared, young boy Lord Debnam must have been made her heart ache. She had looked for portraits of the former earl and his wife in their later years but realized now that they'd never grown old. It was so senseless a crime, she found it impossible to comprehend.

Might the painter have taken license with his portrait of the former earl? Such a work wasn't always a painted replica of its subject. A good portrait painter, as he undoubtedly had been, would try to capture character in the face he painted. And his lordship certainly didn't appear to have been the sort of man destined to play such a grim role in life.

The horror remained to trouble her as she lathered the soap and finished washing. She stepped from the bath and dried herself with a towel. "His lordship must not hear that I know about this," she said as Penny held out her nightgown. "So please don't mention it to anyone below stairs."

"Of course I wouldn't, milady. I'd get into the worst trouble for gossiping about my employer."

"I am pleased you have told me, Penny." She might have unwittingly asked Lord Debnam questions, which would surely have hurt him. Questions he would not want to answer.

Laura slipped on her dressing gown and sat before the mirror, removing the pins from her hair, and picked up her brush, tackling her long, heavy hair with firm strokes. "I am to have dinner in my chamber, although I'm perfectly able to dress and walk to the dining room. Penny, once you've tidied away the bath things, go down and have your supper."

When alone, still heavy-hearted, Laura wished she could see Lord Debnam, even though she could not refer to his family's past. There was nothing she could do or say to make him feel any better. Except to tell him how strong her conviction was that there was no violence in him. That he could not become like his father. He would not believe her or welcome it. Lord Debnam had suffered this from a child through all of his adult life. Her mind filled with impressions of him: wading into the river to save Mary and her mother, and then patiently waiting for her to agree to continue the journey here; his kiss when he'd taken her to see the wildflowers, which now filled the vases in the reception rooms; and hastening into the woods to find her without taking time to dress or even grab his hat, and then carrying her all that way home as if she'd weighed nothing at all. No, she saw no violence or madness in him, only profound sadness, which she now understood.

Laura grew sick of her own company. If only she'd taken up his offer of a book from the library. She wasn't ill and disliked the idea of being alone for hours in this chamber with her restless thoughts. She needed something to distract her from the appalling tragedy. But she longed to know more about the earl's past. What had happened to the little boy after his parents had died? Had some good-hearted person cared for him? And loved him? It was unbearable to think the tragedy might have left him all alone. She wished she could ask him.

It was too early to retire. Her long hair in a braid, she rose from the dressing table and roamed restlessly around the bedchamber, rearranging the vases of wildflowers, smoothing her hand over the creases in the silk counterpane, and studying the floral paintings on the walls.

A footman brought in a tray, and she sat at the table to eat her dinner. Broccoli soup, tender roast beef and vegetables, and a delicious caramel dessert, probably with some fancy French name. Her appetite gone, she ate the meal with little enjoyment, then pushed the plate aside, lingering over the glass of fruity, red wine.

Leaving the table, she went to the window. The weather had turned breezy, and shadows danced over the grass like grasping fingers. A long night loomed ahead. Laura knew she would not sleep.

Why not slip down to the library while the earl dined? She could select a book to read from the shelves and be back in her bedchamber before he left the dining room. Deciding, she tightened the belt of her dressing gown and, still in her slippers, left the bedchamber. Although a little sore, her ankle no longer bothered her. The house was quiet. No servants or footmen appeared in the corridors or on the stairs, and the library, when she opened the door and poked her head in, was empty. What a wonderful room. Leather sofas and walnut paneling, many tables and chairs. Bookshelves rising almost to the high ceiling with a ladder, inviting her to climb it to investigate the upper shelves. A room a person could spend untold hours in. More appealing than the formal drawing room, she imagined this handsome room in winter with the enormous fireplace aglow with a yule log, while snow painted the gardens white beyond the windows. Holly decorating the mantel. A tall fir for a Christmas tree like the one she'd seen in a magazine article about Queen Charlotte's, with bright baubles and sparkling tinsel. Wrapped presents awaiting the family on the hearth.

How had Lord Debnam, as a young boy, spent the few Christmases he had shared with his parents? Had he ever enjoyed Christmas again after they'd been gone? She gasped as sympathy for the earl, so strong, it was painful, tugged at her heart. But she must not let him see it. She sensed he wouldn't welcome it.

BRENDAN HAD LITTLE appetite. He finally pushed back his chair and rose, ordering Redfern, who hovered with the wine carafe, to inform the chef his *la fricassée de poulet aux champignons* was superb as always, and he was sorry he couldn't do it justice.

Forgoing his usual lingering at the table with the port, he left the dining room, intending to have a cognac in the library; it was the one room in the house which offered him solace, perhaps because his father's books and letters revealed the words of a rational being and not a raving madman. His actions defied all reason, and Brendan would never make sense of it, but in the library, for a brief time, his father seemed restored to the man Brendan remembered, and the man's erudite letters and journals written in a fine, clear cursive somehow reassured him.

He made his way along the corridor, framing in his mind the missive he must write to Laura's brother. He would advise the baron that while he did not require reimbursement of the monies paid, some urgent, unforeseen matter had arisen which would require him leaving his estate for London. Brendan would invite

Netterfield to come to Beechley Park to take his sister home, as it seemed the most discreet option. It was imperative that he do so quickly before Gaylord caused irrevocable damage, which Brendan suspected he would take a good deal of delight in.

As he walked along the corridor, Brendan found himself reluctant to put pen to paper. Perhaps tomorrow. He found parting with Laura extraordinarily hard to accept. He opened the library door and stood, silenced. Before him, Laura, dressed in a negligee as fragile as smoke, her long hair braided and hanging down her back, stood at the top of the bookshelf ladder, a tome in her hand. Her dressing gown swirled around her ankles, revealing her lovely bare legs above the knee. He caught his breath and then strode forward. The siren! He had thought her safely tucked up in her bed and unable to tempt him.

"Dear lord, Laura. What are you doing here?"

She turned quickly and almost overbalanced. "Oh, my lord— *Debnam*, you shouldn't startle me like that! I expected you to still be at dinner."

"Well, as you can see, I am not," he said, his voice tight with suppressed emotion. The unexpected sight of her, when he'd decided they must part, sent a heated yearning through his body. Intent on returning her swiftly to her chamber, he moved to the ladder to help her down. "What the devil are you doing climbing that ladder with an ankle strain?"

"I wouldn't have attempted it if I thought my ankle wouldn't support me," she said reasonably. "It does very well, as you can see."

The book in one hand, she descended slowly, backward, the shape of her deliciously rounded bottom showing through the delicate silk of her dressing gown, while he waited, his pulse beating hard.

When she reached the lower rungs, he caught hold of her and swung her away to place her safely on her feet. He kept his hands at her waist, anchoring her there, enjoying the sight of her, the closeness.

She clutched the book against her chest and smiled up at him. "Are you cross with me?"

He returned her smile with a shake of his head.

Their smiles fell as they studied each other. His gaze roamed her face, marveling at her delicate features, her small nose and full-lipped mouth. He placed a thumb and finger on her firm chin to raise her eyes to his, her skin as soft as a rose petal. "But you are stubborn."

"Unfair," she murmured and she reached up to stroke his jaw. "Your bristles are soft. I expected them to be scratchy."

"I've had no complaints." He swallowed. At her touch, insistent need rocketed through him, demanding more of her. Every inch of her. "I shave twice a day. But I didn't expect to see you tonight."

"But here I am," Laura said inconsequentially.

"Yes," he said slowly. "Here you are." He ran a finger along the collar of her dressing gown lingering above the channel between her breasts. "And you in your night-rail."

"Mm." Her blue eyes darkened with desire, pinned him, as his good intentions threatened to crumble.

He took the book from her and tossed it onto a table. Then he pulled her slowly toward him, his hands on the small of her back until they touched chest to hip. Until his hard cock pressed against her.

Laura's eyes widened, but she didn't move away.

A moment passed between them. He was acutely conscious of her unfettered breasts in her night attire, pressed against him. He fought to contain his raging emotions while his body clamored to take her to bed, and he feared his mind and his noble intentions were losing the fight.

She seemed so unaware of the effect she had on him. He was more convinced than ever Laura was a virgin. *If I had known,* he thought, *would I have resisted the temptation to bring her here?* No, he would have done it anyway. Even if this was all there was. It seemed so right, he and Laura. Had done so from the moment he'd met her. And yet they were not lovers, and if he kept to the promise he'd made to himself, they never would be. But it was difficult, and growing more so. He should send her to her bedchamber. But perhaps not yet…

His mouth covered hers. She raised her hands to his shoulders and her sweet, feminine scent enveloped him, threatening his decision to write to her brother immediately. He saw no reason why they couldn't enjoy each other's company for a day or two. Taking her hand, he drew her over to the sofa.

Seated beside her, he raised the thick rope of dark-blonde hair to breathe in the scent of violets, wanting to unravel it, and undress her. To see her naked, her tresses adorning her curves like Botticelli's painting of the goddess of love and beauty, *The Birth of Venus.*

Heaven help him, he had to taste her. He'd at least allow himself that. *"Sweetheart."* He pulled her onto his lap. She came willingly, coiling her arms around his neck, and he kissed the velvety skin of her neck, the tender sweet spot beneath her ear, and with a sharp intake of breath claimed her lips. His mouth toyed at the seam of her mouth, then entered the dance with her tongue.

Laura moaned, her fingers tugging his hair. Brendan eased away the dressing gown to expose the creamy rise of her breasts and sucked a nipple through the cloth.

She wiggled on his lap, making him patently aware of how little fabric stood between her soft body and his demanding cock. In one breathless moment, he could have what he fervently desired. And he doubted Laura would stop him.

"Oh, that feels so…"

This wasn't going to happen, not if he wished to look at himself in the mirror tomorrow. He moved her off his lap and put some much-needed distance between them. "You should go to bed, Laura. Rest your ankle."

Laura's eyes glazed with desire, settled on the bulge in his trousers. He swiftly turned away. He must tell her now! And write to Netterfield in the morning.

"I am sending a note to your brother to come get you," he said, dragging out the words reluctantly.

Laura's eyes widened. "Have I done something wrong?"

"No, of course not." He raked his hands through his hair. "I believe it's best for you, that's all. If you leave before things go too far between us."

Laura stared at him, surprise in her eyes. "If that is your wish, Debnam—*my lord*," she said crisply.

"Tomorrow after breakfast, we might go for a drive if the weather is fine. Didn't I promise you we could visit the harbor?"

"Yes, I believe you did," she murmured. She turned away and briskly gathered up the books from the table. "But I shan't hold you to it."

Aware he'd hurt her feelings, he held out his hand to help her up.

That dashed harbor. Right now, he could only think of one thing: Taking her to his bedchamber and loving her until dawn.

"I shall go up alone. Good night."

Laura slipped out the door.

There should have been some kind of medal awarded to him for resisting her.

Chapter Seven

LAURA KNEW DEBNAM didn't really want to send her away. She spent another sleepless night confused and uneasy about what she wanted, and what her future now held for her. Noticing the dark shadows beneath her eyes as she brushed her hair, she sighed. Would he do as he'd promised and summon Robert? How long before her brother arrived? When she'd first come here, she would have been relieved to be sent home. But now, knowing what she did about the earl changed everything. She thought over the few glimpses he had given her into his life—his disinterest in his home, being shut away from society. Even in London, he was reclusive. Wasn't that why they called him the "Phantom Earl"? His reluctance to name his horses, and his grim acceptance he would never marry and have children, reinforced her opinion that he was a wounded soul, and not the careless rake she'd first thought him to be.

Perhaps he didn't know himself what he wanted from her. Not marriage. But surely not just a passionate affair, which he could easily have in London with the company of whichever sort of woman he fancied. It remained unclear why he had invited her here. And until it was, she wanted to stay, while accepting she must leave him when the time came and never see him again.

Her future ceased to matter. It was this moment that was important. She believed she was here for a reason. Call it fate, or pure foolishness, but she couldn't dismiss it.

She hurried down to breakfast, hopeful Debnam had undergone a change of heart during the night, while not really believing he would. In the library last night, he'd been so determined that she leave, it seemed impossible to change his mind. She'd worn her prettiest negligee, and yet he'd sent her away. But not without a struggle, she had been pleased to see.

Heavens, how much she had changed within such a short space of time. A prim, going-on-spinster tempted to become an earl's plaything? Nothing had the power to shock her anymore. Uppermost in her mind was Debnam's personal torment. She needed to understand it. To help him before she went away.

The breakfast room was empty, but for the footman waiting to serve her.

"Has his lordship been down for breakfast, Charles?"

"Yes, and he has gone riding, madam."

Debnam had not seen fit to invite her to join him. He'd left the house before she'd risen from her bed. Coward. She drew in a breath. So, he planned to avoid her until Robert arrived. She was not about to give in like a frightened titmouse. He didn't really want her to go.

It became important to understand him. To learn why he had brought her here and now spurned the idea with such fierce determination. If nothing else, he owed her an explanation. She would endeavor to spend the rest of the time allotted to her in Debnam's company as much as possible until Robert arrived. Debnam was going to find it difficult to avoid her.

After she nibbled a piece of toast and drank two cups of tea, she rose from the table. "Where on the estate might Lord Debnam ride this morning?" she asked Charles as he stood to attention beside the bain-maries filled with hot, tasty dishes she had no appetite for.

"His lordship is unlikely to have gone far afield this early, madam. He is alone. Perhaps he rode to the top of Green Hill, which offers a good view of the estate."

"In which direction is the hill, Charles?"

"As the crow flies, it is due north. If you take the path past the stables, you'll find it leads directly there."

She smiled. "Thank you. You have been very helpful."

"I hope I haven't sent you on a wild goose chase."

"I shall enjoy the ride, in any event. It is a lovely morning."

"It is. But it promises to grow hot later on. Perhaps that is why his lordship went out so early." The footman bowed.

"Then I must make haste."

It wasn't the weather which had driven Debnam outdoors. Was he avoiding her? They must talk. Last night, she'd been rocked by his decision and hadn't known what to say.

Laura hurried upstairs to change into her habit, hoping to meet him, and rehearsed what she might say if she did. It was foolish to try to protect her reputation now. She had to make him see it.

Once the stable staff had assisted her to mount Honey, she followed the footman's directions. She rode her mare along the bridle path toward the hilltop in the distance. As she and Honey climbed a slight incline, her bold plan began to seem unwise. Had she no pride? It would amuse Debnam to see her trailing after him. Especially now, when he'd made it clear he didn't want her here.

Was it mere vanity that made it so difficult to accept his change of heart? Or was it this absurd notion, which strongly persisted, that he needed her? It wasn't as though he'd reached out to her and sought comfort. Far from it. It was clear he preferred love affairs with no strings attached. But his sad past affected her soft heart. He'd been a boy when his parents had died; however, he was a grown man now. A rake, while not a heartless one. He feared for her reputation? It had been clear from the outset that her reputation, indeed her future, had already changed irrevocably.

Laura suddenly couldn't face him. Not if she wished to keep a shred of her dignity intact. When another path presented itself through the trees, she directed Honey onto it. Did she really imagine she could make a difference to Debnam's life in the few weeks they might spend together? It hardly mattered now. Robert would waste no time in collecting her and taking her home. He might even insist she return to London to find a husband. Especially as the money Debnam had paid him was safe. *Safe?* Or had Robert rushed straight to the gaming tables and lost a good deal of it? The thought made her stomach roil, and she groaned.

The path petered out onto a long stretch of open meadow bordered by large shrubs. "Come on, Honey, let's stretch your legs." Honey obeyed, breaking into a canter. As if eager to show what she could do, she responded when Laura urged her to gallop.

The soft, foliage-tinted breeze touched Laura's face as they flew over the daisy-strewn meadow. A low fence loomed up, and the horse didn't hesitate, sailing over. "Well done, Honey." Laura patted the horse's glossy neck.

She heard a horseman coming up behind her and turned, expecting to see Debnam. It wasn't him. Lord Gaylord, with his insolent smile, rode up to her. "Well, Miss Peyton. You ride exceedingly well. You must have spent time in the country."

"I grew up on my parents' country estate," Laura said, doubting her status as a gentleman's daughter would work to ensure he kept his distance. But she was wrong.

He frowned. "A gentleman's daughter should not be here without a chaperone. I believe your parents have not joined you."

How had he heard of that? He must have questioned Debnam's servants. "My brother has been held up. He will be here very soon." She hated how hot her cheeks felt and his piercing gaze taking note of it.

"How careless of your brother. We can't expect Debnam to care, but your family should. Does your brother not worry about your reputation?" He shook his head. "You should leave here, Miss Peyton. There is madness in Debnam's family, and he is eccentric, to say the least."

"I am aware of the earl's history, but it doesn't mean we should judge him by his father's actions."

"Do you know that his great-grandfather was mad too?" Sly amusement pulled at Gaylord's thin lips.

"If you wish to believe old stories embellished over the years."

"No. It is quite true. The fourth earl abandoned his family and took to the roads. He was hanged."

Laura shrugged with indifference, but she was interested. She planned to search for the fourth earl's portrait in the gallery. "Are you always on Lord Debnam's land, my lord?"

He chuckled. "You are on mine, my dear. As soon as you crossed that fence."

"Then I beg your forgiveness. I shall return the way I came."

Lord Gaylord angled his horse in front of hers. "Don't rush off. I'd like to talk to you. I rarely have the chance to enjoy a pretty woman's company. Why must Debnam have all the pleasure?"

Laura backed Honey away. "I am expected at the house, my lord. Please remove your horse."

He tutted. "When you tire of Debnam, and you will—he's a surly fellow—you might take tea with me." He turned his horse's head and rode away.

Laura's heart pounded, her face so hot, she thought she'd explode. After several deep breaths, she calmed down enough to take Honey back over the fence.

Before she'd covered half the long stretch of meadow, Debnam appeared, galloping Bruno toward her. When he reached her, her heart sank. He looked angry.

"What were you doing on my neighbor's land?"

"I wasn't aware it was his land when I crossed that fence," she said, feeling she'd had enough of both of them.

"Have you forgotten I told you not to roam about the estate on your own?" he asked, his voice strained. His shoulders looked stiff as he turned and rode back toward the trees.

Laura nudged Honey and followed. "I wouldn't have if you'd invited me to join you," she called. "But please don't feel obliged if you have no wish for my company. I will leave here in a day or two, so it hardly matters."

Debnam wheeled his horse around and rode back to her. "Don't think I am eager to see you gone. I'm not, Laura." His deep voice lowered as if he struggled to admit it. He looked miserable, and while it lifted her spirits to hear him say it, she was sorry she'd worried him. She was too independent. Didn't Robert always say so? But there was so little time for them together. Laura didn't want to waste it. She resisted the urge to question his reasons but no longer believed he didn't want her. She'd seen the evidence of his desire for her in the library. And she wanted more. "I met Lord Gaylord."

He tensed, his mouth a hard line. "Gaylord spoke to you?"

She quaked. "Yes. He pointed out that I was trespassing, but he wasn't angry."

"Did he act appropriately?"

Serious, gray eyes stared into hers, making it difficult to obfuscate. She was determined not to mention Gaylord's cruel words about the earl's family. "He invited me to tea."

"He *what*?" Debnam's dark eyebrows lowered, his expression thunderous. "What the devil did he mean by that?"

"I don't think he meant tea, Debnam. But what he did mean was clear." She suddenly wanted to cry. "Nonetheless, I find myself in desperate need of that cup of tea." She nudged Honey's flank and galloped her over the grass toward the trees. Reaching the path, she heard Debnam riding behind her. Ignoring him, she rode back to the stables. He didn't overtake her, but when they reached the stable courtyard, he dismounted and came to help her.

Laura felt unusually fragile as she leaned down to him. She wanted to draw strength from him, for them to be friends, at least, before she left. But somehow, even that seemed impossible.

His hands remained for a moment on her waist as he gazed

down at her. "Laura, I hate that he said that to you. He's a nasty fellow and I'll ensure he doesn't come onto my land again. But I told you, I cannot..."

"Marry," she finished for him. "I don't expect you to marry me, Debnam. I never did."

"But that is the reason why you must leave."

"If nothing has changed, why must I? I don't understand."

He ran a hand over his face as if to wipe away the pain. "Nothing must prevent you from making a good marriage."

"Oh, Debnam," she murmured. As if it were so easy. Did he really think her attractive looks would be enough for her to marry well? Without a decent dowry and a few years off thirty? She was no bargain, but she wanted to hear him say he desired her so she might go home with her dreams intact. "Then please tell me why you brought me here."

"Because I wanted you. I still do." He took off his hat and pushed his dark-brown hair back from his brow. "It was wrong of me. I must have been out of..." He shook his head. "I hope you'll forgive me once you are safely home. And I intend to keep my distance until then, Laura. I am only a man and you're too dashed seductive."

She smiled a little at that, before reality struck. His words had a decided ring of finality.

After they saw to the horses, they walked to the house together in silence, with Laura wanting to tell Debnam he wasn't wicked, and certainly not mad. He was just deeply unhappy. If only he would tell her of his fears. A problem shared is a problem halved, her mother used to say. But she held her tongue, deciding to wait until the chance to change his mind presented itself. It seemed unlikely to happen. Robert could arrive as early as tomorrow.

BRENDAN STRIPPED OFF his coat and shirt in his bedchamber. In his riding breeches, he sat to pull off his boots. Gaylord had discovered Laura was here alone and become far too interested. This should have occurred to him. What a fool he'd been. His Uncle Ralph had never liked him, and that was mutual. He had hated Brendan's father, blamed him for the death of his sister, Brendan's mother. It was all still raw, despite the passing years. Perhaps because Brendan had been away for years, sent first to boarding school at ten, then Oxford and a tour of the Continent, while his trustees had run the estate and investments. The solicitors, Hillwood & Brown, had done an excellent job. He was beholden to them, and their senior partner still wrote often wishing to discuss new possible investments. But Brendan couldn't stir up enough interest himself.

When he'd returned here four years ago, he'd found Gaylord had treated Beechley land as his own. Rather than start a feud he'd had no energy for, he'd allowed his uncle to continue. It troubled him to return to the home he'd avoided for years, because everywhere he turned was the stark memory of his parents' deaths. All the happy times they'd shared as a family, blotted out forevermore by the inexplicable actions of his father. That shattering day had etched itself in his mind when he'd discovered their bodies. His mother had been pregnant.

He put a hand to his forehead, which tightened ominously. *Don't let his cursed malaise return. Not now!* He didn't want to deal with a nasty piece of work like his uncle. Let him do what he liked. But if Gaylord overstepped the line, he might find Brendan capable of great anger. He had been angry since he'd been ten. Finding it impossible to hate his father, he had no one to blame for his tragic loss. At first, he'd tried to bury those feelings, and to lead the sort of life his mother would wish for him. But in the last few years, he'd come not to care. Apart from the few good friends who stood by him no matter what, he kept his own counsel and sought no other friendships among the *ton* or country society. Until Laura had come into his life. He should resent her awaking these feelings in him. Yet he felt only a deep respect for her and cared for her, while heartily wishing it weren't so. Otherwise, he would have had her in his bed days ago.

Chapter Eight

CHARLES BROUGHT LAURA'S afternoon tea to her bedchamber, where she pondered her predicament alone. Several hours passed, but nothing helpful came to mind by the time she'd dressed to join Debnam for dinner. She took extra care with her appearance, choosing her pale-lilac evening gown trimmed with three bands of satin ribbon around the hem and on the puffed sleeves, and Penny revealed a remarkable talent, braiding Laura's hair in the Grecian style.

Debnam waited for her in the drawing room, a gracefully proportioned room with a fireplace at each end, richly decorated in the chinoiserie style with red-and-gold-patterned wallpaper and deep-red curtains caught back with gold ropes and tassels at the tall windows.

He crossed the Persian carpet to greet her. "Would you care for a sherry before dinner?"

"Yes, please."

Freshly shaven, his sideburns neatly trimmed, and his cravat fashionably tied, he wore a dark-gray tailcoat and buff trousers. She admired his waistcoat with cream-and-pale-blue stripes and pearl buttons. For a moment, his dapper appearance made him more like the man she'd met in London ballrooms. She had forgotten that man. Debnam no longer seemed anything like him.

She sat on the sofa upholstered with damask, gazing around at the magnificent room. Every reception room at Beechley Park was beautiful, if a little dated, as if some magic wand had cast a spell over the house and kept it exactly the way it had been in the last century.

"You look lovely tonight, Laura."

When Debnam handed her the glass of sherry, she breathed in his cologne and her heartbeat quickened. As it did whenever he was near. Would she always feel this way about him?

"Thank you." She took a sip to settle herself. He did not want to discuss his decision with her.

"Would you care for a game of cards after dinner? Or there is chess, or perhaps billiards?" He seated himself a distance from her in one of a pair of gold, silk damask chairs.

"Robert taught me to play billiards."

He smiled. "Then I shall enjoy the game."

She raised her eyebrows. "You're thinking I'll be no match for you?"

"Can you read my mind?"

"I can read your overly confident expression. My brother said I was a natural."

"I shall find out after dinner."

The butler came to the door. "Dinner is served, my lord."

They finished their wine, and he stood to offer her his arm. "Shall we go in?"

A splendid Italian crystal chandelier hung overhead, spilling light over the long dining room table laid with a white, linen cloth. Sparkling, crystal wineglasses; silver candelabras; a low bowl of red roses; fine china plates monogrammed with the earl's crest; and gleaming silverware awaited them.

A footman seated her to one side of Debnam, who sat at the head. It was terribly formal. She viewed the acres of white tablecloth and imagined it filled with guests, laughing and talking. As it should have been. But he'd said earlier that he didn't receive guests.

Redfern poured the wine, then he and the footmen left the room.

"You've never invited anyone here for dinner?" she asked, to ensure she hadn't been mistaken.

Debnam raised his glass, the candlelight flashing off the crystal. "You already know the answer, Laura."

"But I don't know *why*," she persisted. "If you won't tell me, I'll have to guess. And that might be worse."

A smile lit Debnam's gray eyes. Not his cynical smile, but warm and intimate. Laura experienced an odd little thrill. As if she'd vaulted over some sort of obstacle, although many more awaited. She didn't want to lose the mood and so she chose her words carefully. "You were very kind to Mrs. Joyce and Mary. It is obvious you care about people."

Debnam's mouth quirked. "I am filled with the milk of human kindness." He shrugged carelessly, quoting from Shakespeare's *Macbeth*.

Laura slowly shook her head, her eyes admonishing him. Picking up her wineglass, she took a sip of the superb vintage. "If you open your mind and heart to others, it might surprise you to find you enjoy it excessively."

"'Excessively'? Let's not get carried away. There are admittedly some people I like very much, but also many I have met whom I detest."

"And you liked me? That's why I'm here?"

Debnam rubbed his hand over his eyes. "Laura, of course I do. Despite you reminding me of a bird tugging at a worm it can't pull out of its hole. And like the bird, you persist undaunted."

She laughed. "I am pleased to be likened to the bird and not the worm. What kind of bird am I to be?"

He studied her. "Metaphorically? A robin. A jaunty, determined, little robin redbreast."

"And you a lonely falcon flying high above the ground, swooping down only to snatch up your food."

Debnam's eyes widened. "Ah, Laura." He turned the glass in

his fingers, making the crystal flash in the candlelight. "Perhaps we may talk of something more pleasing?"

"I agree. You talk and I shall listen."

His appreciative glance roamed over her. It lingered on the low neckline of her gown before he met her gaze. "I must confess, I will miss your company."

"I will miss your company too, Debnam," she said, suddenly sad.

"Will you? Just for tonight, will you call me by my given name?"

She drew in a breath as another obstacle fell away. "Brendan."

"I like the sound of my name on your lips."

It was a surprising confession after he'd been so formal. Elated, she hoped they might stop avoiding the topic which hovered unspoken between them. What had made him change his mind and send her home? She couldn't believe he wanted to. One look from him made her yearn to be closer. And he felt that way too; it was apparent in every heated glance.

The footmen entered with the first course filling the room with flavorsome aromas. Redfern appeared from the cellar with another decanted bottle of white wine.

Conversation ceased while Redfern replenished their glasses, although she'd drunk only half a glass, intending to be careful. Just being here with Brendan made her head swim.

"Leave us," Brendan ordered the footmen, after the oyster soup had been ladled onto their plates and side dishes placed on the table.

Laura drank a spoonful of the soup, then licked a droplet from her lip. It had a subtle, delicious flavor. "Mm. You have an excellent cook."

He gazed at her mouth. "I'm pleased you approve. This morning, the oysters were brought fresh from the harbor. Shall we go there tomorrow? Your maid can accompany you. That's if your brother doesn't arrive. Although I think it too soon."

"I would like that." Would Robert come? He would hasten here as soon as he got the earl's note. Her brother, now his debts were settled, would be at pains to see her home safely again. *Home?* The thought of leaving made her shoulders droop. Left to roam around Longworth or sent back to London to the marriage mart? She couldn't decide which was worse.

"What are you thinking about, Laura?" Brendan asked. "For a moment, you looked sad."

She couldn't tell Brendan it involved him, so she chose the next thing of concern on her list. "I worry about my brother."

"His gambling habit?"

Laura nodded, unwilling to admit to the rest. How Robert had threatened to end his life. She glimpsed sympathy in his eyes, but he said nothing. What was there to say? Tomorrow or the next day, she would be off his hands. The prospect dampened her appetite for the tasty array of dishes brought to the table.

BRENDAN WATCHED LAURA push away her plate. She had only picked at the dishes. Arnaud would despair at his creations returned to him unappreciated. Brendan disliked how worried she seemed. What did he send her back to? He had been blind to the problems she faced. Her brother could have ratcheted up more debts in gaming hells in the last few days. It would take little for his estate to end up in the hands of creditors, if he didn't learn economy and employ a good estate manager.

He wanted to cease this polite conversation and speak truthfully. To say he longed for her to stay. He wanted to leave his chair now and pull her into his arms. To take her upstairs to his bed. None of which he said, or had any intention of doing. At the temptation, Gaylord loomed large in his thoughts. The man would stop at nothing to discredit him, and although he cared little for himself, he cared for Laura. Enough to sacrifice that which he wanted very much to hold on to.

Salmon followed the soup. "Caught here in the river on the estate," he said. "My chef makes an excellent sauce."

She tasted it. "The sauce is superb."

"Laura…"

She looked up. "Yes?"

"I'm sorry for bringing you here. Profoundly sorry. I hope you believe me."

Laura put down her knife and fork. "I don't regret it, Brendan. You came into my life at a time when I was at my wit's end. I shall go back to that life, a little stronger, after I've been able to view my situation from a distance."

"Am I to believe that? Or do you wish me to feel better?"

"It's true. I have come to terms with reality."

He frowned. "And what might that be?"

"I shall spend the rest of my life at Longworth."

He thumped the table, causing the cruet set to fall over. "Nonsense. You must marry. Many men would want you for their wife." His reaction was not because he thought her wrong, but because he was urging her to marry while selfish enough not to want to see her with any other man.

Laura calmly restored the silver cruet set. "I don't wish to marry someone I don't care for, just to have a roof over my head."

Brendan huffed out a humorless laugh. "So you plan to sink uncomplainingly into spinsterhood?"

"I would have liked to be a mother. But it isn't as bad as all that. I have my horse, my cat, the garden, and my books."

That was *if* Robert hung on to Longworth. Brendan had never felt so helpless. If only…but no, he must not think of it. The life she spoke of was better than an existence with a man who could lose his mind and turn violent at any moment. What if he hurt her? And what if they had children? He would never leave a child alone in the world, as he had been.

But what Laura saw as her future was wrong. There would

be a very good reason why she hadn't married. It wasn't just her beauty or her kindness and gentle nature, which made her special. It was her courage and determination to overcome anything life threw at her. She would make a success of marriage, but he hoped she would marry a man who appreciated her.

After the dessert course, a fragrant delicate syllabub, Brendan rose from the table. "Shall we have coffee in the drawing room? Or go directly to the billiard room?"

"Let's begin the game," she said. "I enjoy it and haven't played for some time."

He drew back her chair. While engrossed in the game, he might keep control of these rampaging emotions and send her safely to her bedchamber when it was over. Alone.

They entered the billiard room. He came in here sometimes to play. The dark-paneled room was a man's domain with its leather sofas and emerald-green, velvet curtains at the windows. His favorite spirits were on a tray. Before the fine green baize table, they chalked their wooden cue sticks. Laura chose the yellow ball, and he chose the white.

He glanced at her. "Shall we agree on fifty points to win the game?"

When she assented, he stepped back to allow her to take a shot to see who broke first. Laura bent over the table, giving him an enticing view of her creamy bosom in the low-cut gown. Unfair! He tamped down a groan as she focused and hit her cue ball. It ran the length of the table, hit the cushion, then rolled back toward her and settled six inches from the baulk cushion.

"Well done." Brendan's attempt to get his mind off Laura failed. Her perfume, the pleasing shape of her slender body in the clinging gown, was a distraction. He struck the white ball, which fell short by a foot.

"I get to break, sir." Laura smiled impishly.

He raised an eyebrow and adopted a stern expression. "You are remarkably confident, Miss Peyton."

"Ha! And you don't think I should be?"

"Why don't you show me?" He grinned as he placed the red ball and his cue ball into position.

Laura worked the angle, then shifted to take her shot. Her ball struck the red and rolled against the cushion. "Oh, bother."

"Bad luck."

His cue ball struck the yellow before rolling into a pocket. "Darn," he muttered, then he retrieved it. A shot he would make nine times out of ten, not that miserable effort.

"I thought it well done," Laura said.

"Mm. Two points." He wrote it in the book, then flubbed his next shot completely.

Laura stepped up to the table, studied it, then took her shot. Her cue ball struck the white and the red before it rolled into a pocket. She turned to look at Brendan, eyebrows raised.

"Great shot," he said with an approving nod. "Three points." He picked up the pencil.

"It was a lucky shot," she said, but he noticed her smile.

His mouth quirked. "Maybe, maybe not."

She laughed. "I fear I have provoked your competitive spirit. There's no hope for me now. Watch as I sink the white with the red ball, Debnam."

"Please proceed. I'm riveted," Brendan said.

Laura's cue slipped, sending the white ball careering across the table to bounce uselessly against the cushion. She turned to him and burst into laughter.

Damn the game. Brendan removed her cue from her fingers and placed it with his on the rack. Laura's eyes widened as he pulled her into his arms. His mouth covered hers.

She sighed. Her arms crept around his neck. Her breasts pressed against his chest, and her warm, feminine fragrance made him moan against her lips.

He kissed the hollow at the base of her throat, feeling her tremble. *Hell*, he knew this was unwise, but he battered the thought away as he lost himself in the pleasure of her scent, her soft skin, and the flame of desire in her beautiful, blue eyes.

Chapter Nine

THEIR PANTING BREATHS filled the quiet room. Brendan's mouth sought a response she was only too willing to give. His hands, on the small of her back, settled her against the length of his hard body, his arousal pressing against her stomach. The intent in his eyes thrilled her. It was as if they couldn't get enough of each other. As if a dam had broken. They clung to each other with unrestrained passion. Laura breathed him in and stroked her hands over his muscular back and shoulders, wanting his naked skin beneath her fingers. To see and touch every part of him. Her legs became unsteady.

With a quick gesture, he flicked the balls to the other end of the table, then lifted her up and laid her down gently on the baize surface. He leaped up to join her there.

His eyes dark with passion, locked with hers. A sensation spiraled through her middle at the potency of his gaze. He smelled clean, of the soap he used and a hint of musky cologne. Her breast pressing against his muscular chest, his mouth found hers. Their kisses deepened and his tongue plundered her mouth, tasting of wine.

"*Laura.*" His husky voice was a mere whisper. His hands cupped her breasts, then he pulled the lace on the neckline of her gown down to expose more of them, bending to kiss her skin. When he rolled her taut nipples between his fingers, more tingles raced through her body.

"Oh, how…" Laura lost herself at the fierce rush of need, tightening her belly.

Leaning over her, Brendan mouthed her breasts, drawing gently on each sensitive bud. An urgent throb and moisture gathered between her legs.

Laura stilled, unsure what he might do but unwilling to stop him as he grasped the hem of her gown and eased the material up over her leg, past her ribbon garter.

His fingers found that special place. At first, embarrassed by the slick sound of her damp skin, she moaned at the tantalizing friction his fingers caused. When he slipped one finger inside her, she tensed at the extraordinarily tight sensation, but he kissed her, delving into her mouth as he worked magic with finger and thumb. Laura was lost. Lifting her hips toward him, she panted, moaned, and sought something. She wasn't sure what, only that she needed it badly.

Brendan's lips found that tender spot on her throat. "I want to be here, inside you," he murmured as he withdrew and pushed inside again.

Nothing in her life had prepared her for this. Laura wanted him. Knew for the first time in her life that this was what she needed from a man. To give herself up to a man. To experience passion. Laura arched her back as a current of heated sensation shot through her. She threw back her head, murmuring meaning-less words, as the crescendo of feeling built. Was that she who called out?

The waves eased away, leaving her melting, mindless, and yet still needing more. To have him inside her. To feel his naked skin against hers. She opened her eyes. Brendan watched her, with a heavy-lidded expression, his chest rising and falling with each quick breath. With a thrill, she knew he wanted her too. She reached out to touch him, but he rolled away.

He leaped down from the table and then scooped her up, placing her on her feet. Still aroused, Laura clung to his coat, unsure of her legs.

"I hadn't intended for that to happen," he murmured. "I think we should stop, Laura."

Abandoned so abruptly, Laura dropped her hand from his coat and stared at him. She swallowed sharply on a protest. He didn't intend for them to be lovers. She would never forgive him for this glimpse of what life as his lover would be like before he sent her away. He'd denied her those memories. But his expression was resolute, his mind made up, and to press him would only embarrass them both.

"We must stop," he said. "This isn't wise."

"It wasn't wise when you asked me to come here. But you did."

"You've never lain with a man, have you, Laura?"

She frowned. "And you thought I had."

"It doesn't matter what I thought. Your lover should be the man you marry."

"According to the dictates of men. What about my feelings on the matter?"

He smiled. "Sweetheart, I *am* thinking of you. If I were the selfish rake society paints me to be, you would be in my bed right now."

His eyes still burned with desire. He wanted her as much as she wanted him, but still held to this ridiculous notion that sending her home untouched would make everything all right, when the slightest rumor led to discovery. And she knew the *ton* found everything about Lord Debnam a fascinating topic of conversation. It was nonsense to think otherwise, but it was as if he needed to believe it.

How quickly he gained control of himself. If she were familiar with the ways of seduction, could she have touched him there, aroused him and made him want her too much to turn her away? Then they would confess their most intimate secrets and she could help to make him see how wrong he was about himself.

What folly!

"No need to escort me. I should go alone. We don't want to draw attention to ourselves," she said with bitter irony, and the stark expression in his eyes told her he knew it.

He nodded. "Perhaps it is best."

Debnam opened the door.

"Good night, Debnam."

She refused to call him "Brendan" again, even in her thoughts. It hurt too much. In his determination to do the right thing, he was further away from her than ever. She fled from the billiard room as his quiet "Goodnight, sweetheart," reached her. The corridor was shadowy with candles guttering in the wall sconces. She darted quickly across the hall where a footman would be stationed, and thankfully, met no one on the stairs.

In her bedchamber, she slumped against the closed door. Her trembling fingers stroked over her sensitive nipples where he'd touched them. She closed her eyes, but the tears still escaped to run down her cheeks.

Laura drew in a shaky breath. She would not allow him to see how he affected her. She would leave here with Robert and put an end to this affair that never was.

WHAT A MESS he had made of this. At the drinks tray, Brendan poured himself a large brandy. Holding the tumbler, he moodily leaned over the billiard table and flicked the white ball with his fingers. It rolled across the baize to strike the red, and both slid into a pocket.

He could always bed a woman if invited to do so, and he was just as capable of forgoing the pleasure if needs required it. Why he had almost broken that rule tonight eluded him. Nor could he make sense of how drawn he was to Laura. So much so, his willpower deserted him. It had been that way since he'd first seen her seated in the ballroom, looking bored stiff. He'd enjoyed the challenge of making her laugh, but as they'd danced, he'd caught a glimmer of yearning for life in her eyes; it had drawn him like a moth to a candle flame.

Laura was like a sleeping beauty, and he wanted to be the one to awaken her, to make her come alive to passion. While selfishly making his dark corner of the world a little lighter. Well, he had done a splendid job tonight. Laura had responded to him with all the passion a man could wish for. He'd lost himself in her kisses, her soft body, and had come within an inch of possessing her completely when it had become clear how much she'd wanted him to.

Brendan groaned. No matter how much he wanted her, he would not take her innocence and send her home to face whatever that might entail. Trouble was, Laura made him desperate for something he had no right to. Yearning for something more pulled at his heart. But dammit, he refused to damage her more than he had already. She would be gone within a few days. Out of the way of temptation.

Even after she'd gone, he didn't fool himself. A strong sense of her would stay with him. He refused to believe it was love. His heart had hardened against such an emotion years ago, but it was powerful all the same.

The clock in the hall chimed three o'clock when he retired to bed. Once he closed his eyes, morning would be upon them, and this interlude, which gave him a glimpse into how things might be should she stay, would be a mere memory. His life would continue as it had before. He could find another woman to fill his empty days and his bed but knew that wasn't the answer. It wasn't only the physical release he craved. It was the companion-ship of a woman capable of understanding him. Of accepting him. And he sensed that lady was Laura. But how unfair it would be to draw her into this uncertain future he called his life.

In the morning, when he entered the breakfast room, it was empty. He hadn't expected to find Laura there. The footman told him she had come earlier, and after a brief repast, had gone to arrange for her luggage to be brought down to the hall.

He'd upset her. Brendan went in search of her. He found Laura in her bedchamber with her borrowed maid, who bobbed and left the room. He stood watching Laura fuss with her reticule. "Isn't it a little precipitous to pack so soon?"

"It's best to be prepared."

"Your brother is unlikely to come today."

Laura turned to look at him, her eyes sad. "I believe he will."

He caught his breath, wanting to catch her up in his arms, hold her, and ease her unhappiness. To be where he longed to be, loving her, making her his own. And he tried not to glance at the bed, which loomed out of the corner of his eye. "How can you be so sure?"

She rummaged in the reticule in search of something and removed a small square of lace-edged handkerchief. "Because he will want me to come home. It's hard for him to manage the servants without me."

Brendan took the reticule from her, forcing her to look at him. "I am sorry about last night." He tossed the beaded bag onto a chair. "It seems I am always apologizing, but I can see it has upset you."

She raised a slim shoulder. "You're quite wrong. I am not upset. You were right to end it before…" She flushed. "I am ready to return home."

He didn't believe her but resisted drawing her close. To know she felt more for him than that slight shrug of her shoulders implied. He deserved it. And he must allow her to leave, then endeavor to forget her. His heart strangely heavy, he nodded. "I'm glad we agree it's best."

"Now, if you'll forgive me, I must see to the rest of my packing."

He couldn't bear the finality of it and reached out to keep her there for a moment longer. "Don't do it now. I promised you we'd go to the beach. Let's have a picnic, make it our last day together."

Laura's frown cleared. "I should like that. If you really want to."

"I do. We'll take your maid with us."

A reluctant smile lifted her lips. "Penny will enjoy that."

"I'll see you downstairs when you are ready. Mrs. Brandt will organize a hamper."

He left her to go down and give the order. A day at the seaside was a safe choice. There'd be no opportunity for a seduction. He sighed. The maid's presence would make sure of it.

"We go to West Wittering," Brendan said as he assisted Laura and the maid into the carriage.

"Is there sand there, milord?" Penny asked, looking wide-eyed. "I've always wanted to see sand and the water."

"Indeed there is. You may walk down to the sea, if you wish," Brendan said as he settled with his back to the horses. Which would give him and Laura time alone together.

At midday, having driven through several small villages and verdant landscape, the carriage came to a stop. Laura gasped at the beautiful vista. "How glorious!"

It was high tide. Spread out before them, the long sweep of sandy foreshore, dotted with tuffs of scrubby vegetation, stretched down to the rippling sea. Above, in the azure sky, gulls soared and dipped, while waterbirds gathered together on the sand like ladies at a tea party.

Frederick, his second footman, took the large hamper from the coach, while Charles put down the steps.

Brendan assisted Laura and the petite, excited maid onto the grass.

"I have seen pictures, but this is nothing like I imagined. One gets a sense of infinite space, and the air smells so different to Surrey," Laura said as the brisk, salt-laden breeze toyed with her bonnet ribbons.

Charles placed a rug on the grass and began laying out plates, cutlery, napkins, wineglasses, and the dishes. Then he settled a bottle of iced champagne and a plate of oysters among them.

Ordinarily, such an affair would be arranged with a seduction in mind. Brendan had certainly lost his touch. With regret, he watched the maid, having begged permission from Laura, dance over the sand to the water's edge.

Laura met his gaze, her blue eyes rivaling the sky. "I would love to walk barefoot over the sand and feel it on my toes."

"And I should like to watch you," he said with a sigh. What a sensual woman she was.

Her eyes danced. "But of course, I'll resist."

He could have offered to remove her stockings. "Shame," he said, eyeing an angler throwing his line in farther along the shore. "Shall we eat?"

"Oh, yes. I'm famished."

Laura sat down on the rug, arranging her skirts around her. Brendan joined her as Charles served champagne, while Frederick brought out the dishes: cold breast of fowl, ham, mustard, salad, bread rolls, small pork pies with crusty pastry, grapes from the hothouses, and lemon syllabub.

As they ate, Penny joined the footmen and the coachman to eat beside the coach.

Brendan put down his knife and fork, wiped his hands, and leaned back on his elbows to watch Laura sip her champagne. "Tell me about Longworth. What it was like there when you were a girl."

She frowned, as if wary to divulge some secret. "I had a wonderful childhood. My brother and I rode our ponies, and we told stories to entertain each other." She shrugged. "After Robert went to boarding school, I was left to my own devices. I rode, read books, and helped Mama in the house. Papa tutored me in science and Latin, which my governess didn't teach. He believed a woman had as much right to an education as a man."

"Your father had a strong influence on your life?" Brendan asked, understanding why she seemed so different to the women he had known.

She screwed up her nose. He wasn't sure if it was at him or

the champagne bubbles in her glass until she spoke. "He urged me to pursue those things which interested me. I wanted him to be proud of me."

Brendan hated how hampered she was. He'd never thought about it before, but Laura made him want to roar at the unfairness of life. He wanted to be there to encourage her and help her. The power of his feelings surprised him. "You're a kind person, Laura," he said finally. "One who cares very much for her brother, whom I doubt deserves it."

Laura selected a grape from the bowl. "Robert lived a wild life in London, as many young men do. Sowing his wild oats, they call it," she said wryly. "He has found it hard to adjust to the demands of an estate after my father's death."

"You make excuses for him, Laura."

She shrugged. "He's my only sibling. We are a small family, with just us and Aunt Gertrude." She popped the grape into her mouth, drawing his attention to her lips. He fought a powerful urge to lean over and kiss her to taste the grape on those sweet lips. "Now it's your turn, my lord," she said, distracting him from his thoughts. "I should like to hear about your childhood."

The question unsettled him. He feared his voice would betray him. It was still difficult to talk about his past without giving in to melancholy, and he didn't want to be sad today. Laura deserved better than that. "Not much to tell, really. No brothers or sisters. I went to boarding school at ten, then Oxford."

Her blue eyes looked grave. "And after that?"

"I toured the Continent, Italy, Greece, and on to Constantinople. My tutor and I were in France when Bonaparte escaped from Elba, and we had to come home." He had wanted to join up and fight for his country, but his health had prevented it.

"And then you returned to Beechley Park?"

He swallowed as he watched a flock of birds in a tree making a great fuss about something. "Yes."

Laura waited for more and when he didn't offer it, she turned to look at the sea, and thankfully, asked no more questions.

He rose and offered her his hand. "Shall we take that walk?"

She reached up to take it, and he helped her to her feet.

They walked over the grassy verge, saying little.

With a peal of laughter, Laura pointed. "Look at Penny!"

Brendan swung around. The maid had removed her stockings and, holding up her skirts, waded in the water. He laughed. "Good thing she won't be a lady's maid for long. I don't know if a proper mistress could handle the scandal."

As the meaning behind his words became clear, he swung around to meet Laura's eyes. She shrugged. "I think Penny makes a perfect lady's maid. I envy her the freedom to do as she likes."

Falling silent, they walked on while Brendan tried to remember when he'd laughed so heartily before.

Silences with Laura were comfortable and companionable. He glanced around to discover the carriage and his servants were out of sight. No one was about. He took Laura's hand and drew her in among the trees, which hid them from the row of shops and houses over the road.

Easing her back against the smooth bark of a birch, he looked into her eyes. "I will miss you. This time spent together has been special for me. Has it been for you?"

"Yes," she whispered, her gold-tipped lashes hiding her expression from him.

What would he find in her eyes? Regret? Sadness? Had she come to care for him? Did any of it matter? With a sharp breath, he bent his head to hers and kissed her.

Laura grasped his shoulders to stay upright on the uneven ground as he angled his mouth over hers. He nibbled her full bottom lip, drawing a sigh from her. His hands slid down her back and over the curve of her hip and pulled her against him, as need, unfulfilled, made him hard.

He drew away, searching for that elusive control which threatened to desert him, and with a deep breath, smiled. "Shall we play cards or a game of chess after dinner?"

"Chess," she said. "Papa and I played regularly. I can give you a good game."

He raised an eyebrow. "Your competitive spirit coming to the fore?"

She laughed, acknowledging she'd accused him of precisely that when they'd played billiards. As the memory of last night hovered between them, Laura's eyes grew sad. She reached up and stroked lightly over his cheek.

He could bear anything except to see her sad. Brendan caught her hand and kissed her fingers. He was about to say more when a voice hailed them. He sighed. "My servants think we have become lost. We'd best go back."

As Brendan and Laura walked toward the coach, Penny appeared from behind it, wearing her shoes and stockings again, a huge grin on her face. *At least one person got what they most wanted today*, Brendan thought.

In the midafternoon, the coach deposited them back at Beechley Park.

"I still expect Robert today," Laura said before she left Brendan to go upstairs to change her gown.

Netterfield! It brought Brendan back down to Earth. He went to his library, his place of solace. But today, the somber room offered him nothing, apart from the loud ticking of the clock on the mantel. A damnable quiet which left him alone with unwelcome thoughts. He sat in a leather armchair, and Hunter, sensing his low mood, came to lick his hand. As he patted his dog's silky head, his thoughts remained on Laura. Her warm gaze as she leaned back against the tree. How he wanted to make her his. Tomorrow, she would be gone.

Laura was correct to assume her brother would arrive today. For an hour later, through the library window, Brendan saw a coach with the baron's crest on the door drive past. He braced his shoulders and left the room to greet Netterfield.

As Brendan entered the hall, Laura hurried down the staircase. He waited for her, met her serious gaze, and they went outside together.

The coach pulled up. The groom jumped down and went smartly to the horses' heads while the footman rushed to open the coach door and put down the steps.

Netterfield leaned out of the coach door, making no attempt to alight. "You devil, Debnam!" he yelled, waving a pistol about. "You promised to take good care of Laura."

"And that I have done." Brendan stared at the dissolute baron. What the devil had gotten into the fellow? He needed to get him safely inside and learn what had caused this startling change.

"I am packed and ready, Robert," Laura said, anxiety shaking her voice. "We can leave immediately."

Netterfield ranted and took no notice of her. When she moved to go to him, Brendan held her back, a hand on her arm. The pistol Netterfield handled so carelessly alarmed him. He wanted to take her inside and shut the door on the disgraceful fellow.

"Put down the gun, Netterfield."

If the man didn't drop it immediately, Brendan would take it from him. He was reluctant to haul him out of the coach by his cravat in front of Laura, but he was prepared to do precisely that.

Fortunately, as Brendan started toward him with that aim, Netterfield, a foot on the top carriage step, lowered the pistol. Holding the gun against his chest, he fumbled in his pocket and with drunken glee, produced a piece of paper. "Then why have I received this from your neighbor, Lord Gaylord? He writes that you have mistreated my sister, that you have failed in your promise to behave discreetly."

"That is nonsense. I am perfectly well, as you can see," Laura said, a catch in her voice. "Please come inside, Robert. We can sit and talk. Make sense of this."

The brave footman made another attempt to assist him but was waved away again. With the letter in one hand and the pistol in the other, Netterfield yelled, "I insist on a duel. You will pay for your dishonor."

"Don't be absurd." Brendan had no intention of humoring

the foolish fellow. But it did not surprise him about Gaylord. He had done exactly what Brendan had feared. Why his uncle hated him so much, he could only guess. It was time the man was dealt with.

"I won't rest until…" Attempting to climb down, Netterfield stumbled on the steps and fell heavily to the ground. The sound of a gunshot exploded into the quiet air. The pistol clattered away on the gravel. The baron lay with his arms flung out. He didn't move.

With an anguished cry, Laura rushed to him.

Stunned, the footman stood helplessly as Brendan crouched beside the fallen man. He was still breathing. "He still lives," he said to reassure Laura.

Laura knelt in the gravel and took her brother's hand. "Robert!"

Netterfield's eyelids flickered but failed to open. Blood seeped with alarming speed from a wound in his shoulder.

Brendan removed a handkerchief from his pocket and tucked it in firmly against the wound as he called to Redfern, who waited by the door. "Have the baron taken to a bedchamber. And tell them to do so with care! Summon Dr. Phillips. Advise him it's urgent."

Brendan patted the man's pale cheek, not too gently. "Robert!"

Netterfield moaned but didn't stir.

As the footmen ran to obey the butler's orders and carry the baron inside, Brendan assisted Laura. His arm around her, she trembled against him as he led her into the house. He cursed the drunken idiot. Anger churned in his gut at Gaylord's sly act. What had driven him to write that letter?

In the hall, tears blurred Laura's eyes as she looked up at him. "Will he live?"

"The ball appears to have entered high on his shoulder and lodged there." He squeezed her arm. "Don't worry. Your brother's young, healthy body is in his favor, and he obviously has a fighting spirit."

She wiped a tear from her cheek. "But he doesn't. A few weeks ago, he threatened to shoot himself." Her voice broke. "I don't think he cares whether he lives or dies."

Could this have been the means her brother had employed to force Laura to come here? Guilt twisted Brendan's stomach.

"I must go up to him," Laura said, straightening her shoulders.

"A footman will undress your brother and put him to bed. Dr. Phillips is a capable surgeon. He will be here soon."

Distressed but evidently calmer, Laura nodded. She turned away and hurried up the stairs.

What would happen to her if her brother died? Deeply concerned for her, Brendan put a hand to his forehead. *Damn it! Don't let this be the onset of one of his strange spells.* They crippled him, despite liberal doses of feverfew and laudanum. His father had suffered from the same affliction. No fuss had been made of it. He'd merely retired to his suite for a day or two. Was it a sign of the madness which could one day strike Brendan?

Life was so damned unfair. He tasted bitterness on his tongue.

Chapter Ten

FORTUNATELY, AS DEBNAM had surmised, the pistol ball had missed an artery and bones, lodging high in Robert's shoulder. But there was often the risk of fever with such an injury, the doctor warned Laura. "Nothing is certain with a gunshot wound. We must stay on guard," he said, promising to return tomorrow.

After Dr. Phillips had left, Laura remained at Robert's bedside. Her brother had endured the pain while the doctor had probed the wound to remove the ball and suffered a couple of stitches without complaint. Robert was braver than she'd expected, although Phillips had said it helped him to be the worst for drink. And now, after a small dose of laudanum, Robert drifted into what she hoped was a restful sleep. He looked so pale and young, with his overly long fair hair spread on the pillow. She tended to forget he was a year younger than she was when her destiny lay in his hands. Losing their parents in such quick succession and inheriting the estate had rocked him. He resented the burdens it presented, while most of his friends from university enjoyed their freedom in London. And his way to deal with it was to gamble and drink too much.

Laura sipped the cup of tea a maid had brought her and settled back in the comfortable padded chair placed beside the bed for her use. She put the cup in its saucer on the table and closed her eyes, expecting Robert to sleep for at least an hour or more.

"Laura?"

She sat up straight and saw him gazing sleepily at her.

"You must rest, Robert."

"We must go home."

"You cannot, before you heal, or the wound will start to bleed again."

"I had to come save you from that devil. It horrified me what I learned about him. Do you know he is called 'the Phantom Earl'?"

"Of course. It has hardly been a secret," she said. If he ventured out of the card room occasionally at balls, he would hear of these things. "Who told you?"

"Lord Gaylord wrote of it in his letter."

What a horrid man. "I have been perfectly safe. Lord Debnam is a gentleman. Robert, I implore you, please believe nothing Lord Gaylord wrote. None of it is true. The earl sent a letter asking you to fetch me. Did you not receive it?"

"I left before the post arrived. Are you sure he sent it?"

"Quite sure."

"Why does he wish to send you home? Did you argue? Was he cruel to you?" he asked, his voice becoming slurred. "I haven't forgotten about the duel. We shall meet when I've recovered. He won't get away with treating you so shabbily."

"You are wrong about Lord Debnam," she repeated. She sighed, fearing he didn't want to believe it. "He has been nothing but kind." She rose to tuck the blankets around him, smoothing the pillows while carefully avoiding his bandaged shoulder. "Let us speak of this later. When you feel better. You must sleep now."

"And that's not all…" He groaned, but his eyes closed, and he slipped into a deep slumber.

What else did he wish to tell her? More of the same nonsense? Laura's ribs ached with compassion as she watched his chest rise and fall, thinking of the good times they'd had when their parents had been alive. Memories she chose not to share with Debnam.

Robert had been away for months, first with boarding school and then university, but he'd come home for the holidays, and they'd spent the days together. Edward would come over from next door to join them, and they'd ridden, played quoits and badminton on the lawn on fine days, and played board games when it had rained. They'd attended dances at neighbors' parties and the assembly rooms. She had been blissfully in love with Edward then and believed he'd loved her.

Once Laura had turned nineteen, her mother had taken her to London for a Season, to gain a little of what Mama had termed "Town bronze." But, as it was understood Laura would marry Edward, her father had declined any offers from suitors. That had not dismayed her. None of the gentlemen had appealed to her. Her head had been filled with thoughts of Edward, who in her mind at the time had encompassed everything she wished for in a husband. But Edward's father had wished his son to wait until his majority before he gave any thought to marriage.

When Laura had turned twenty-two, Mama had fallen ill after visiting an orphanage with some ladies from a charity she'd supported. It had quickly became serious, and Papa had rarely left her side. Soon afterward, he had been struck down too.

Edward had been a wonderful support in those days. But as she'd embarked on a period of mourning, he'd come to tell her with shame in his eyes that an announcement of his engagement to Miss Felicity Bloxham was to appear in *The Morning Chronicle* the following day. It had been his father's decree, and Edward had had no say in it. Naturally, Miss Bloxham came from a wealthy family. While Laura had understood the way these things worked, the pain had been so intense, she'd wondered if she could survive the horrendous sense of loss of those she'd cared most about. But she'd rallied because Robert, shattered to find himself the third Baron Netterfield, with an estate and tenant farmers to care for, had needed her.

She remembered the despair which had claimed her when Robert had seemed to give up. He'd turned his back on his responsibilities and joined his ne'er-do-well friends in the fleshpots of London. Alone, she'd managed the house as best she could, until their Aunt Gertrude had arrived. Their aunt had insisted Robert come home from London. And when he had, she'd given him a stern talking to, warning him in no uncertain terms he must do the right thing by his sister and manage the legacy his father had left him, or she would cut him out of her will.

Robert, apparently incensed at being ordered about by his aunt like a stripling, had finally agreed that Laura should marry. And so began another Season spent in London, which had ended when Robert's money had run out. The best part of that time had been meeting Debnam. He had shocked Laura into facing what she still longed for: a husband she could love and children, although as the days passed at Longworth, she feared it was unlikely to happen.

Laura leaned back in the chair and closed her eyes, listening to Robert's soft moans.

The door opened and Debnam entered. "How is the patient?" he asked quietly. "Dr. Phillips is confident he will survive."

She put a hand to her hair, aware it unraveled from its pins. "He woke for a brief time. He would like to go home."

Debnam drew up a chair to sit beside her. He rested his hands on his knees and studied the patient. "That will not be possible for a while."

He seemed so mature and capable compared to Robert. Her desire to climb into his arms and rest her head against his broad chest almost overwhelmed her. "But we mustn't rely on your hospitality…"

"I believe we've moved on from polite courtesies, Laura." Debnam took her hand and enveloped it in his large, comfortable palm. "There's no reason for you to leave now your brother is here. My neighbor can hardly make an objection."

Her heart beating fast, she withdrew her hands. "Why did he write that atrocious letter?"

Debnam shrugged. "He carries a grudge against my father and because my father isn't available, I suppose he takes it out on me." He searched her eyes. "Let's forget about Gaylord. I intend to make your stay here as pleasant as possible."

The nearness of him, his familiar male scent, and something intrinsically him made her yearn to be close to him. She swallowed, her throat tight. "Thank you, Debnam. Caring for Robert will leave little time for anything else. We'll leave as soon as he is well enough."

He stood and moved the chair back into place. "You should spend time outdoors to get some fresh air," he said with a hand on the door latch. "A walk tomorrow? You could accompany me on a ride once your brother is over the worst."

"We must wait and see."

He opened the door. "Will you join me for luncheon?"

It was hard to be near him, to gaze at his handsome mouth and remember his kisses. She shook her head. "No, thank you. I expect Robert will wake soon."

"I'll have Redfern order a tray."

When the door closed, Laura sniffed back tears. What a watering pot she'd become. She pushed a wispy lock of hair back from her brow. She must stay strong for Robert. His recovery would depend upon it. She tried to ignore the disappointment she felt at not joining Debnam at luncheon. "Incurable!" she said aloud, annoyed by her weakness.

Robert groaned and stirred. He opened bleary eyes. "Oh, you're here, Laura. I'm glad."

"Of course." Laura smiled. "Where else would I be?" She silenced her unruly thoughts and leaned over him, pleased to find his face a better color and his breathing steadier.

IN HIS BEDCHAMBER, Brendan changed into riding clothes. He'd decided against luncheon. His anger at Gaylord had robbed him of appetite. He came downstairs, the crop tucked under his arm, pulling on his gloves. In the hall, Redfern instructed a new underfootman. He turned as Brendan came in. "How is the baron, milord?"

"Not in any immediate danger, thank you, Redfern." Brendan settled his hat on his head. "I won't be in for luncheon. Please order a tray for Miss Peyton. She wishes to remain with her brother."

"Certainly, milord."

Brendan strode along the gravel drive to the stables with Hunter at his heels. In the courtyard, waiting for his horse to be brought out, he walked over to where the young, fair-headed stableboy swept the cobbles. "Jeremy, has Lord Gaylord been here in the last few days?"

"Yes, milord."

"Did you speak to him?"

Jeremy shook his head. "Devon had a word with him."

Devon, his head groom and stable manager, emerged from the stable interior, leading Bruno by the reins. He bowed his gray head. "Milord."

"I believe you had words with Lord Gaylord a day or so ago." Brendan patted his horse's glossy neck.

"Yes, milord. He inquired about Miss Peyton. I said I knew nothing. Didn't like it, got short with me."

"Did he indeed? See that the staff don't divulge any information to my uncle should he ask, no matter how trivial."

He mounted Bruno and rode out of the stable yard, Hunter running behind. Someone in his household must have talked to Gaylord. But who? Did his uncle have an ally at Beechley Park, supplying him with information? The lengths to which the man would go to discredit Brendan were both disquieting and unfathomable.

Turning Bruno's head, he rode toward the front gates. It was time to pay the man a visit and have a chat on Brendan's terms.

As he rode down the drive of Camelia Grove, his mother's childhood home, he viewed it with a sense of nostalgia and deep sadness. She had told him delightful stories of her life here before she'd married his father. His mother had loved her elder brother, Simon Mather, who'd died when he'd been twenty-four, but she'd rarely spoken of Ralph, his younger brother by two years, who'd inherited the title of Viscount Gaylord along with the estate. Back then, Brendan had never taken to his uncle. He'd sensed Gaylord had disliked him. Gaylord hadn't remained long in England after Brendan's parents' funeral, soon departing for a lengthy stay in France.

Brendan's father's trustees had taken control and while they'd dealt efficiently with the distressed and frightened boy he must have been, they'd lacked any understanding of what Brendan had really needed. Someone to hug him and explain why his parents were gone. Bewildered and grieving, he'd struggled to adapt to the unforgiving life at boarding school while left to deal with the tragic circumstances his father's apparent murderous rage had dealt him.

He dismounted and tossed the reins to a groom. "Look after my dog, Hunter."

"Aye, milord. Come, Hunter." The groom led the horse away. Hunter remained at Brendan's side until the groom's shrill whistle sent him bounding after him.

Brendan crossed to the front door of the pretty, pale-stone Georgian building. A butler, whom Brendan didn't know, answered the door. Brendan stripped off his gloves, aware of an ominous tightness at his temples. "Earl of Debnam. I don't believe we've met. Is your master in?"

The butler bowed. "Wallace, milord." He gestured to an upright chair. "Please be seated. I will advise Lord Gaylord you are here."

Forgoing the seat, Brendan strolled the length of the great hall. How odd the charming portrait of his mother had been removed from its usual place. It portrayed her barely out of the schoolroom, with a red ribbon in her hair, as she sat on a garden bench. The renowned artist Sir Joshua Reynolds had painted it. When Brendan had returned to live at Beechley Park four years ago, he had asked Gaylord if he might purchase it, but his uncle had refused, saying he was too fond of the painting to part with it. Brendan wondered if they had hung it in some other room.

With a discreet cough, the butler reappeared.

Brendan turned to address him. "Wallace, where is the Reynolds portrait of my mother dressed in a white gown, a small dog in her arms? It used to hang here. Is it now in the portrait gallery?"

Wallace looked mystified. "No, milord. I didn't find a portrait of your mother here when I first came several years ago. Nor can I say I've seen it anywhere else in the house."

Had Gaylord sold it? Brendan followed the butler to the library, attempting to quell the anger building inside him.

His uncle stood as he entered. He gestured to a chair. "Well, nephew, what has prompted this visit? It's been some time since we spoke, as I'm never invited to Beechley Park."

Brendan loathed his smug smile. Gaylord thought himself in the right, and to a certain degree, he was. "You wrote to Netterfield. Why stir up trouble?" Brendan asked, taking a seat. He had not intended to stay long, but he sank into a chair as his stomach roiled and his head throbbed.

Gaylord scowled. "Someone as gently bred as this young lady should not ride about your estate without a chaperone. Goodness knows what goes on behind closed doors."

Brendan clamped his jaw. He wasn't about to defend himself. It wasn't why he'd come here. "Her brother has arrived."

"Do you intend to marry Miss Peyton?"

"That's none of your business." Flashes of colored lights distorted his sight. His vision seemed to shrink, making it seem as if he gazed through a tunnel. He put a hand to his head. Why had he ignored the signs?

His uncle's voice seemed to come from far away. "You seem

out of sorts, Brendan."

"Just one of my headaches."

Through a distorted haze, Brendan saw Gaylord give a know-ing nod. "Your father suffered the same strange visions. You are wise not to marry. The madness could come upon you."

Brendan struggled to his feet. "Damn you, Gaylord. Keep your nose out of my business or you'll be sorry."

He heard Gaylord's scathing laugh as he flung himself out of the library. The throbbing pain and flashes of light strengthened. Somehow, he found his way to the stables, where a groom assisted him to mount.

Brendan remembered little of the ride home, but Bruno knew the way. Reaching the house, he slid from the saddle and was vaguely aware of Redfern's barked order and the two footmen running to catch him before he fell.

Chapter Eleven

DEBNAM HAD NOT visited the sickroom for two days. As her brother rallied, Laura knew that the time she and the earl could spend together ebbed away. Laura wanted to talk to him. Now that Robert needed less of her attention, she hoped to have a quiet moment with Debnam before she and her brother left.

She read to Robert as he sat propped up in bed with pillows, his luncheon on a tray before him. His appetite hadn't improved, and he was still unwell and querulous. He shoved the tray away. "I am sick of soup. Inform the cook I want meat for dinner."

Laura rushed to take it before the soup spilled. "The doctor said light foods are advisable. Perhaps tomorrow—"

"Tomorrow, we go home. I want to recuperate in my own bed. I don't want to be beholden to the earl a moment longer than I have to be."

Laura suspected his behavior stemmed more from guilt about sending her here. She wasn't about to mention it, though, aware of how sensitive Robert was to criticism. Any bad feeling would upset him and delay his recovery. She set the tray on the table. "You are making an excellent recovery. We might leave at the end of the week."

"Not soon enough. I said tomorrow. Where is Debnam? I thought he might have called in to see how I was."

Laura widened her eyes. "You want to see him?"

"I don't. But it's the decent thing for him to do, is it not?"

She was glad Debnam hadn't come. Robert was still ready to argue with him. Best he and Debnam saw little of each other before they left. She pushed back her hair with her forearm and sighed. What did they go home to? She wanted to ask Robert if he had paid his debts but was afraid to. Had he gambled away the money Debnam had given him?

A servant took the tray and Robert settled down for a nap. Laura left him and went downstairs, hoping to see Debnam. Redfern was in the great hall overseeing a maid who flicked a duster over the portraits. He turned to greet Laura with a smile. What a nice man he was, with nothing snooty or condemning in his manner. And there well might have been.

"How is your brother, Miss Peyton?"

"A little better today, thank you, Redfern. Has Lord Debnam gone away?"

Redfern hesitated, an eye on the maid, who had paused to listen. "Go to Mrs. Brandt, Beverley. She will have other chores in mind for you."

Once the maid had gathered up her box of cleaning materials and hurried out, Redfern turned to Laura. "His lordship suffered one of his attacks and took to his bed. They usually last a day or two."

"Oh, no. I am sorry." Shocked, Laura stared at the butler. "What form do they take?" she asked, deeply concerned for Brendan.

"Milord doesn't say, but his head aches and I believe his sight is affected."

"That sounds most unpleasant."

"Indeed, Miss Peyton. But his lordship is stoic."

Troubled, Laura left him and went outside for a walk. She breathed in air scented with summer greenery and flowers. The sun warmed her shoulders as she donned her bonnet, but she barely noticed as her thoughts remained on Debnam and his malady. Serious enough to strike a vigorous man down and send him to his bed for two days. Was he suffering still? She wished she could see him. Or perhaps help in some way. Penny had told her Debnam's father had suffered from spells. Was it the same complaint? Could it be a megrim? Her mother had suffered from them. She'd found some relief with a hot bag applied to her neck and a dose of feverfew.

Was this another reason Debnam might believe he took after his father? If only she could send word to him, suggest the heated poultice, but she couldn't. He would not appreciate her prying. He was a proud man, and, as Redfern had said, bore his affliction without fuss. What made her heart sore was how terribly alone he seemed. She knew only too well how that felt, with so few options available to her.

She returned to Robert, finding him awake, instructing a housemaid from his bed, who packed his few things in a portmanteau.

"It's a little early for that," Laura said. "I am hopeful you can get up tomorrow. We could go for a stroll together. The weather is glorious."

"We are leaving tomorrow. You must see to your luggage, Laura."

Alarmed, she worried he exhausted himself. But it was useless to argue with him. "Very well." She left him and went to her bedchamber. Would she see Debnam again before they departed? She hated to leave like this, without the chance to speak to him. He would be relieved to see the back of Robert, who was hardly an ideal guest. As for her, well, there really was nothing left to say.

While the afternoon stretched slowly toward dusk, Laura, frustrated and feeling helpless about a future which never lay in her hands, left her bedchamber and returned to the gallery to search for Debnam's ancestor, the fourth earl, whom Lord Gaylord had said had suffered from madness. She found his portrait easily. He stood out among the sober-faced portraits of his ancestors, with his broad smile and head of wild, curly, black hair. Portrayed in the dress of the times, he wore knee-length breeches, boots, and a cape. His stance, with a hand on his hip and that wide grin, made it appear as if he laughed at something—the painter, society, or life? Had he been a madman, as Gaylord had suggested? More of an adventurer, perhaps. But what had made him turn his back on his family to become a lawless criminal? His eyes, of an indeterminate color which might have been gray, seemed full of lively intelligence. Intrigued, she wished she could learn more about him. But she could hardly ask Debnam. Where might she find the family history? The library? If only she had more time.

On the way back upstairs, she first entered the library for a book on the family history which might mention the earl in question. She found one and carried it upstairs. When she entered Robert's bedchamber, she crossed to his bed, where he appeared to be deeply asleep, his face flushed. She touched his shoulder. "Robert."

He didn't respond. His skin burned hot when she touched his forehead, his breathing labored.

Laura gasped and ran to pull the bell. A footman answered promptly.

"Lord Netterfield has taken a bad turn," she said. "Please ask Redfern to send for the doctor."

BRENDAN OPENED HIS eyes. A gray light flooded the chamber, the curtains closed tight. He remembered taking the opiate, something he always tried to resist because he hated how it robbed him of his senses. How long had he been unconscious? He sat on the edge of the bed, holding his head in his hands, fuzzy with the effects of the drug. When his eyes cleared, he rose and rang for a footman.

"What time is it, Frederick?" he asked when the young footman entered carrying a tray.

"Past eleven o'clock, milord."

"In the morning?" Brendan took the coffee and drank the rich brew down. He winced as the footman pulled the curtain cord. "Leave the curtains." The light still hurt his eyes.

"Have I been here since yesterday?"

Frederick's smile faltered. "The day before, milord."

"Aah. I'll bathe, then. Bring hot water."

A half hour later, Brendan rapidly improved. He lay back in the hip bath, his head resting on a towel, thinking about Laura. He wondered how she and her brother fared. His absence would have surprised her, no doubt. Would Redfern have told her the reason behind it? He wasn't sure how he felt about that.

He quickly finished bathing and dressed, then went to knock on the baron's bedchamber door.

Laura opened it. There were dark circles beneath her lovely eyes, but she looked relieved to see him. "Robert has developed a high fever."

Brendan crossed to the bed. Her brother tossed restlessly, his face and neck flushed. "The doctor has been to see him?"

"Yes. He promised to return after attending to another patient. He expressed the view that the popular practice of bloodletting would not aid him. There is nothing to be done except to apply cool compresses, which I have done. We must wait for the fever to break."

"When did this fever develop?"

"Yesterday."

He took hold of Laura's hands. "I'm sorry I wasn't here."

"I understand. Redfern told me of your malaise."

Dash it all, it made him seem like a cursed weakling. He shrugged. "Just a damnable headache."

She studied his face. "And it has gone now?"

"Yes. You are too pale, Laura. Have you slept?"

"I grab a few hours when I can."

"Go out into the fresh air. It will make you feel better."

She shook her head. "I can't."

"A walk before luncheon, please."

She shook her head. "I don't like to leave him, Debnam."

"I'll stay with him. Go."

She nodded, warm gratitude in her blue eyes. "That is good of you. I shan't be long."

"The rose garden is in full bloom."

"Is it? I am very fond of roses."

But he doubted she'd walk that far. Or be in the right mood to enjoy it. "Robert is in good hands. Promise me you'll take your time."

"I will. You'll send for me if his condition changes?" She put a hand to her disordered locks, loose strands curling against her neck. As if she'd only just become aware of it. He found it infinitely attractive, as if she were rumpled from sleep, and it made him think of her waking in his bed after a night of passion.

At the door, she turned. "You are a good man."

It wasn't what he'd wanted to hear from her, but he smiled. "Go."

She closed the door behind her.

Robert moaned and turned over in bed, dragging the covers down. Brendan rose and went to straighten them.

"Water!"

Brendan raised the man's head and held the cup to his dry, chapped lips. After Robert had taken a few sips, Brendan settled him down again. "Try to sleep."

"Is it you, Father?" Robert asked.

He was delirious. A worrying sign. Brendan laid a hand on his forehead. It was fiery. A bowl of water and a cloth sat on the table beside the bed. He wrung it out and placed it on Robert's forehead, only to have him whip it off again. Brendan replaced it and this time, the cloth stayed. Deeply concerned for the young baron, and especially for Laura, he prayed the doctor would soon return. Did Phillips have nothing in his bag of tricks to ease this man's suffering?

A short time later, while Brendan observed the patient, the doctor hurried in, with Laura following.

"He drank a little water." Brendan stood, relieved to see him. "I'll leave him in your capable hands, Dr. Phillips."

Brendan enjoyed Laura's warm smile of gratitude before he went out the door. He doubted she'd walked as far as the rose garden. Perhaps he'd have the chance to show it to her himself.

As soon as Brendan stepped from the staircase onto the tiled floor, Redfern approached, as if he'd been lurking. "Are you well, milord?"

"I am, thank you, Redfern."

"The steward called yesterday. He mentioned a fence down in the south pasture. He has sent workers to mend it."

"I'll ride over and inspect their work."

Redfern's eyebrows rose, but he recovered himself. "Certainly, milord."

Brendan fought an amused smile threatening to lift his lips. His sudden interest in the actual workings of his estate seemed to have taken his butler by surprise. "Have a light meal sent to the library, will you?"

"I'll instruct the chef, milord."

The earl sat at his desk with the post and the newspapers, a ham and cress sandwich and an ale in front of him. He felt edgy, wondering what might be occurring upstairs. If only he could hold Laura close and ease her fears. But Robert's life was in the doctor's hands, and ultimately, God's.

The ride over the estate, with Hunter loping along behind him, cleared Brendan's mind of everything except for Laura, who, it seemed, still filled his every thought. She grew dearer to him with each day. Admitting it made him groan. But Gaylord, for all his sins, was right. Brendan could not consider marriage with Laura or any other woman. He would not bring a child into the world when they might be cursed, and pass it on for generations. It must stop with him.

Riding to the south pasture, he jumped Bruno over a hedge, and they cantered across the meadow to where two men dug holes in the ground for new fenceposts. They stopped to greet him. Brendan dismounted and rolled up his sleeves, glad of some good physical work, while Hunter dug his own hole in the dirt.

Brendan watched a worker dig a hole, then stepped closer to where the air smelled of moist earth. He grinned. "Let me know when you reach Australia."

The man stared at him. "Milord?"

"Too deep." Brendan took the spade from him and partly filled the hole. Then the three of them planted the post in the soil. Brendan turned to dig the next one, enjoying the stretch of muscles on his arms and back.

Two hours later, the fence mended, he rode home feeling better for the exercise, and something more vital too, which touched his heart and soul and seeped into his bones. He gazed around at the green pastures, flowering hedges and towering trees of his estate. Despite everything that had happened here to his parents and to him as a lad, he had come to love Beechley Park.

At the stables, Hunter yawned and stretched out on a sun-warmed patch of grass. "What a disappointment you are, Hunter." Brendan laughed to himself as he unbuckled Bruno's saddle.

"Care to share the joke, milord?" Devon asked as he took Bruno's saddle from him.

"A fox and her cubs crossed the meadow while Hunter slept the afternoon away."

Devon chuckled and shook his head.

"I'll leave you to see to Bruno," Brendan said. "Come on, Hunter, let's have a drink."

When he entered the house, he did not wish to intrude, so he sent a servant to inquire about the patient. The news came back. No change.

At his desk, a coffee cup at his elbow, he wondered what he might do to help Laura should Robert die. Cursing, he ran his fingers through his hair. Beyond offering his support, there was little. Her fool of a brother had better pull through.

Chapter Twelve

Laura spent the night in the chair beside Robert's bed. While her brother slept, she settled down with a book about the Debnam family history she'd found in the library. The writer had devoted a few paragraphs to the fourth Earl of Debnam, which convinced her he had not been mad, as Gaylord had suggested, but had lost his fortune when he'd fought the Roundheads. A Cavalier, he'd left his wife and son to fight for Charles II. The clever fifth Earl had restored the family's wealth.

Laura finally fell asleep curled up in the chair with the candles guttering. She woke at daylight when a maid pulled the curtains back and put a cup of chocolate and a plate of buttered bread on the table.

"The doctor is downstairs, madam."

Had she slept through a crisis? Laura jumped up and leaned over Robert. The sheets were soaked through. His fever must have broken during the night. He mumbled something while she checked beneath the bandage, which was damp and sweaty and needed to be changed. But there was no sign of infection. He was still very unwell and difficult to rouse, but she, so thankful for the improvement, let him sleep. The chocolate revived her as she waited for the doctor.

Dr. Phillips came in shortly afterward. He examined the patient and reassured her the worst was over. It looked like

Robert was on the mend.

Tears of relief filled Laura's eyes, and she quickly dabbed them away. When the doctor left, she attempted to tidy herself before the mirror, despairing at her badly creased dress. As she scrubbed a spot of chocolate from her lip, someone knocked on the door.

The housekeeper entered with two housemaids in tow. "I'm ordered to change his lordship's sheets, Miss Peyton."

"Good, Mrs. Brandt." The direction must have come from Debnam, who would have spoken to the doctor.

"I've brought a fresh nightshirt for the baron," the house-keeper said. "Can you change him? Or do you need help?"

As Robert had no valet, she would have to manage. How enraged he'd be to find a strange footman or young maids attending him. "No, thank you. I'll need a bowl of hot water, soap, and towels."

"I've sent for them." Mrs. Brandt approached the bed and drew down the covers, exposing Robert's long legs and big feet. Laura hurriedly pulled down his nightshirt, which rode high on his thighs.

The housekeeper addressed the two maids, who stood gazing at Robert. "Close your mouths, girls. Have you never seen a man in his nightshirt?"

"I've seen me pa and me brothers," one of the maids said. "Cared for them when they was sick."

"Then your help will be invaluable," the housekeeper said, sounding unconvinced.

"I hope 'e gets better. 'E's that handsome." The younger maid put a hand to her mouth.

"He's a body in need of care, Cathleen," Mrs. Brandt said sharply as she rolled Robert onto his side. He grunted but fortunately didn't wake. They rolled him back the other way and pulled away the damp bottom sheet, then adeptly removed pillow cases and the top sheet.

Marveling at the housekeeper's efficiency, Laura assisted her while they remade the bed around him.

As they firmly tucked the blanket in, Robert opened an eye. "Tell them to go away, Lolly."

"Mrs. Brandt has changed your sheets. You will feel much better in a little while," Laura said as a maid brought the bowl of hot water, soap, and towels.

"There," Mrs. Brandt said with a satisfied look about the room. "Shall I leave you to wash and change him?"

"Yes. Thank you, Mrs. Brandt. My brother will be much more comfortable. I know he'll be grateful when he is fully awake."

Left alone, Laura went about her task. Robert drifted off again as she washed his face, neck, and hands and dried him. She struggled to dress him in the clean nightshirt, admitting she was not as competent as the housekeeper. While attempting to get Robert's arms into the sleeves, he stirred and tried to push her away.

Debnam came in and joined her at the bedside. "Let me help you."

As it always did when he was near, Laura's heart skipped a beat. She puffed away a wisp of hair and wiped her forehead. "I would appreciate it."

Together, the task was quickly done, and Robert settled back into the clean linens.

"Thank you, Debnam. I could not have managed alone."

"His fever has broken. A promising sign."

"Yes. During the night. Dr. Phillips is pleased."

She sank into the chair and looked at Robert, who frowned. His eyes opened, and he stared blearily up at Debnam. "Why is the earl here?"

"Lord Debnam helped me to change you. Without his care, you would have died, you ungrateful wretch," Laura said crossly, out of patience with him.

Debnam put a hand on her shoulder to shush her. He glanced at Robert, who continued to glare at him. "You don't deserve your sister, Netterfield."

Debnam's eyes, when he looked into hers, grew gentle with understanding. "I'll leave you to it. Don't forget the rose garden."

When the door closed behind him, Robert groaned. "He's right. I don't deserve you, Lolly." He gave her a soul-searching look. "Am I about to die?"

"No. You are improving, according to the doctor."

Robert yawned. "I am dreadfully tired."

She urged him to drink a little water. "Sleep. When you wake, you might like some food."

Robert fell asleep again, and Laura tiptoed from the room, thinking of Debnam as she returned to her bedchamber. She'd gone through so many changes since she'd come here, from anger and suspicion to a deep attraction and sympathy for his plight, and now admiration. He was brave and considerate, and something she hadn't expected: honorable. But was that all he meant to her? She dared not dwell on her feelings too deeply. It would only hurt more after they left. Now Robert was on the mend, their departure would be soon. They could not in all conscience continue to enjoy Debnam's hospitality.

While Penny was downstairs at luncheon, Laura enjoyed the quiet. She washed and changed into her muslin gown embroidered with pink flowers. She tidied her hair as best she could, vexed by how tired she looked. In her jewelry box, she selected dainty, pearl earrings in a gold setting and the matching locket to make herself feel better. Then she went downstairs, hopeful of some luncheon. She'd eaten little at breakfast.

Debnam emerged from the library as she passed. "Good to see you downstairs, Laura."

Could he really be pleased to see her when she hardly looked her best? She couldn't help but smile, thinking of what he'd initially planned for the two of them, and what he'd gotten instead.

Amused, gray eyes met hers. "Why the smile?"

"My brother is rallying," she said to put him off.

"Mm. Not in the best of tempers, is he?"

"No. I'm sorry. But if he continues to improve, we shall be able to leave within a few days."

"I am not eager for that to happen, Laura," he said. She found herself pleased that he felt that way. "Will you join me for luncheon?"

"Thank you. I will. Now that Robert improves, I find so has my appetite," she admitted.

At one end of the long dining table, everything necessary for a light meal had been laid out. A joint of cold lamb, sliced ham, cheese, bread rolls, butter, salad, and plum pie and cream.

After serving them, the footmen left the room. She wondered if Debnam had banished them.

"Wine?" he asked.

"No, thank you. If I drink wine, I shall fall asleep at the table."

"You are tired."

Not quite the glamorous mistress he envisaged, she thought with regret. A failure all around.

His eyebrows rose. "Did you go to bed at all last night?"

"Now that Robert is gaining in strength, I shall sleep well tonight."

He nodded and attacked the leg of lamb with a carving knife, cutting neat slices.

"Lamb?"

"Yes, please." She put a little mustard on her plate and buttered a roll. Adding a slice of lamb, she took a large bite. "Mm. Heavenly," she said, chewing, a hand to her mouth.

He laughed. "My chef, Arnaud, will be pleased. After we eat, will you come for a walk? We can visit the rose garden."

She lifted her eyebrows. "You first ordered me there some days ago." She wanted to tease him. To make him laugh again. His laugh was infectious and made her grin. And he so rarely laughed.

"I ordered you?"

"You are inclined to order me about. How do you know I

didn't go to see the roses?"

He narrowed his eyes, then smiled. "And have you?"

"No," she admitted with a grin.

"I know this much about you, Laura. You would never leave your brother if he needed you. Not for such a frivolous reason. Or am I wrong?"

"I suppose you are right," she admitted. While a little flattered, she disliked how easily he saw through her when he himself remained a mystery. And he obviously intended to keep it that way. She had hoped they might talk about what troubled him, but he clammed up when she gently prodded. Accepting it, Laura felt happy just being here with him.

"I always know when you're unsure, or in doubt," he said softly. "You catch your bottom lip in your teeth."

It sounded so intimate, which was absurd, but she ducked her head and continued to cut her meat. He could read her like a book. It didn't seem fair. "I shall be careful not to do so in the future," she said. She looked up and saw he watched her, his gray eyes troubled. The light-hearted moment they had shared vanished, as fragile as a bubble that floated away and burst too soon.

"Well, as I clearly haven't seen the rose garden, will you escort me there?" she said, a lift in her voice, wanting to regain their earlier lighthearted banter.

"Delighted." He smiled. "You have mustard on your mouth. Here." He gestured to the corner of his well-formed mouth while his eyes met hers, so sensual. A lick of flame warmed her from head to toe. When she removed the spicy mustard with her tongue, she thought he sighed.

She questioned him about the estate, and he seemed happy to talk about it. It appeared to be very large and exceedingly well run.

They left the dining room after their coffee, walking out into the garden. They neared the rose garden, the air scented with their sweet perfume. The glorious display made her catch her breath. Walking along the rows, she bent to study a red rose. "Such a lush bloom, and what a beautiful color," she murmured.

"The gardeners have surpassed themselves this year." He leaned over and picked the rose, presenting it to her. "A rose for a rose, whom I shall miss."

Laura's chest tightened. She wanted to say so much and yet must not. Debnam brushed a lock of her hair away from her cheek. A good hand, well-shaped with long fingers. The hand that had touched her body in places no other man had done, or was likely ever to do. Was it only she who felt the air become hushed with wanting? She wished he would kiss her, enfold her in his arms, but knew he would not. If she had lain with him, could she ever have left him?

She distracted herself by recalling that Robert was alone in his bedchamber and still far from well. It helped to pull herself together. "I must return upstairs."

He sighed audibly, the magic broken. "Yes. I suppose you must."

Laura left him at the staircase and hurried up, her heart still beating too fast. Why must she be made to feel shame because she wanted to feel passion? To enjoy a man's love? To be happy? She took several deep breaths to calm herself before she entered Robert's room, unsure of what she would find.

"There you are." Robert sat up in bed with a sling on his right arm, which the doctor had put on earlier. His luncheon tray, stacked with the empty plates, sat on the table. "You've been gone for hours."

She smiled and shook her head. "Am I not also allowed to eat?" She glanced at the tray. "I'm pleased to see you have regained your appetite."

"I ordered meat for supper. They would like to turn me into a milksop, eating their soft food."

"It would have been on the doctor's orders." She sat on the edge of the bed. "I am very relieved to see you're getting better."

Robert nodded his head. "Friday, Laura. We finally go

home."

"If you are well enough, Robert."

"I will be."

Two more days, Laura thought. *And then this will be all but a memory.*

"You will be glad to go, too," Robert said. "It must have been difficult here for you while I was ill."

That he gave any thought to her at all surprised her. "Lord Debnam has made us very comfortable. You must thank him, Robert. Or your bad manners will embarrass me."

"All right. But it wasn't my fault. Lord Gaylord sent that letter to rouse me to anger. Anyone would have acted as I did."

"Not everyone, but I imagine he wrote it with that aim."

"Why would he? A person doesn't say such things unless there is some truth to it."

"There isn't. I took it upon myself to roam the estate grounds alone, although Debnam wished a maid to accompany me. And I met Gaylord twice. I suspect he had some axe to grind. We certainly cannot blame Lord Debnam."

Robert shook his head. "According to Gaylord, Debnam is likely to become mad and dangerous at any time. Naturally, it brought me here in a hurry, determined to defend you, as any brother would."

"He said that, exactly?"

"Yes." He groaned. "I can't wait to have you safely home again, Lolly."

"It was cruel of Gaylord, and utter nonsense," she said. "But we shall leave as soon as it's safe for you to travel." Robert nodded and leaned his head back on the pillow. It appeared he had forgotten the appallingly selfish way he'd acted when he'd sent her here.

IN THE LIBRARY, while awaiting his steward, Brendan thought of those precious moments spent with Laura. When he was with her, life seemed more normal, just a man enjoying a comfortable conversation with a beautiful woman. He didn't have to flatter her or make promises, which mistresses demanded. Laura took him as he was and often made him laugh. How long had it been since he'd laughed, really laughed, with a woman? He joked with his friends, Tate and Hart, when they rode in Hyde Park or played cards, and he enjoyed their companionship, but once he returned home, the low mood enveloped him. Refusing to burden those two happily married men with his concerns, he rarely spoke of his past. Even though it caused a wall between them, and they were observant enough to recognize it.

A knock sounded on the door.

"Come."

His steward entered.

"Take a seat, Crosby. We have quite a few matters to discuss."

"Yes, milord." As Crosby covered concerns pertaining to the estate, Brendan listened and made the odd comment, welcoming the distraction. His recent interest in how the estate was run, and how his tenants fared, had come as a surprise even to himself. It heartened him because it seemed the life he had feared he would never enjoy was not entirely beyond him. Since Laura had come, he'd traveled down a different path. Not what he wished for, but one he might find rewarding all the same. He glanced up at his father's portrait. He had died at thirty-three years of age. If Brendan had only those few years until he reached the same age left, he would make the most of them.

Chapter Thirteen

LAURA ROSE FROM her bed, the sky beyond the window a vast, blue landscape dotted with white clouds. The early morning sunlight reflected off the glass into her chamber.

When donning her dressing gown, Penny came in with a tray and set Laura's chocolate, a buttered roll, and a pot of jam on the table. While the maid scurried about preparing the bath, Laura sipped the hot beverage. Would she see Debnam this morning? Alone? She decided to broach the subject of his parents. He needed to know that she knew about them. And that she would always think of him and hope he was happy.

After Laura saw to Robert's needs, she left the house for a brisk walk and her last glimpses of beautiful Beechley. She chose a different direction to avoid Lord Gaylord. Should he lurk about. She strolled along the avenue beneath aged, gnarled oak trees, their branches a leafy arch overhead. When she walked out into the warm sun, the ornate front gates and gate house were ahead of her, the gates standing open. An old man sat on the ground with his back against one of the tall, stone pillars, his head bowed.

Laura approached him. "Are you all right, sir?"

Unfolding his long legs, he climbed to his feet and removed his shabby beaver hat. The man's curly, brown hair was gray at the temples. His craggy face broke into a smile. "Now, why would a young miss concern herself about me?"

"I'm happy to assist you, if I can."

His old-fashioned, charming bow made her smile. "Wagstaff, miss. I came to see the steward seeking employment. But I'm told there is nothing to suit the likes of me."

"Miss Laura Peyton." She offered her hand, and he hesitated before he shook it firmly. He reminded her of their butler, who had passed away several years ago, never to be replaced. Wagstaff wasn't as old as she'd first thought. Although shabbily dressed, he looked neat and clean, his hair and whiskers trimmed. "What sort of work, sir?"

"Sadly, my standards have been lowered by necessity."

"What did you do before?"

"I was butler to Lord Gaylord. He put me off a few years ago. I found temporary work in one of the big houses in the district while they were shorthanded, but now..." He spread his arms and shrugged. "I am here, as you see, seeking a new position."

Gaylord! That ghastly man. She wondered if Mr. Wagstaff had a pension. It could not have been generous. "A butler? That is an important position within a household."

He straightened and pushed out his narrow chest. "Indeed, it is."

"What occurred with Lord Gaylord? Do you mind telling me?"

"No, but ah, it's a long story. Lord Gaylord took a set against me and refused to give me a reference. Something I said and shouldn't have. But that's me, cannot keep my mouth shut to save my life. Or to keep my position." He frowned. "But when something needs to be said, one must speak. Do you not think so?"

Laura nodded, wondering what it had been about. He seemed reluctant to tell her. "I doubt he's a nice man."

"That he is not."

"What will you do now, Mr. Wagstaff?"

"I'll walk back to the village, although it will do me little good. There's no work for me there." He smiled. "You are a kind lady, Miss Peyton. But you mustn't worry yourself about an old fellow like me."

While they talked, Laura walked part of the way along the road with him. It was at least a ten-mile walk to the village. An idea formed. She stopped and placed a hand on his arm, upset by how thin he was. "My brother and I are guests of the earl's, Mr. Wagstaff. Lord Netterfield and I return home to Longworth, my brother's estate in Surrey, tomorrow. We don't have a butler. Nor, I must admit, do we have need of one. But I'm sure there's other work you could do there. That's if Lord Netterfield agrees with the arrangement," she added hastily. She would have to be careful how she put this to Robert for him to see the sense of it. "Could you remain here while I ask him?"

His twinkling, blue eyes brightened. "Happy to. I sincerely thank you, Miss Peyton."

"Don't thank me yet," she said with a smile. "My brother might not agree." She turned and retraced her steps, hurrying back to the porch and the front door. Before she reached it, Debnam rode around the corner from the direction of the stables. He reined in Bruno and leaned down to her. "You look more rested today. You've been for a walk?"

"I met an old gentleman at the front gates. Mr. Wagstaff was once Lord Gaylord's butler."

Debnam raised his eyebrows. "Wagstaff? I remember him many years ago. A kindly fellow, as I recall."

"I appreciate your endorsement."

He raised his dark eyebrows. "You wish to engage him? He must be at least sixty."

"I like him. He's fallen on hard times and is too thin. But he is keen to work. I hope to convince Robert."

Debnam's gaze roamed her face. "So, you leave tomorrow?"

"Yes, Robert believes he is well enough. He is determined."

He nodded. "Would you ride with me this afternoon?"

A swift rush of pleasure sent tingles racing down her spine. "Of course. I would enjoy one more ride on Honey."

"Two o'clock." Debnam nodded to her and rode on. Laura stared after him. He seemed intent on them being alone. And while she knew whatever happened between them wouldn't change anything, she wanted to be with him very much.

Laura was pleased to find Robert had left his bed. He sat in a chair reading a periodical on estate management, a subject which surprised her. If only it could be a sign of better things to come.

"Where have you been this morning?" he asked.

"I went for a walk."

"Why you enjoy roaming for miles in the summer heat is a mystery to me."

She sat in the chair beside him, carefully forming her words in her head. "Robert, I have something important to ask you."

He raised his eyebrows, then tossed the magazine onto a table. "That sounds serious. What is it?"

"You know how hard it is for me to manage at home with so few servants."

He nodded. Was that shame which flittered across his face?

"Robert, I want to employ a gentleman I met this morning."

He stared at her. "Another footman? I admit we have needed a housekeeper since Mrs. Finch left. But I don't see the necessity of..."

"Mr. Wagstaff was once butler to Lord Gaylord," she said hurriedly. "He is looking for work. He would make an excellent addition to our household."

Robert shook his head. "We have no need of a butler."

"Mr. Wagstaff is prepared to do any kind of work. He could help you sort your books. You've wanted to restore order to the library for ages. It's difficult to find servants who can manage that kind of work."

Robert scratched his cheek, looking pensive. "I suppose that's true."

"Shall I tell him?" Laura asked, encouraged. "Mr. Wagstaff waits for me at the gates. He can accompany us to Longworth tomorrow in the coach. I am confident he will make a perfect factotum. You will be impressed, Robert. He is such a well-mannered gentleman."

Robert shook his head. "Although financially, we're out of the woods at the moment, I have plans. There is work to be done to the house, the woodlands, and the home farm, not to mention the tenants. I will engage an estate manager. So it's doubtful we can stretch to—"

"Have you visited London since I've been away, Robert?"

He scowled at her. "No. If you think I've returned to the card tables again, you're wrong." His eyes pleaded forgiveness. "It's my intention to improve the estate. I won't place it in jeopardy again."

"I'm sure you will succeed if you set your mind to it." While she still didn't trust him, she couldn't help but be caught by his enthusiasm. "Please, Robert. You owe me this."

He shrugged, his gaze darting away from hers. "Very well, if you must," he said after a moment. "But you have a history of bringing home strays, Lolly. That deer with the injured foot, and the bird with the broken wing, not to mention the cats! One had six kittens in the kitchen and nearly gave Cook the apoplexy."

"Mrs. Amery has grown fond of the cats. She always has one on her lap when she's sitting by the kitchen fire in the evening."

"She complains they run away with her wool."

"But she thinks they are exceptional ratters."

He sighed heavily. "Dare I hope your collection of homeless creatures ends with Tibby? And that goes for the human variety as well."

"You love Tibby. You allow him to sleep on your desk while you work."

"I have grown fond of the animal," he said with a soft smile.

She picked up her bonnet. "I'll tell Mr. Wagstaff the good news. Oh, and I'm riding after luncheon."

Robert frowned. "The devil you are. With Debnam, I suppose."

"He wishes to show me a little of the estate."

"I can't fathom the earl. He seems to like you. I've noticed the way he looks at you. But it is passing strange that he now wants to send you home." Robert frowned, and she sensed he wanted to order her to take a groom along with them, as he once would have. But those days were gone. He must have been curious about what had occurred between her and Debnam.

"You know, Debnam has never touched me inappropriately," she said, running her bonnet ribbons through her fingers. Not quite true, but it would do.

Robert drew in a sharp breath. "Naturally, I'm pleased to hear that. But his actions are hardly those of a rational being, are they?"

She loathed his suggestion that Debnam might not have been normal, but then, he did not know the circumstances. "It hardly matters now, does it? After tomorrow, I shan't see him again."

Laura left the room, relieved her voice hadn't given away her despair. But she had won a minor battle with Robert. She only hoped Wagstaff would prove a sound investment. Her instincts told her he would. She was good at summing up people she met. It was only Debnam who had fooled her. But she suspected he'd had a lot of practice at hiding his true self from society.

Mr. Wagstaff stood at the estate gates, his hat in his hand. Expressing his delight at the offer, he promised to be at Beechley Park at first light. She wondered where he would spend the night and hoped he didn't have to trudge for miles carrying his luggage. But she didn't ask, unable to offer anything more for the fear that Robert would change his mind.

Laura ate luncheon with Robert in the dining room to keep him company and ensure he said nothing untoward to Debnam. But they dined alone when Debnam sent word he could not join them. After the meal, she ran up and changed into her habit. Penny assisted her with her boots. "I am that sorry you're leaving tomorrow, milady," Penny said, giving a last-minute polish to the footwear with her sleeve. "I wish I could still be your lady's maid. You've been kind to me."

"I wish you could too, Penny, but unfortunately, it's not possible." To suggest to Robert that they take the maid along would be the last feather to break the camel's back.

Laura came downstairs to find Debnam waiting in the hall, hat and crop in his gloved hands. How the clothes suited him. Her gaze wandered from his broad shoulders to his narrow hips and powerful thighs. She glanced quickly away from the shape of his body in the snug-fitting breeches.

As they left the porch and walked to the stables, she smiled at him. "Where are you taking me?"

His answer was swift. "Where I will have you to myself."

The desire and purpose in his eyes made Laura's breath catch.

At the stables, she patted Honey. The horse seemed to recognize her and nudged her with her nose. If only she could save the mare from Tattersalls auction and an uncertain future.

On the mounting block, Laura accepted Debnam's hand. She placed her foot in the stirrup and swung up onto the saddle. Tucking her leg around the pommel, she arranged her skirts. "I hope Honey's new owner will be gentle with her," she said as she took up the reins.

Mounted on Bruno, he smiled. "You have a soft heart, Laura. I don't wish to breed with her. If I kept her, she would languish in the paddock. Would that be kind?"

She sighed. "No, I suppose not."

Honey followed Bruno along a bridle path, through the woods. They emerged where a few willows leaned gracefully over the water. Beyond the river were distant, green hills, and sheep in the meadow. When he helped her down, his large hands and familiar manly scent reminded her of how big and powerful a man he was. And yet he could be gentle. She thought of the first time he had kissed her. It seemed longer than a few days ago.

When he'd tied up the horses, Debnam turned back to her. "I wanted us to have time alone before you go."

"And I." How much should she tell him? She had decided and now almost lost her courage. Would he welcome what she had discovered about his parents? With so little time, was there nothing she could say to alter his perception of himself? She knew him to be a rational man. He would require evidence, not supposition. And apparently, no one had an answer for what had caused his father to kill his mother and then turn the gun on himself.

Debnam's eyes were the color of clouds before a rain burst. "I want you to know how much your company has meant to me these few precious days."

"I shall never forget my time here with you." Laura stroked a finger along his jaw. "Debnam, I know about your parents. A servant told me what happened." Tears filled her eyes, and she blinked them away. "Such a dreadful tragedy."

His eyebrows lowered. "I saw no sense in telling you, Laura. It is in the past."

"But the past can have a way of informing the present and the future. It must not ruin your life. You are an honorable man."

"My father was a man of integrity and high moral character." A muscle jumped in his jaw.

"Will you tell me more about it?"

His eyes turned bleak, unfocused, as if he were back there, in that moment. "My parents were in my father's private sitting room. I was on my way to join them when I heard Father yell, and then the sound of two shots. I ran in and found them. They were alone, crumpled and bleeding on the floor, and the gun, part of my father's dueling set, lying close to his hand."

"Oh, Debnam. Could someone else have..." She hated that she'd stirred these shocking memories up again.

He shook his head. "Impossible for anyone to shoot them then flee unseen. My father must have lost his mind with rage over something. There had been no sign of it beforehand." He raised his sad gaze to hers. "It's been said he was mad."

Laura moved to touch him, to try to banish all the times he had needed loving and had so little.

But Debnam shook his head. "I will not chance bringing a

babe into this doomed family. Nor will I risk a wife."

She saw how impossible it was to change his mind. His belief was too indelibly ingrained in his psyche. And there was nothing to refute it. She bowed her head and fell silent.

When she raised her face to him, his eyes still revealed his torment. But his voice was controlled, resigned. "I have come to terms with my lot, Laura. And so must you. Promise me you will not live out your life as a spinster in your brother's house."

A sudden thought leaped to her mind, one she'd never voiced before, but she knew to be true. "I'll just go on loving you for as long as I live, so it matters not whether you send me away."

Once Robert married, she doubted he and his bride would welcome her at Longworth. Debnam was right. Such a life would be insupportable.

Debnam groaned. "Sweetheart, knowing you love me means so much to me." He hesitated, and she waited for him to say he loved her too. But he merely shook his head. "It is what it is. We must endure."

"Then kiss me goodbye."

He framed her face in his hands and kissed her with a fierce passion. Breathlessly tearing his lips from hers, he buried his face in the warmth of her neck.

Laura flung her head back and clung to his coat as her knees weakened. His arms tight around her, he molded her to his hard, heated body. Held within his muscular arms, they kissed again. Their panting breaths mingled. Desire and need settled heavy and low in her stomach. She never wanted him to stop. For this to never end. That *he* should be the one. The thought of any other man touching her was an abomination.

With a groan, he pushed away from her, leaving her chilled and bereft. "Choose a good man who will love you and treat you well, Laura," he said, his voice husky. He didn't want that any more than she did.

And she hated to hear those words and might have shaken her head, but he raised her chin with his finger, lowered his head, and kissed her mouth again, then proceeded with tiny kisses across her cheek and beneath her ear. His soft, warm breath stirred the fine hairs on her neck and made her shiver. When he was near, that low throb in her stomach began and she lost her breath. Pressed against him, a hand at his nape, she pulled his head down to kiss him passionately. As if she could change everything by the sheer force of her will.

"*Laura.*" He broke away with a groan. The despair in his eyes mirrored her own.

"You mustn't worry about me. I'm stronger than I look."

With a small smile, he searched her eyes for a sign of her determination. "I know that. I'm counting on it."

The idea of facing the *ton* again was abhorrent, but she was determined not to say so. It would be unfair to leave him concerned about her.

"We'd best go back." Debnam took her hand, and they walked along the path to the horses, while Laura, conscious of his strong, long-fingered clasp, bit her lip and tried to hold back the tears.

The time they'd spent together hadn't been nearly enough. It wasn't fair. It had only left her wanting more.

BRENDAN WOKE BEFORE dawn. He lay in his bed with an arm over his eyes, dreading the coming day. Then he rose and dressed and walked out into the cool, morning air to the stables. Bruno whinnied when the horse spied Brendan, while Honey watched him with her soft, dark eyes. He stood watching Netterfield's coach horses put in their traces for the journey and stayed to talk to the coachman until he, the footman, and the groom mounted the box and ordered the horses to walk on. Then Brendan followed it back to the front of the house, where Laura, Netterfield, and Wagstaff had gathered on the drive for the journey home.

As the footmen strapped the luggage to the back of the coach, Netterfield strolled over and offered his hand. "Well, Debnam, I must thank you for your hospitality."

Obviously, the baron had no wish to take responsibility for his appalling behavior, the result of his self-inflicted injury, and his prolonged stay at Beechley Park.

"No need." Brendan shook his hand. "I would do anything to help your sister."

The baron flushed deep crimson. "Yes, well. This didn't turn out quite as planned. I'm sorry, but mistakes were made."

Brendan turned his back on him. He walked over to Wagstaff, who stood a little apart.

"Good to see you, Wagstaff." Brendan offered his hand.

"I remember you well, milord," Wagstaff said, giving it a hearty shake. "Those times as a lad you visited Camelia Grove with the countess. When Master Simon was alive, that was."

"I haven't forgotten the chocolate drops you gave me." Brendan grinned. "I didn't tell my mother. She would have confiscated them until after dinner."

Wagstaff chuckled. Then his expression saddened. "My lord, I wasn't able to offer my condolences—"

"No need," Brendan hastened to say. "A long time ago now." He turned to Laura. "Thank you for your delightful company, Miss Peyton. Most especially the night we played billiards, and your skillful game was my undoing."

She knew only too well what he really referred to, and for a moment, their gazes lingered. Then she shook her head with a smile. "Not so. You were gallant, Lord Debnam. And an excellent host. I have enjoyed our stay here in your beautiful home."

Her eyes told him what she could not say. She remembered as he did the night they'd come so close to becoming lovers. It would have been the act of a scoundrel, but he couldn't help wishing there could have been more between them. More to remember of her.

The footman stood ready to assist Laura up the steps. She turned back to Brendan, her eyes suddenly wide with concern. "Might you have altered your plans about Honey? Is she still to be sent to auction?"

He came forward and gestured to the footman to step aside. "I have other plans for Honey. I believe you would approve."

Laura raised her eyebrows in evident query, then rewarded him with her sweet smile as he assisted her into the carriage.

Netterfield, then Wagstaff, joined Laura inside. The door closed, and the coach rattled away along the drive.

Brendan saw her face at the window, her hand raised in farewell. He watched until the coach had disappeared. Strangely empty, as if his future had gone with Laura, and fearing all that was left was a dry husk of a life, he went back inside. He whistled for Hunter. "I'll go for a ride before breakfast, Redfern," he said to the butler as the dog skated around the corner of the hall, his big feet sliding on the marble tiles.

Some hours later, he rode out of the woods, the dog panting behind him, having exhausted himself in his determination to keep Bruno in sight. Brendan had ridden far and fast while he'd come to terms with his life. Whatever that might hold for him.

Chapter Fourteen

Fortunately, Robert slept for most of the journey to Longworth. It allowed Laura and Wagstaff to have a long chat. Laura thirsted for anything that concerned Debnam, and Wagstaff seemed happy to talk. He told her about his work as butler to the previous viscount at Camelia Grove, at the time when Debnam's mother, Constance, and his father had married. "It was an excellent position while the old Viscount Gaylord lived. The staff were treated well in those days." Wagstaff stroked his chin, appearing to gaze back into the past.

"How did the older brother, Simon Mather, die?"

"They found him dead of knife wounds in the lane behind the tavern in Chichester. No one knows why he went there. Some at the inquest suggested his lordship might have been involved in smuggling bolts of silk, brandy, and tea across the Channel from France. But I never believed it and no evidence of his association with smugglers was ever found."

"Was his brother with him at the time?"

"No. The brothers were very different and not close. When Master Ralph inherited the title, the mood of the house changed. He treated his servants shabbily and some left. And after the viscountess passed, and Miss Constance became Lady Debnam, she seldom came to Camelia Grove." He sighed. "Such a sweet lady. The servants missed her visits. She always brought a treat for the staff, some who had been in service since she'd been a girl."

They talked on as the miles passed, breaking the journey once to water the horses and take luncheon at a coaching inn. Robert stirred himself and joined them for the meal, but his mood had not improved. He was clearly irritated with her for engaging Wagstaff, but despite his objection, she was pleased with the arrangement. She liked the old butler and the small window he'd opened into Debnam's life fascinated her.

"The current Lord Debnam was a lively lad. I used to watch him on my days off when he played cricket on the village green with the other children, while his mother shopped. There was nothing uppity about the countess or the earl. And neither is his lordship prideful, I'm pleased to see.

"But that all changed with the tragic death of the earl and the countess," Wagstaff recalled as the coach continued the journey. Robert appeared to be listening but made no attempt to interrupt. "I heard his lordship found them dead of gunshot wounds. Ten years old, and known to be fond of both parents—the shock would have crushed the poor lad. Then, soon afterward, to be sent away to boarding school. So very hard on Lord Debnam. The tragedy must have had a profound and lasting effect on his life, for I'm told he failed to come back to live at Beechley Park for years, having spent a lengthy time on the Continent. I'd left by then and a new butler had taken my place, so I hadn't set eyes on him until today. A housemaid I met in the village told me they seldom see the earl there, nor does he attend church." He paused. "Lord Debnam appears a strong man, and I wish him well."

Robert, finally becoming bored, interrupted to question Wagstaff about his experience. While her brother was still wary and critical, it pleased Laura nevertheless to see him taking an interest. The discussion soon turned to the needs of the library and the changes Robert wished to bring about.

"The books are to be catalogued," Robert said, eyeing Wagstaff.

"I am sure I can manage that to my lord's satisfaction," Wagstaff said with confidence.

Robert raised a skeptical eyebrow, but said nothing.

Dusk had fallen as they approached Longworth's gates. Coach lanterns sent swaying halos of warm light over the graveled drive as they traveled through the park. When the coachman pulled the horses up before the house, Peter, one of their two remaining footmen, rushed to open the door and helped with the luggage, while Ellen, the upstairs maid, hovered in the great hall to attend to coats and hats.

When they entered the house, Robert disappeared into the library, after ordering the footman to take hot water to their chambers.

Laura took Wagstaff down to the servants' hall, where the staff ate supper.

The delicious aroma of beef pie and potatoes wafted out from the room. When she entered, the servants put down their knives and forks and moved to rise. Laura gestured for them to remain seated. "I shan't keep you from your tasty meal. This is Mr. Wagstaff, a new member of the household. His duties will be varied." She addressed their senior footman. "Please help him settle in, William. And once supper is over, show the gentleman to his chamber."

A rumble of welcome passed around the table, and Betty, the kitchen maid, gestured to the vacant chair beside hers with a friendly grin.

Laura nodded to Cook. "Mrs. Amery, would you prepare a meal for Mr. Wagstaff? Lord Netterfield and I will take a light supper in our bedchambers."

Their plump, cheerful cook put a hand to her light-brown hair, rose, and smoothed her apron. "Certainly, milady."

Laura climbed the stairs wearily. Above her, on the landing, a whiskery face gazed down at her. "There you are, Tibby." She scooped the soft body up in her arms and took the cat to her bedchamber. Shutting the door, she sat in a chair with Tibby purring on her lap. A small coal fire burned in the grate. The nights were still cool here, and it helped remove some of the chill and damp of the old house, but it failed to warm the icy knot deep inside. Although she'd promised Debnam she would consider marrying, right now, it seemed impossible. There would never be another to equal Debnam in her eyes. She questioned her feelings, at first wondering if sympathy drew her to him. Robert considered her soft heart a flaw in her character. But as she'd gotten to know Debnam and had been drawn to him, Laura knew it to be much more than that. She loved him.

Trying not to think of him, she drew her mind to more practical matters. Her bedchamber had not been dusted in her absence, nor the stairs or the carpet runners in the corridors. There was much to be done before she could consider leaving for London.

As the weeks passed, Wagstaff settled into the household remarkably quickly and soon became a favorite of the staff. Under his supervision, the cobwebs disappeared from the great hall, the stair banister polished, and the hall rugs were taken up and beaten. The rooms smelled of lavender and beeswax. Wagstaff restored the silver in the old butler's pantry, and with some secret ingredient he'd fetched from the kitchen, disclosed to him by the old viscount's valet, he'd buffed Robert's boots to a mirror shine. No job seemed too menial for Wagstaff. He mended a strap on Laura's dancing slipper, saving her the cost of a new pair, and made himself useful in the kitchen without getting in Cook's way. In the evenings, he and Mrs. Amery sat together after dinner with the four cats at their feet. While she knitted, and the staff noisily played snap or gossiped in the staff hall, Wagstaff told Cook about his life at Camelia Grove.

Laura, having come down to fetch her slipper, paused outside the door to listen as Wagstaff vividly described life, not only in Camelia Grove, but Debnam's family on the neighboring estate, making them come alive for her.

Even Robert seemed satisfied with Wagstaff, who worked

diligently in the library, cataloging the books, directing the maid, dusting the shelves, and restoring order.

More at peace with himself, Robert made no trips to the gaming hells in London, nor did he drink to excess. Perhaps, as a semblance of order returned to the house, his fear of failure eased, and his confidence grew. He engaged an estate manager, and after lengthy discussions, they rode over the estate together. Heartened, Laura allowed herself to hope they might have turned a corner, and her brother could be all she'd once expected of him.

Aunt Gertrude surprised them with an invitation for Laura to stay in her London townhouse. She'd even agreed to chaperone Laura at balls and other engagements. While it pleased her that Robert would not come to London and be exposed to the temptation of the fleshpots and gaming hells, her aunt wasn't an easy person. Her sharp eyes missed nothing, and she didn't hesitate to express her opinions. That would not go well with the *ton*, who considered politeness and manners to be important, and as her own return to London could raise questions, it made Laura uneasy.

The day before she departed for London, Laura busied herself packing her trunk in her bedchamber. She would spend the last six weeks of the Season there. Although disliking the very thought of it, she accepted she must do as Debnam had suggested and think of her future, as it did not lie in this house. Robert seemed to have gained some sense since his rash actions at Beechley Park and worked at improving his estate. But she felt sure he would eventually tire of the solitude of country life and may soon consider marrying. She hoped he would choose wisely. The right wife could be a beneficial influence in his life.

When Laura went down to the library to return a book, she found Robert seated at his desk, having just come back from a trip to the village.

He looked up, a speculative gleam in his eyes. "Ah, there you are, Laura. I've heard some interesting news."

"Oh?" Laura waited for him to embellish on it. "Are you

going to tell me?"

"Edward's wife died in childbirth."

With a gasp, Laura put her hands to her cheeks, her eyes filling with tears. "Oh, no! Poor Edward. Did the baby live?"

Robert shook his head. "Apparently not. It was over six months ago. I don't know why the news didn't reach us before this."

"They lived in York."

"Yes. But Edward's widowed mother still lives on the adjoining estate. Apparently, she told the postmaster she expects a visit from him soon." He glanced at her. "It would be polite to invite him to call. You will receive him, won't you?"

Laura wondered if Edward would call on them. "I doubt he will want to." But for welcoming an opportunity to offer her condolences, she didn't wish to see him again and was glad to be going to London. It wasn't because she hated him for how he had treated her. She had long since come to terms with that. He simply represented a sad time in her life she did not wish to be reminded of.

A WEEK AFTER Laura and her brother had left Beechley Park, Brendan rode over to visit a tenant farmer. With the help of the neighbors, Ben Shipton constructed a new barn.

When Brendan arrived, the men were hard at work, pausing briefly to hail him while their wives laid out a lavish luncheon on a long, wooden table. Their merry talk washed over him as he stripped off his coat and rolled up his sleeves to join the men. Hammers and saws filled the air with noise and the smell of cut wood as the construction of the barn framework took shape.

Brendan sawed a wooden beam as a fine baritone burst into a rendition of the haunting ballad "Early One Morning." While he hammered in the nails, he and the others joined in. It felt good to open up his lungs and sing. He had missed singing in the church choir as a boy, and even though his friends sometimes broke into song when swigging ale in some tavern, Brendan never sang along. It was good to be among folk who, while they treated him with the respect his title afforded him, accepted him as one of them.

By mid-afternoon, they'd completed the frame. The workers put down their tools, surveyed their handiwork, and sat to eat.

"Yer father was a good man," Shipton said, chewing on a slice of ham. "He'd be mighty pleased to see his son helpin' folk like he did." Consternation entered the heavy-set man's eyes. "If you don't mind me saying so, milord."

"I'm pleased you told me, Shipton." Brendan smiled, glad that although it had obviously occurred to him after he'd spoken, the farmer hadn't referred to his parents' deaths. It was understandable that Shipton and many others who'd liked his father found it hard to believe him capable of such a horrendous act. They had told him so when he'd first returned here to live.

Brendan remembered going with his father to visit tenants and the villagers in need, while his mother had taken nourishing food to the sick and the poor. His mother had told him they were good people, whatever had gone wrong in their lives, and deserved help. Why had he forgotten that? He would try to emulate them to honor her. Laura, who was such a caring soul, would have been the same as his mother had they… He shook his head and rose with the others to pick up their tools. There was still much to do before night fell.

At dusk, Brendan rode home welcoming the weariness and the ache of unused muscles after a satisfying day's work. He was keen to have a bath. As he neared the woodland path which cut a few miles off his journey, Gaylord rode out of the shadows and drew in beside him.

"I told you to stay off my land." Brendan's fingers tightened on the reins, fury lowering his voice.

"I heard Miss Peyton and her brother have departed. I suppose wedding plans are not on the agenda?"

He ignored Gaylord's snide reference to marriage. "Who told you they had gone?"

The viscount shrugged. "That's not important. But is it true they hired my old butler, Wagstaff?"

"Yes. Whom you let go without an adequate pension."

Gaylord scowled. "I ordered him to leave the area. He is a menace. Indiscreet and prone to gossip, and he likes to make up stories." He nodded his head. "Netterfield will come to regret it."

"Your father must have been pleased with him."

"He was too soft. As was my sister."

Fury rushed fiery blood through Brendan's veins. To disparage Brendan's mother in that manner. He feared if he got his hands on Gaylord, he'd beat him within an inch of his life. "Get off my land, now, Gaylord," he said through his teeth. "Or I won't be responsible for my actions."

"What? Will you shoot me?" Gaylord sneered. But he backed his horse away. "Runs in the family, does it not?"

As Brendan began to swing his leg over the saddle, ready to dismount, no longer caring what he did to the man, Gaylord took note and turned his horse. He galloped away.

Brendan watched him go. Fighting Gaylord wouldn't give him satisfaction. He was much older and not as big as Brendan. But why had Gaylord expressed an interest in Wagstaff? The man had nothing to do with Brendan or Beechley Park. And what Netterfield did was none of his concern.

Gaylord's unusual interest in the butler stayed with Brendan as he rode home.

By the time he sat in his library, he'd put Gaylord's attitude down to the man's pettishness. He didn't like to be bested. And certainly not by a butler. It wasn't the first time Gaylord seemed to have knowledge of what happened at Beechley Park. What interested Brendan was which member of his staff supplied Gaylord with information.

Chapter Fifteen

London, July

"MISS GERTRUDE PEYTON and Miss Laura Peyton," the Brookes' butler announced.

Laura took several quick breaths to calm herself and smoothed the skirts of her pink-and-white gauze gown before she entered the ballroom. While Laura and her aunt made their way along the crowded periphery, several of her friends and acquaintances came to her to welcome her back, including Her Grace, the Duchess of Lindsey, whom Laura had met years ago during Ianthe's first Season.

Laura curtsied low. "Your Grace."

"It is nice to see you among us again, Miss Peyton," the beautiful, fair-haired duchess said. Her Grace might have heard the gossip concerning Robert's financial troubles, but surely nothing of Laura's stay at Beechley Park. But for such an important personage to show her favor, it would stop gossip from spreading. "We must take tea together soon. I should like to hear all your news."

Laura curtseyed. The duchess had always been kind. "I would love to. Thank you, Your Grace."

In her lavender, silk gown and pearls, Aunt Gertrude settled herself on a sofa placed against the wall, where she arranged her fan, shawl, and reticule around her. Donning her spectacles, she turned her short-sighted attention on the *ton* and, after a moment, leaned over to Laura, who sat beside her. "Some of these women dress like trollops." Her aunt did not try to lower her voice as she pointed her fan toward a woman on the dance floor. "Mrs. Dewsbury's big bosom is about to fall out of her dress!"

Laura glanced around at those seated nearby, fearing her aunt's words would be overheard. But a sudden commotion at the entrance of Prince Edward, Duke of Kent, whose duchess had given birth to a daughter, Victoria, drowned everything out. The noisy welcome continued for the tall, dark-haired, dashing Duke of Wellington, who walked in behind him.

"Ah, there's Marion Hislop. I haven't seen her for an age." Aunt Gertrude waved her fan at her friend, who saw her and beckoned.

Her aunt stood and collected her things. "I hope you're asked for the next dance, Laura. It doesn't do to sit alone. You will resemble a wallflower." With that deflating comment, she and her friend strolled away, chatting.

Aunt Gertrude was so alarmingly unpredictable. Laura tried to ease her tense shoulders as she viewed the new arrivals cramming into the ballroom and the adjacent salons. The Brookes had refurbished the ballroom since she had last been here. An elegant row of marbled columns lined the walls and arched windows opened onto a wide balcony overlooking the garden. The scent of a multitude of sweet-smelling flowers fought with the candle smoke and the less pleasant smells of sweat and perfume. Crystals from the twin chandeliers sprayed twinkling lights over the dance floor, where dancers performed the quadrille. The dance suddenly came to a halt and a collective gasp went up as a middle-aged gentleman stumbled and almost fell while attempting an overly enthusiastic execution of the *jeté assemblé*. Clearly a little embarrassed, he righted himself, fortunately, and the dance continued.

When the quadrille ended, Laura's friend Emma Burton left

the dance floor with the other couples. She spied Laura, and parting from her partner, hurried over to her.

"How wonderful to see you here, Laura." Emma seated herself beside her. "I've looked for you everywhere. I doubted I'd see you again in London this Season."

Her friend was too polite to ask the reason which had kept her away, but her green eyes were curious.

"My brother suffered a hunting accident. A wound to his shoulder," Laura said, giving her a briefer version of the truth. "It kept us in the country."

Emma's eyes widened. "How dreadful." She gazed around. "Is Lord Netterfield here in London?"

"No. Robert is still not well enough to return to the city. My Aunt Gertrude kindly chaperoned me." She laughed. "Not that I need one at my age." She remembered how young and lovely Debnam had made her feel. Desired.

Emma frowned. "You talk as if you are old, Laura. In that pink gown, you're prettier than many debutantes here tonight. And so much more sensible."

"How kind you are, Emma." Laura leaned over and patted her hand. But it seemed wisdom didn't necessarily come with the years, or protect her from hurt. "How are you? What has occurred in my absence?"

"Mr. Lang is courting me." Emma grinned, tucking a dark curl behind her ear. "He has been to dinner, and Papa seems to approve of him."

"I remember how you liked the Scottish gentleman! That is wonderful news. I am so behind the times! Are you to announce your engagement?"

"Not officially. But we talk of an autumn wedding," Emma said. "I would love you to come, Laura."

"I wouldn't miss it." Laura smiled, pleased for her, and a little envious.

Emma rose. "I must go. Mr. Lang has claimed the country dance."

Sitting alone again, as no gentleman had approached her, Laura returned to viewing the interesting personages among the milling crowd, including the Prime Minister, Lord Liverpool, and some of his cabinet.

A man caught her attention when he emerged from the throng. He made his way purposefully toward her, the candlelight shining on his fair hair. She drew in a sharp breath. Her old neighbor and suitor, Edward Ryland.

He stood smiling before her. "It is a great pleasure to see you again, Laura."

They were of a similar age, but she thought Edward looked older, with deep lines bracketing his mouth. They had both been so young when he'd courted her. And much had happened to them both since. Back then, she'd anticipated a rosy life ahead for them. How naïve she'd been.

She smiled up at him. "Please sit down, Edward, or I shall get a crick in my neck."

He laughed and sat beside her.

She gazed compassionately at him and reached across to touch his gloved hand. "I've only recently heard the sad news. I am dreadfully sorry for your loss."

Edward's brown eyes darkened. "Thank you. It was an awful shock, but some months ago now." He gave a half-hearted shrug. "I've grown tired of my company and thought it time to return to society again." He smiled. "I'm delighted to find you here, Laura. According to my mother, you have not yet married. Is there someone special in your life?"

"No," she said, hating to have to lie. Edward must have been surprised to find her still single after all this time. When they had been together, he'd liked to say how lucky he had been to beat the other men and claim her as his. Well, that was in the past.

"I hadn't forgotten how lovely you are," he murmured, his gaze roaming her face. He rubbed the back of his neck, looking awkward. "Have you forgiven me, Laura? I hated hurting you. You believed me when I said it was my father's wish, didn't you?

He always aimed high. Had some financial troubles."

And your marriage solved them nicely for him, she thought. "I knew he disapproved of us, Edward. But perhaps he was right."

His fair eyebrows drew together in a pensive frown. "I didn't love my wife when I married her. I was as angry and hurt as I'm sure you must have been. But I came to love Felicity."

Laura was pleased he'd been honest with her and hadn't spun some tale about always having loved her, which she would have doubted and disapproved of.

The musicians gathered on the podium and took up their instruments. Those intent on the country dance drifted onto the dance floor. "Are you free for this dance?" Edward asked.

"Yes, although I see Mr. Rowntree approaches." She would prefer not to dance with Edward, but Mr. Rowntree had changed direction and veered toward another lady.

Edward stood and held out his hand. "Then say you will dance with me. Please."

She rose and took his arm.

While they danced, she discovered she felt no animosity toward him. It was as if what had happened between them had never been. Since meeting Debnam, nothing else seemed to have the power to hurt her. She gazed into brown eyes not far above her own and tried to recapture the fever of anticipation he had caused once when he'd been near. It was absent, and she wondered if he felt the same.

When she and Edward approached her seat after the dance ended, Aunt Gertrude sat observing them. Laura silently groaned as her aunt donned her spectacles.

Edward bowed before her. "Miss Peyton. I hope you are well?"

Her aunt regally inclined her head. "How are you, Mr. Ryland? You look older. Well, you're a man now. Married too, are you not?"

Her aunt had either missed Edward's black armband or ignored it. "Aunt, Mr. Ryland is recently widowed." If Laura hoped to head her aunt off before she got into her stride, she failed.

"Of course. How sad, so early in the marriage." Her aunt nodded. "I remember now. You married after you reneged on your promise to marry my niece."

"We were never engaged, Aunt Gertrude," Laura hastened to say as Edward's clearly embarrassed gaze sought hers.

"Your relationship was of long standing, however," her aunt continued, undaunted.

"It was not Edward's fault, Aunt." Laura's face grew heated. "His father insisted."

Fortunately, her aunt appeared to have said as much as she cared to. She tapped the seat beside her with her fan. "Well, don't stand there as if you're growing roots, Mr. Ryland. Sit down and tell me about yourself."

Edward obeyed and Laura breathed more easily. Perhaps he was nervous. She certainly couldn't blame him, for he spoke fulsomely of his estate in York.

When he drew breath, Aunt Gertrude turned to Laura. "Very impressive, don't you agree, niece? I seem to recall you saying how much you liked York after you visited there."

Laura cringed. "York is a fascinating old town: York Minster, the Roman ruins and the Shambles." Now she rambled. When she felt brave enough to meet Edward's eyes, she saw him smiling.

After Edward had excused himself and left them, Aunt Gertrude turned her full attention on Laura. "If you have any sense at all, my girl, and don't look to your brother, who is in short supply of it, you will grab Mr. Ryland before someone else does, and the chance of a good marriage slips by you."

"I doubt he is still interested, Aunt."

"It's as plain as the nose on your face that he is. And there won't be many more of his ilk coming along."

Laura had to agree with the last bit. "But I no longer feel the same way about him."

"Of course you don't. Not after what his wretched family did to you. But you were a silly chit then, barely out of the school-room. You've matured and are better for it. You used to get on well, and you will again. A marriage based on mutual interests is to be wished for."

Laura smiled. Despite everything, she was fond of the irascible old lady. And grateful to her for going to the trouble in helping her. Her father's sister had never married, and Laura wondered why. Was she in danger of becoming a lonely, old spinster like her aunt? It made her slightly ill to think about it. Women depended upon men so much. Without a husband, there would be no children. That possibility stirred her on to find, if not love, then a companion in life and a father for her children.

As the night passed, Laura danced several times, while Edward partnered with different women. He had smiled at her from across the dance floor. Although he'd been complimentary, it was unlikely he would want to marry her. But what if he did? Her throat tightened. To consider him, she would finally have to accept she and Debnam would never be together.

ON SUNDAY, BRENDAN attended church. It was the first time he'd been in the building since he'd been a lad. As he took his seat on the family box, the parishioners' interest in him burned the back of his neck. As the vicar's voice droned on, the meaning of his message evaded Brendan. He felt uncomfortable and missed the thrust of the vicar's rather rambling sermon. When the service ended and everyone filed out of the church, the vicar warmly shook his hand and welcomed him back into the fold. Others from the area gathered around him to follow suit. It was pleasant to be among friendly faces and that made Brendan feel a little less guilty at having been absent for years.

In a burgundy, silk pelisse and a floral hat, Mrs. Gould, the wealthy banker's widow who lived in one of the big houses in the district, came up to him as he prepared to leave.

The brunette had an attractive smile. She offered her gloved hand. "How good to see you here, my lord. You have satisfied our rampant curiosity. How unfair it was of you to return these four years past and then leave us wondering how you fare." She studied his face, then looked down before meeting his gaze. "But I see you fare exceptionally well."

Brendan laughed. "You have praised and condemned me in the same sentence, Mrs. Gould."

Her smile became flirtatious. "I warn you, Lord Debnam, that you shall not be allowed to disappear again. I believe invitations to dinner and card parties are being organized among your neighbors as we speak."

He drove the curricle home, surprised he'd enjoyed the morning. Mrs. Gould was charming. In her early to mid-thirties, he guessed. Would the widow want to marry again? Or did she merely seek a lover? An affair might suit them both. But he felt no eagerness or rush of excitement at the possibility. He wondered why that was. Dash it all, he knew. Laura refused to leave his thoughts, but that was because he didn't want to let her go.

In his library chair, Brendon gazed out of the window at the night sky. He mulled over his new social activities. As Mrs. Gould had predicted, by mid-week, several invitations to dinner and a card party had arrived in the post, including another from Mrs. Gould. He had ordered Thornton, his secretary, to send acceptances. Being around people helped to lift his mood, so perhaps he needed the company more than West Sussex society needed him.

He would have to host himself at some point, perhaps a dinner, or a shooting party in autumn. Mrs. Brandt would know if they needed to hire more servants for the occasion. Might a servant feel some loyalty or have a connection to Gaylord? His jaw tightened to think that a member of his staff might be disloyal to him. But someone had informed Gaylord that Netterfield had hired Wagstaff. There had been no time for gossip to spread about the butler. But who had it been and what could have been their reason?

Movement in the gardens drew his gaze to a spare figure kneeling in a flower bed. The head gardener, Fenchurch. He'd been at Beechley Park back when Brendan's father had been alive. But it could have been anyone. It was impossible to discover what had taken place here during the years he'd been away.

The trustees had forwarded a list of new employees who'd replaced the skeleton staff when Brendan had first arrived. So cast down was he to return to the home of his parents, he'd left it to his secretary. He would get Thornton to ferret it out.

Any newly employed servants would not know Gaylord. And Brendan found it difficult to believe any of the older servants could be capable of such disloyalty. What relationship could any of them have with Gaylord? Would Gaylord have offered them money? While it seemed unlikely, something drew Brendan from his chair. He left the library and went to speak to Fenchurch.

The old gardener climbed as quickly as he was able to his feet. He removed his hat. "Milord?"

"I wanted to offer praise for the rose garden, Fenchurch, a fine display this year."

Fenchurch's craggy face broadened into a smile. "Thank you, milord. I believe it is the best for some years."

"Good man." Brendan nodded and left him. Fenchurch had been with them since Brendan had been a boy. He struggled to suspect a loyal servant with no obvious reason to turn against his employer. But if it could not have been Fenchurch, who the devil was it?

Chapter Sixteen

BENEATH HER UMBRELLA in Richmond Park, Laura stifled a yawn. Beside her on a similar wicker chair, Edward handed his empty champagne flute to a footman and turned to her.

"You look sleepy, Laura. Shall we join the others for a stroll? Someone spied a big stag among the deer in the copse of trees on the hill. It's wisest not to get too close, but we can walk to the pond."

"Yes, let's. I am a little tired and a walk will refresh me." She took Edward's hand and stood. "It's been a busy week. So many late nights, and the sunshine doesn't help." She dabbed her perspiring forehead beneath the brim of her bonnet with her handkerchief. The midsummer day had become too hot to be outdoors. Many of Mrs. Fleming's guests wisely sought the shade.

Laura took his proffered arm. They followed the path through the grass, scattering a flock of birds that flew into the trees. Since she and Edward had met in London, they had spent time together at the same dizzying round of engagements, including luncheon at Mirvat's Hotel and dining with the Grenvilles before the theatre, where Edmund Kean had performed in *The Fatal Accusation*. She was comfortable in his company. Discussing past shared experiences, they seemed like an old married couple. There were no breathless silences, no pounding of her heart, or the urge to draw closer to him. No warmth rising to her face at his touch. No thrill of desire. It made her wonder if she had ever been passionately in love with Edward. Had it been a girlish infatuation? She feared so, and now because of Debnam, she knew what it was to be passionately aroused and desperately wanting another's touch. She couldn't bear to think she might never feel that way again.

"If things had been different, I know we would have been happy together," Edward said.

Laura supposed he was right, although she suspected she would have yearned for something more, while unaware of quite what that was. Since she'd met Debnam, she better understood herself. She had a passionate nature. And still longed for him. Especially in the quiet of her bedchamber at night. It made her horribly restless. Was he well? Might he have found some measure of contentment? It had occurred to her Debnam could return to London, and she searched for him at every venue but failed to find him. Her stomach churned with jealousy at the thought of him flirting with some woman on the dance floor. But she reminded herself sternly that she had no claim on him.

She'd come to understand Edward was a conventional gentleman. He had not fought for her all those years ago, meekly obeying the order from his overbearing father. Perhaps he'd believed his father to be right. Her parents had never been very wealthy.

To be fair to him, he mourned the loss of a beloved wife. She doubted Edward had an ardent nature. Their few stolen kisses were a brief touch of lips, and he hadn't attempted to touch her breasts, although she sometimes wanted him to. Laura couldn't imagine him doing anything outrageous, like seducing her in the billiard room. And she wanted a lover who excited her. It would not be so with a respectable, careful man like Edward. Their life would be different. Laura mourned the woman she might have become, had she and Debnam been able to marry.

Edward cleared his throat, and Laura tensed. He could be about to propose, and she was still in an anxious flurry of indecision. Would it be fair to him to marry him, when she wanted more than he could give? Wanted the man who was a dashing scoundrel and passionate lover, who could be gentle and honorable, and whose slumbering gaze set her on fire? Laura wished she weren't so confused. Why couldn't she use her good sense, as her aunt had urged her? After all, she was fond of Edward, and there could be children.

Fortunately, before he could frame his thoughts into words, a married couple they had met earlier hailed them, and the opportunity passed. It was a reprieve, but not the end, Laura suspected. She bit her lip. She *must* be ready to respond to him with her answer.

When she returned to Aunt Gertrude's townhouse, her aunt hurried to meet her in the hall. "A letter has come from a family friend, Mrs. Purcell. Mr. Purcell has passed away. I am to leave tomorrow for Oxford, to attend the funeral."

"How sad. I am sorry."

"No need to accompany me, Laura, as you've never met them. But while I'm away, you cannot stay in London. Go to Longworth. Within a few weeks, social events will peter out as people depart London for the country. I shall do the same. I cannot abide the city during hot weather." Her aunt appraised her. "I expect Edward will return to Surrey, and you shall see him there." She smiled warmly, obviously of the opinion Edward would propose.

Laura supposed it would disappoint her aunt, and Robert, too, if she refused Edward. And if she did, she would have no option but to become her aunt's companion, should she agree to have her. The burden of choice seemed to settle heavily on her shoulders.

Home beckoned. Clear skies and fresh air and Tibby curled up on the end of her bed. It had been so long since she'd ridden over the green meadows. The frenetic, frivolous pace of city life bored her. The humid weather seemed trapped beneath a solid bank of unshifting clouds, everything coated with soot, the roads clogged with traffic, and the unrelenting noise from dawn to dusk. Even a promenade in Hyde Park was unappealing at the height of summer.

Robert worried her. What had he been up to in her absence? He used to turn to her for guidance. Had it been foolish of her to leave him to his own devices?

At the desk in her sitting room, Laura wrote a note to Edward to explain why they could not meet tomorrow. And how sorry she was their plan to visit the Dulwich Picture Gallery in Southwark must be abandoned.

Edward's prompt reply arrived before Laura left London. He intended to go to Surrey, to see his mother, and hoped he might call, as he had a particular question to put to her.

No further along with her decision, Laura groaned.

In the late afternoon of the following day, her hired carriage pulled up outside Longworth house. The front door opened, and Wagstaff welcomed her, resplendent in butler's garb: a neat, dark-blue tailcoat and gray trousers. With a rush of pleasure, she hurried up the steps and smiled at him. "How fortunate we now have you as our butler, Wagstaff."

His craggy face beamed, and he gave a brief bow. "But I'm happy to keep my position as a general factotum. Welcome home, milady."

Laura laughed. "It seems to agree with you."

While Wagstaff gave orders to the footmen to pay the driver and collect her luggage, a neat, middle-aged woman entered the hall and stood with her hands clasped. "Mrs. Smythe, milady," she said. "His lordship has engaged me as housekeeper."

Laura hid her surprise with a smile. "How do you do, Mrs. Smythe. Welcome to Longworth. Please come see me about anything you wish to know."

"Thank you, milady."

"We shall have a good, long talk tomorrow," Laura promised.

She knocked on the library door.

"Come."

Robert sat at his desk, his bailiff in the chair opposite. He dismissed Mr. Maddox, who greeted her with a gap-toothed smile before leaving the room.

When the door closed, Robert looked at her in surprise. "Why have you come home?"

Desperate for a cup of tea, she sat down and explained about Aunt Gertrude.

Robert leaned back in his chair and nodded. "You will notice how smoothly the house is now run. The housekeeper I engaged, Mrs. Smythe, is most efficient."

"I have met her." Why had Robert, who never took an interest in such things, taken the matter in his hands with such urgency?

"Has Edward also returned home?" he asked, studying her.

Laura stared at him. "You knew Edward was in London?"

"He came to see me before he left. He wished to advise me of his intention to court you. Thought it the correct thing to do, as I'm your guardian."

Edward was always so careful not to offend. What had passed between them about her? "You are not my guardian, Robert. I am two years older than you. And my own woman."

He scowled. "That blasted book by Mary Wollstonecraft. You should never have read it. There are murmurs about women's dissatisfaction reported in the newspapers. Why should women be unhappy to have men in charge? We shoulder all the responsibility." He leaned forward. "Let's not argue anymore. I have met someone."

So it had happened. She hadn't thought it would be so soon. "That's splendid, Robert. Tell me all about her. Where did you meet?"

"Bart Wilson dragged me to an assembly dance. Miss Aurelia Laverty is the sweetest girl, Laura. I know you will like her."

So this had prompted the necessity for a housekeeper. They would soon entertain the Lavertys. "I have not heard of the family. But as you love Aurelia, I'm sure I will too. Have you made wedding plans?"

"I've not yet proposed. Mr. Laverty is a wealthy gentleman, so I must have something to offer. Our revenue has increased since I hired more workers. New spring plantings and improvements to the tenant farms. And I took out a small loan to broaden my investments."

She stilled. "Oh?"

He scowled. "Must you always think the worst of me? The bank. Not a shylock. It is perfectly legal. I dealt through Father's broker."

"I can only take you at your word, Robert."

He flushed. "Well, you will revise your poor opinion of me when you see how prosperous we become."

As if it were just about money. Relieved and hopeful, Laura pushed back her chair and stood. "I need to wash off the travel dust and change my gown. Please tell me more about it at dinner."

Laura climbed the stairs to her bedchamber. Robert seemed determined to make amends and improve Longworth after his experience at Beechley Park. Longworth could soon have a new mistress. Would they like each other? Or would the new Lady Netterfield want her gone?

Another reason to accept Edward should he propose. She drooped with tiredness but laughed when a furry, dark body leaped out and tangled in her skirts. "There you are, my pet." She scooped Tibby up in her arms and rubbed the soft fur against her cheek.

ACCORDING TO REDFERN, two members of staff, as well as Redfern himself, had been at Beechley Park since Brendan had been a child. Mrs. Wilson, formerly a kitchen maid and now a cook, assisting his chef, Arnaud, and Fenchurch, the head gardener. Pratchett, the gamekeeper, had passed away several years ago. And now his young son, John, had stepped in to admirably take it over.

When his investigation failed to point to any member of the staff, he felt restless and sleep eluded him. A usual occurrence since Laura's lighthearted spirit had vanished from Beechley Park and from him. He missed her. Her lovely face filling his thoughts, he gave up trying to rest and remained in the library until late, a book in front of him he failed to read. He rose, stretched, and strolled about the long room, which caused Hunter's ears to twitch, although the dog didn't wake. In the cloudless sky outside the tall windows, the light from a full, yellow moon painted the gardens.

Brendan recited a favorite poem from the mystic poet, Rumi, causing Hunter to raise his head.

"Escape from the black cloud that surrounds you.

Then you will see your own light as radiant as the full moon."

While Brendan considered whether Rumi's message was even possible, the wavering light from a lantern appeared. It brought him closer to the window. A housemaid's white mobcap peeked above a hedge, moving along at a slow pace. She left the gardens and appeared in the drive. Brendan idly watched her making her way, the lantern held high. He expected her to be on her way to the stables to see one of the staff, but she crossed the drive and disappeared into the woods.

"What the devil?" Brendan left the library, closing the door smartly behind him before Hunter joined him. Outraged woofs followed him as he ran down the corridor. He ordered the sleepy footman to stay put and bolted out into the cool night and across the lawn, following the girl. When he entered the woods, he saw the fiery light of her lantern move in among the trees ahead of him. She had quickened her pace. But he knew where she went. There was only one place which lay in that direction.

Brendan now followed more leisurely so she wouldn't spot

him, cautious of his footing with no light to guide him except intermittent moonlight through the trees.

He reached the clearing and hung back. Ahead of him, the maid stood before the cottage. When she knocked, welcoming candlelight flooded out as the gamekeeper's door opened to admit her.

Once the door had closed, Brendan picked his way across the leaf- and twig-strewn ground to the timber cottage. Outside, a row of pelts had been strung up on a line. Smoke wafted from the chimney.

He peered through the un-shuttered window to see the couple in a passionate embrace before the fire, where a big, black pot boiled. Smiling, he turned and made his way back to the house. The gamekeeper was in love, and that could mean trouble if the girl fell pregnant. Brendan supposed he should offer advice to the young man, who was not yet twenty-five.

If only life were as simple for him and Laura.

Chapter Seventeen

MID-MORNING, LAURA WENT downstairs to the kitchen to have a cup of tea with Mrs. Amery, who was always good for a chat, even when up to her elbows in flour.

Laura hoped to hear what had occurred among the staff in her absence, and their cook was the one to ask. Laura poured her tea from the brown kitchen pot while Cook deftly made scones.

"A light touch is the secret to a good scone." Cook's skillful hands shaped each one before placing them onto the greased tray.

"How fortunate Wagstaff is now our butler." Laura put down her teacup and took a bite from a delicious tart filled with jam from the strawberries in the garden.

Cook blushed and bent to place the tray in the oven. "It was cruel of Lord Gaylord to treat him that way."

"I wonder why he did?"

Cook's usually cheerful face turned grave. She glanced at the door before speaking. "Wagstaff has made a confession which troubles me, milady. He suffers from dreadful remorse. I want to tell you about it. But I wonder if I should."

"Oh?" Alert, Laura put down her teacup. "Is it something Robert and I should know about?"

"I cannot say, milady."

"You'd best tell me, Mrs. Amery, then I can decide what, if anything, must be done."

"It was back in the days when the former Earl of Debnam and the countess were alive." Cook scattered more flour over the table, added dough, and picked up her rolling pin. "When Mr. Wagstaff was butler to Lord Gaylord."

"Do continue," Laura urged her.

"The day of the shooting, it was. Mr. Wagstaff was in the great hall at Camelia Grove when Lord Gaylord entered. When his lordship removed his gloves to put in his pocket, he had blood on them. There was more blood on his coat. He said to Mr. Wagstaff he'd shot a fox, but he had no gun with him. Mr. Wagstaff said Lord Gaylord couldn't have gone to the gunroom to replace it before entering the hall."

Laura took a quick breath. What did this mean? "Why didn't Wagstaff mention this to the constable or the magistrate investigating the murder at Beechley Park?"

"Mr. Wagstaff said that Lord Gaylord might have told the truth, so he couldn't take the chance. He was that frightened he'd be let go, so he held his tongue. Years later, a housemaid came to him in tears after Lord Gaylord had assaulted her. He went to face his lordship about it. Mr. Wagstaff was that angry. Everything boiled up and spilled out; his lordship's ill treatment of the maids—another girl who had been let go earlier for the same reason, as well as the blood on Gaylord's clothing the day Lord and Lady Debnam died."

Cook put down the rolling pin, her large bosom heaving. "Lord Gaylord was furious. He accused Mr. Wagstaff of mixing up the days deliberately to cause trouble. Gaylord said he'd killed the fox the day before Lord Debnam had shot Lady Debnam. Although he never produced the animal at the time, and it was customary to use the fur. He fired Mr. Wagstaff, then spread lies around the district warning the owners of the big houses not to hire him because he was unreliable. Mr. Wagstaff says little about those times, but I know the last few years have been very hard for him. That is until you came along like an angel from heaven, milady."

Laura put her cup and saucer in the scullery sink. "This could be important, Mrs. Amery. I must speak to Wagstaff about it."

Cook sniffed and wiped her eyes with the corner of her apron. "I daresay he will be angry with me for telling you."

"Wagstaff will be relieved once the matter is dealt with. It must have distressed him for a long time."

Cook nodded. "Aye, there is that."

Laura ran upstairs, tempted to tell Robert, but she was unsure of what his reaction would be. He might forbid her to act. She would write to Debnam.

At her desk, she finished her letter, blotted and signed it, and read it again. Would Debnam think she grasped at straws? And consider it to be of no relevance? It could have been a fox Gaylord had killed. As much as Debnam appeared to dislike Gaylord, he would find it difficult to believe the viscount had shot his sister. What reason could he have had to do so? And just supposing Gaylord had done it, it would be impossible to prove after all these years. But if it caused Debnam to doubt his father's madness, it might ease his anguish. She took up the pen, and with a deep breath, steadied her hand before adding another line.

I hope this is of help to you, Debnam. The letter folded in her hand. After a glance out the window at the pouring rain, which wasn't about to ease, she ran downstairs to get her hat and an umbrella. If she left now and took the trap, she could reach the village before the mail coach arrived.

Laura returned to the house after her successful mission, soaked through to her chemise, and ran upstairs to change. When she came downstairs in a fresh house gown, she found Wagstaff and told him what she had done. He scrubbed a hand over his face. "It may not have any significance, milady, but I'm glad the weight of it is no longer on my shoulders."

Laura went to look for Robert. As she entered the hall, Robert came through the front door in his riding clothes, water dripping off his hat. He shrugged out of his oilskin and handed it to the footman. "Dashed rain is persistent. The river is high and could flood the lower meadows. If it keeps up, we will have to move livestock."

"I have something important to tell you," Laura said as he walked to the stairs. "It can wait until you come down."

A hand on the banister, he turned to look at her. "I wonder what that might be, Laura. I fear I may not like it."

His voice was mild. His manner had improved of late, perhaps because of the young woman he courted, whom Laura had yet to meet.

When Robert reappeared, Laura joined him in the dining room for luncheon.

Slicing a piece of mutton off the joint, he cut pieces of it to put on their plates. He put a piece in his mouth and chewed thoughtfully. "Tough." He shook his head without further comment.

"Robert." Laura tried to gauge his mood while she shifted a parsnip to the side of her plate. "Something has occurred."

He looked up at her. "So you mentioned. What is it?"

She quickly told him what Wagstaff had said, and how she'd dealt with it.

Robert frowned, his knife and fork poised over his food. "You wrote to Lord Debnam?"

"Yes. It was the right thing to do." She took a sip of the tart wine, her throat suddenly dry. "He needs to hear about it."

"You might have discussed it with me first." He sighed. "Very well. It is done but no longer concerns you, Laura. I don't want you getting involved in anything unsavory. Not while I'm working hard to make us appear an attractive proposition to the Lavertys."

"Why should this concern them?"

"I don't know, but I'm worried because it might. You have a history of disrupting the household with your heartfelt schemes." He looked up at her with a smile. "But I shan't go over old ground."

She put down her knife and fork and glared at him. "That is

unfair, Robert, and you know it."

He shrugged, unapologetic. "And then there's Edward. Where does he fit into all of this?"

"It was only a letter. The matter has nothing to do with him."

Robert paused from buttering a roll. "I am not blind, Laura. I know how you feel about Debnam. You must banish him from your mind. He had his chance to marry you and chose not to. To be perfectly honest, I'm relieved he didn't ask you. I found him a troubled man, and after that letter from Lord Gaylord, well… I believe Edward would ask you, if you play your cards right."

Laura fell silent. Robert, for all his blustering, spoke the truth about Edward, even though she didn't want to hear it.

"Oh, and there's a more important matter I want to discuss. I intend to hold a party," Robert said. "I've alerted Mrs. Smythe. Bedchambers need to be readied. Those traveling from some distance will require accommodation for the night, and Mrs. Smythe and you must discuss the menus with Cook."

This explained the sudden need for a housekeeper. "When? And how many do you plan to invite?"

"Fifty guests, should they all accept. I will hold it in three weeks' time." He smiled, further warming to the idea. "We'll hire musicians. Guests can dance in the great hall. Perhaps archery on the lawn if the weather is fine. Think, Laura, it will be like old times when Papa and Mama were alive. Do you remember when we were children and Nanny let us stay up late to watch the dancers from the gallery?"

"I do." Laura couldn't help smiling at his boyish enthusiasm. But only three weeks to prepare for such a large undertaking? Laura was relieved to have Mrs. Smythe.

MRS. ANNABELL GOULD's dinner party ended, and the guests, full of good cheer and too much champagne, departed into the night.

Brendan stood at the front door waiting for his curricle to be brought around from the stables. He turned as Annabel entered, carrying his hat and gloves. While he put them on, they stood together alone in the black-and-white marble hall, the footmen still in attendance on the drive as several carriages rattled away.

Annabell came closer, smiling slightly. She gazed up at him and smoothed his lapel with her hand. "Will you stay awhile and keep me company?"

She invited him into her bed, and she was most appealing in a deep, wine-colored lace dress which displayed her figure to great advantage. Once, he would have accepted her offer in the blink of an eye. But oddly, becoming Annabel's lover didn't sit well with him. He recognized it as some misplaced sense of loyalty to Laura and grew annoyed with himself.

Annabel stepped back, wrongly interpreting his expression. He reached for her hands and held them in his. "Forgive me, Annabell. I wrestle with a problem which seems to have no solution."

Her brown eyes softened, and she reached up to touch his face. The briefest stroke, but it carried a depth of meaning. "There is nothing to forgive." She tucked her hand in his arm, and they went out through the front door to where his curricle waited with Keagan.

"If you ever feel the need to talk, I am here. I have been through troublesome times myself, milord. I make a good sounding board."

"Thank you for that." Brendan, grateful for her exquisite manners, kissed her cheek and left her. He climbed into his curricle and took the reins from his groom, who jumped up beside him.

"How was your evening, Keagan?"

"Not bad, milord. I won a few shillings at cards. I don't think they'll welcome me back for another game."

Brendan chuckled. "Well done."

As they drove home, Brendan tried to make sense of his stubborn determination to become a monk. Annabel was a sympathetic, generous woman. Perhaps in time, he might feel differently, although he did not relish becoming the subject of gossip here. Leave that to London and the *ton*. He would return to the city in two days' time to attend the House of Lords. Perhaps there, he might settle into his old habits. But knowing Laura had turned his life upside down, and nothing was certain anymore.

The next morning, Brendan took his usual morning ride before breakfast. Dark clouds banked up in the sky overhead, and he smelled rain in the air as he rode through the woods in search of the gamekeeper. He found him removing a poacher's trap. John looked up as Brendan rode out of the trees.

Brendan dismounted, secured Bruno's reins, and came over to him.

"Seems the rascals are chancing their luck, milord."

"Keep an eye out," Brendan said as drizzle dripped down through the trees. "Would you inform the bailiff?"

"I will, milord." John looked awkward as he stood with the trap in his hands. He cleared his throat. "Miss Beverley Walcott and I wish to marry and we seek your blessing, milord."

"You have it, of course." Glad he didn't have to suggest it himself, Brendan led his horse by the reins, and they walked between the trees. "Beverley is an upstairs maid at Beechley Park, is she not?"

"Yes, milord."

"I expect she tells you much of what goes on up at the house."

John looked at him, eyes wide. "Only news of the staff. We didn't know it was wrong, milord."

"I am not angry with you, or Beverley, John. I merely wished to know."

Relieved, John nodded, taking scant notice of the weather as the pitter-patter of raindrops struck their hats.

"Have you seen anything of Lord Gaylord?" Brendan asked.

"As you know, he had my permission to shoot a partridge or two in the past."

"Why, yes, he is often about and calls in to the cottage sometimes." John settled his shoulders, looking wary.

"Might you have passed on anything to him Beverley told you?"

John gazed down at the trap in his hand. "Lord Gaylord is an inquisitive man. I might have mentioned the odd thing. But nothing important, milord. I don't know any secrets." He frowned. "Except one, perhaps."

"And what is that? You can tell me, John."

"Beverley and Lord Gaylord are related, although she never speaks of it in his presence."

Brendan turned to him. "The devil they are. Who told you this?"

"Her grandmother told Beverley Lord Gaylord was her father."

Could this be true? Brendan stared at him. "How old is Beverley?"

"Nine and ten years, milord. Born a few months before the…eh, shooting." He hesitated. "Your mother, the countess, allowed Miss Violet Walcott to return to work at the house after she gave birth to Beverley at her mother's cottage. Beverley's grandmother raised her. When she turned sixteen, she came to work here. That was four years ago, during the staff recruitment, which was when they'd opened the house up again for your return, milord."

Brendan rubbed the prickles on the back of his neck. "Beverley's mother isn't at Beechley Park now. Where is she?"

"She died years ago, milord. Beverley was a six-month-old babe when it happened. When the elder Miss Walcott worked at the house, she got hold of a bottle of laudanum and drank the lot."

"When was this?"

"A few days after the tragedy, milord. Miss Walcott was very cast down about it, Beverley's grandmother told her. Her mother said they wouldn't have died but for her."

"How could she possibly be responsible?"

"Never knew the reason, milord. And we can't ask Beverley's grandmother. She has passed away."

They emerged from the trees and looked at John's small timber and daub cottage in the clearing ahead of them.

"Do you expect Beverley to visit you soon?"

The young gamekeeper's face reddened. "She's coming here tonight, milord."

"Assure her she is not in any trouble. I only wish to question her about this matter."

"Yes, milord."

"And arrange your wedding, John, with some speed."

John laughed self-consciously. "That I will, milord."

Brendan mounted Bruno and rode back to the stables. He clenched his fingers tightly around the reins. As slender as this discovery was, what Beverley's mother had said opened a tiny window of doubt about the cause of the tragedy. And it implicated Gaylord. But to find out what lay behind it seemed almost impossible. Memories become uncertain with the passing years. Brendan couldn't be sure what had happened in the short time when he, as a lad, hearing the two shots, had run up that last flight of steps and into the sitting room and found his parents dead. He searched his mind for anything he might have missed. A smell, a sense, a noise? But there was nothing but the two bodies of those he loved, the smell of blood, and the awful stillness. And he casting up his accounts. Brendan would never forget the horror of it. Even now, he sometimes woke in a cold sweat after a nightmare. He wasn't sure this new information was even worthy of further investigation. He doubted Beverley would be of help.

Could he allow himself to hope? Or was it too great a stretch? Hope was a two-faced promise. It could raise you high before you were struck down lower than you'd ever fallen.

Chapter Eighteen

THE HOUSE WAS in an uproar as preparations for the party continued. While Laura worked with the housekeeper, the hope of Debnam's reply remained stubbornly in her thoughts. After breakfast each morning, she waited in the hall for the post to arrive. His reply to her letter should have reached her by now. Concern for him mingled with a deep sense of disappointment. Even should he have considered it of no importance, he could at least send word to tell her so. Had he already forgotten her? She buried the hurt, trying to convince herself for the hundredth time that it was better for him to get on with his life. As must she.

She paused while sorting through the linens, struck by another worrying thought. Had Debnam fallen ill? Could something dreadful have befallen him? The housekeeper cleared her throat. Thrown into a torment of speculation, Laura had failed to reply to something Mrs. Smythe had said.

Laura turned with a look of apology. "I'm sorry, Mrs. Smythe, you were saying?"

The housekeeper held a dozen pillowcases in her hands. "These are the best of the lot, milady."

"Good, Mrs. Smythe. Put aside those with no darns or stains for the maids when they make up the beds."

The linens, like most things at Longworth, were in a discouragingly poor condition, which necessitated recent purchases from the haberdasher.

Laura turned back to the linen cupboard. "I shall have to purchase towels."

Without feeling the need to consult her, Robert had invited Edward to dinner. Drained after a busy day of organizing the rugs to be taken up and beaten, as well as polishing the piano, which footmen would roll into the great hall for the party, Laura wearily dressed to receive him. She chose her lemon muslin trimmed with spring green and arranged her hair in a simple style with green ribbon threaded through it. When she entered the drawing room, Edward stood and smiled. "Pretty as a picture."

"Thank you, kind sir." Laura returned his smile as she sat down.

"My sister isn't merely pretty, Edward," Robert said, waving his arm to encompass the room. "Laura is very competent. She and the housekeeper have worked hard to ready the house for the party." His gesture encompassed the vases of flowers, the gleaming furniture, the bright rugs, and new tapestry cushions on the sofa. "I can't remember the house looking so splendid before."

"It always was when Mama was alive, Robert," Laura reminded him. But back then, it hadn't only been clean and well ordered, but also filled with laughter—and love.

Edward's possessive smile made her uncomfortable. "You will make an admirable hostess, Laura."

Laura forced a laugh. "You two put me to the blush."

"A lady shouldn't spoil her pretty hands with hard work," Edward observed, drawing a scowl from Robert. "My wife will spend her time embroidering, sketching, or arranging flowers and discussing menus with the cook, like my mother. It is to your credit, Laura, that you have performed menial tasks with such good humor."

"I like to keep busy." A little sorry for Robert, she avoided looking into his eyes. She endured sewing, which was a necessity, but embroidery seemed a waste of time. Stuck indoors during inclement weather, she preferred to read. When she had been a child, her father had affectionately called her a "hoyden" because she had more often been found in the stables, or sitting in the oak tree eating an apple and reading a book. Laura did none of those things now, except for reading. Nonetheless, she doubted she'd changed all that much.

After dinner, Robert excused himself, pointedly leaving Laura and Edward alone with their coffee.

Stirring his drink, Edward cleared his throat. "I am pleased we have this moment to talk, Laura. Mother sends her best wishes and hopes you are not overtiring yourself, because you are so short of staff."

"That is kind of her. I hope she is in good health?"

Edward nodded, his expression serious. "As it's my intention to bring my bride home to live with Mother, it was necessary to gain her consent. And she has given it, Laura." He smiled. "Shall we make wedding plans?"

"Oh?" She swallowed. "Isn't it a little soon to think along those lines?"

He put his cup and saucer on the table and edged forward in his chair. "Is it? We have been in each other's company for some weeks now, and I thought... That is, it seemed to me..." He sighed. With a grimace at his trousers, he slipped down on one knee. "Will you marry me, Laura?

"Oh, please do get up, Edward, before you crease your clothes."

Relieved, Edward jumped up and brushed himself down, returning to his seat. "Well? What do I tell Mother?"

Laura gazed at him speechlessly. Now the words were said. She could no longer avoid giving him her answer. Her breath deserted her at the realization she didn't love him, if she ever had. But he was a decent man. Life would hold no surprises. It would undoubtedly be pleasant, living here in the village, which was so familiar to her. She gazed at his face as he sat waiting patiently. Could she devote her life to making him happy? After all, there would be no one else, and Debnam had forgotten her.

Laura put her cup and saucer down beside his cup on the table. Edward's smile encouraged her, but she found no sign of desire in his eyes, or even the fear she might refuse him. Whether or not this proposal was an attempt to make amends for the upset he had once caused her made no difference. She couldn't marry him. They had little in common. Edward lacked humor. She tried not to dwell on Debnam's amused, gray eyes and his teasing smile. With a quick intake of breath, she straightened her shoulders.

"Edward, I cannot..." Laura tried to form the words into a refusal that would not wound him. "I fear we won't suit."

He looked astonished. "Not suit? We've known each other since we were little more than children, and we always got on well, until..." He flushed. "But since we met at the ball, I have become even more certain we are meant to be together."

Laura wondered if he really believed this. He admitted he had loved his wife.

Edward studied her face. "Does something worry you? We can spend a Season in London now and again." The flush deepened on his cheeks. "And should there be a happy event..." He coughed. "Mother is eager to be of help in the nursery."

What did he think of her lack of a dowry? Was he making a concession to marry her? His late wife's family was wealthy. Laura found it impossible to explain what was important to her. He would not understand. "You haven't mentioned love, Edward."

"Well, it's a little soon, Laura, after my dear wife. But I am confident we will come to love each other in time."

She smoothed her skirts over her knees. "But, Edward, please understand. I don't think we will."

"Because you haven't forgiven me? I thought...*hoped* that was in the past."

"Yes, of course, it is in the past. There is nothing to forgive. It might have happened for the best."

"Happened for the best?" he repeated hollowly.

"We were friends, *are* still friends, but I wish for more in a relationship. To be passionately in love."

Edward's nervous fingers fussed with his cravat. "Passion? What does a lady know of such things?"

It seemed they disagreed on the very nature and meaning of love. It surely meant wishing happiness and fulfilment for the one you loved. "Women are also flesh and blood, Edward. Some of us want more from marriage than just to be mothers."

"I never thought to hear you speak this way, Laura. Your mother would be greatly shocked. You were gently raised." He looked at her curiously. "What *do* you want?"

"A husband who loves me and allows me to be myself, and to do as I wish."

"*Do as you wish?*" Edward shook his head. "I'm not sure I understand you. Once married, women see to the running of the house and raise children. A lady supports her husband, and she stands by his side at social engagements. What else is there?"

"I hope to have the freedom to discover it."

"Something has changed you." He looked suspicious. "Was it a man?"

"I suppose I grew up."

Edward stood. "Well, that is that, then. Nothing further to be said."

Laura rose too and came to take his rigid hand in hers. "You will find the right partner for you in life, Edward."

With a half-hearted laugh, he drew his hand away. "I'm sure I will. But what about you, Laura? It might not be so easy for you to find someone to marry you, with your absurd ambitions."

He turned and stalked out of the drawing room. Her hands on her hot cheeks, she heard the front door bang.

A moment later, Robert entered the room. "Why has Edward left so soon? I thought we might play cards."

Laura went to the fireplace and rearranged the china orna-ments on the mantle. "He asked me to marry him."

In the mirror above the fireplace, she saw Robert's eyes gleam. "And you accepted him, of course."

"No. I refused him."

His shoulders sagged. "But, Laura, why?"

She turned to face him. "Because I don't want a loveless marriage."

"How foolish. Edward is fond of you. He offers you a safe, comfortable marriage. Why fill your head with dreams of romance?"

She cast him a level glance. "Does not Miss Aurelia Laverty stir your passion?"

Robert flushed. "But a man's needs differ from women's."

"Once you and Miss Laverty marry, I shall leave this house. It would please me greatly if you would consider leasing a small cottage for me in the village, or better still, a few rooms in London, but if not, I will live with Aunt Gertrude. If she ever forgives me for refusing Edward."

"I doubt she will. Rooms in London? To live alone at your age would be extremely foolish," Robert said, and he stomped out.

Laura glanced back at her face in the mirror. She looked amazingly calm. Her concern about marrying Edward had affected her more than she realized. Whatever lay ahead now, she was free.

BRENDAN SPENT HIS first afternoon in London at the House of Lords, where a discussion of Lord John Russell's speech about the disenfranchising of corrupt boroughs was in progress. Russell expressed the view that it was the duty of the House to rid Britain of any borough convicted of gross and notorious bribery and corruption, and to cease to send its members to parliament.

It was late when Brendan and his friends, Tate, Duke of Lindsey, and Hart, Marquess of Pembury, walked into White's Club to dine and play a game or two of faro. They greeted the Duke of Wellington seated at his table in the bow window with another gentleman, then, awaiting their table, they took leather armchairs near the fireplace while sharing a bottle of claret.

"You seem different." Tate eyed Brendan. "I suspect much has happened of late."

"Is it a lady?" Hart asked.

"An unhappy romance is the most earth-shattering thing, according to Hart," Tate observed with a grin.

Hart chuckled. "And any man who says different lies?"

Sick of how off-kilter he'd felt about Laura, and the quandary of his family situation, he felt the need to unburden himself. He loved her. No matter what happened, he wanted no other woman to fill his life.

Both men would understand. Now happily married with a babe in their nurseries, they had shared their experiences with him. Tate had come close to losing his estate, as well as Ianthe, whom he dearly loved. And Hart had feared he'd ruined his chance for a happy life with his beloved Maddie, while he'd fought to protect her from a villain who'd wanted her dead.

"Hart is partly right," Brendan admitted. "There is a lady, but also a mystery. Although I'm not confident either will reach a satisfactory end." He leaned back in his chair and leveled a glance at his good friends. Usually, while in their company, he kept his problems to himself, reluctant to reveal his worst fears. Perhaps he had changed, for it felt right to tell them what troubled him and benefit from their advice.

"I am all ears." Hart raised his glass.

"And I," Tate said.

"You know, of course, of the circumstances of my father's and mother's deaths," Brendan began. "What I failed to mention was the mental instability in my family's past, or how my father was judged to be mad when he shot my mother and himself."

The two men knew, of course, about the tragedy. Hart swallowed and cast a glance at Tate. They kept silent as Brendan told his heart-wrenching story. "And to add to my concerns are my megrims, which my father also suffered." He shrugged. "So, as you see, my future is uncertain."

"You could never become violent," Tate said, squeezing Brendan's shoulder in sympathy. "It isn't in your nature. Why, the last time we fenced at the academy, I won with ease, and you accepted it like a lamb."

Brendan laughed. As if he'd been carrying around a great weight, lightness settled on his shoulders. "I happened to be late for an engagement with a lady. Otherwise, it would have been a different story, my good fellow." He appreciated Tate's handling of such a sensitive matter, and his kindness, but he resisted pointing out that neither had his father revealed a violent nature until that vile day.

"And what of this lady?" Hart asked. "You need a good woman in your life."

"There is a lady. Miss Laura Peyton, Baron Netterfield's sister. We danced at the Grosvenors' ball. I would very much like to spend my life with her. But we cannot marry. There's a real chance of me being cursed with madness." He took a deep sip of wine. "And I will not bring an heir into the world and pass on this affliction."

Tate shook his head. "While I understand how you feel, Brendan, I can't agree. A wife will lighten your concerns. Miss Peyton seems charming. Ianthe knows her. I saw them talking together at the Brookes' ball."

"The Brookes' ball?" Brendan asked, an edge to his voice. "I suppose there were a dozen men hanging around her?"

"Has it bad, doesn't he?" Hart said. "You can't let her go, Brendan."

"Miss Peyton and Edward Ryland came out onto the balcony when I was there with Ianthe," Tate said. "But I witnessed no flirtation. It was a humid night, and we all sought the cool, fresh air. Why don't you ask the lady and allow her to decide? As you think so much of her, she must be of excellent character."

"Hear, hear," Hart said.

Brendan acknowledged them with a distracted nod. Hadn't Laura's brother mentioned Ryland in his letter? He'd said they had a romance of long standing, which had mislead Brendan into believing Laura had some experience in the ways of love.

Tate topped up their glasses, then held the empty bottle up to a passing waiter. "What about this mystery?"

Brendan explained what he'd learned about Gaylord. How the maid's mother had confessed to somehow being responsible for his parents' deaths, before she'd killed herself the day after his father and mother had died.

"That is strange," Tate said. "There seems to be more to this. Certainly bears looking into. Should you ever wish me to come to Beechley Park for moral support, just send a message."

"And I. Although I prefer to come to your wedding," Hart said as the waiter entered the room.

"Your table is ready in the dining room, gentlemen."

"You are excellent fellows." Brendan rose with a grin. "Allow me to buy you dinner."

In the early hours when Brendan retired to his bedchamber in his Curzon Street house, he went over the evening, recalling how both his friends had urged him to take a chance on life.

"Life is uncertain for all of us," Tate had said as they'd prepared to part ways on St. James's Street.

Hart, enough into his cups to become eloquent, had quoted appropriate words from Shakespeare. *"'Our doubts are traitors, And make us lose the good we oft might win, By fearing to attempt.'"*

"Best you return to your lady wife," Brendan had said with a chuckle, patting Hart on the back.

"And you must pursue the lady of your heart," Tate had said before striding away, his cane resting on his shoulder.

Brendan washed and undressed in the candlelight. Was he right to embrace life as they'd urged him to? He did not fear for himself, but for those who could be hurt by his actions. As much as he wanted a son or daughter, the nightmare which had stayed with him since he'd been a lad would fill him with dread every time he looked at his child.

He sighed. Once he returned to Beechley Park tomorrow, he would attempt to discover what had happened around the time his parents had died. It was possible that the declaration of the maid Violet Walcott just before her death had been misguided, and might not refer to his parents. But as he blew out the candle, the urge to discover the truth gripped him.

The next day, when he'd returned to the country and walked into the hall, a footman handed him his post, which he'd instructed not to send onto him. Sifting through, Brendan found a letter from Laura. Eager to read it at his desk, he sat down and seized the silver letter opener to slit the paper. Unfolding it before him, he cursed under his breath. The missive had arrived the day he'd left for London. She wrote of Wagstaff's anguish in failing to tell the constable of Gaylord's return to the house the day of the shooting, with blood on his clothes. And how Gaylord had insisted he had shot a fox but had had no gun in his possession.

If Gaylord had nothing to fear, why had he gotten rid of Wagstaff, a competent butler who had been with the family for years? Frustrated, Brendan cursed and thumped the desk, making his inkpot jump. Was it possible that Gaylord was responsible? But how? And why? What about Violet Walcott's confession? The more he thought about it, the more the pieces began to fit together, like one of those puzzles his mother had enjoyed. But there were pieces missing. How could he go about completing the picture? Let alone take a convincing story to the magistrate when it had happened so many years ago?

And what reason would Gaylord have had to kill his own sister and Brendan's father?

Chapter Nineteen

TWO DAYS AFTER Laura had refused Edward, Robert proposed to Miss Aurelia Laverty and was accepted. The following afternoon, her brother's betrothed and her mother came to tea.

Aurelia was a pretty eighteen-year-old girl with dark hair. Her mother, a short, stout woman, wearing a hat laden with feathers and flowers, looked around the drawing room with a sharp eye after being introduced.

Laura poured the tea as they discussed the wedding to be held in London.

Aurelia was short and slightly built, and Laura feared her brother would overwhelm her, but as they talked, she revised her opinion. She had a firm chin and exhibited a mind of her own. Perhaps that quality in her appealed to Robert. He would never admit it, but he appreciated strong women.

Her brother didn't insinuate himself into their conversation. He chatted with Mrs. Laverty while watching them with an indulgent smile as Laura and Aurelia discussed a shared love of reading. "Mama and I would love to view the house, Miss Peyton, if you wouldn't mind showing it to us," Aurelia said, smiling sweetly.

"Please call me 'Laura.' And, of course, It will be my pleasure."

After tea, Laura led them into the morning room.

"What a funny old house this is," Aurelia said. "It has none of the clean lines of the more modern houses."

"My family built it in the 1600s," Laura said with a sense of pride.

"Quite ancient," Mrs. Laverty said faintly, the feathers in her hat trembling.

Laura took them upstairs to the baroness's suite.

Aurelia gasped. "It requires a complete renovation. I see the modern chintzes in here. Don't you think so, Mama?"

Laura couldn't bear them discussing renovating her mother's bedchamber, although they had a perfect right to do so. "If you excuse me, I must see Cook. I'll return in a few minutes."

They barely noticed her leave as they discussed rugs and curtains.

Her mother had loved those damask curtains, which she'd made herself. Laura retreated to the landing and took several deep breaths, scolding herself for her foolishness. When she returned, she heard her name mentioned and held back from entering.

"Is Lord Netterfield's sister to live here?" Mrs. Laverty had asked her daughter.

"Well, Miss Peyton isn't married, so I expect she will."

"She's pretty enough. Why hasn't she married? It isn't natural."

"I don't know." Aurelia sighed loudly. "Perhaps she lost her lover in the war."

"You are such a romantic, my dear," her mother said. "There is more than one man in the world."

"Oh, Mama."

"Well, you know my opinion of Lord Netterfield. You could have done much better."

"I love Robert."

"I know, foolish girl. He's very handsome. Your father indulges you and is unaccountably pleased that his girl is to be a baroness."

"Will you come live with us after Papa..." Aurelia's voice grew hushed.

"Of course. You will need my help when the babies come. We must ask Miss Peyton to show us the nursery and the guest chambers. I shall require a better chamber fitted out for me. I refuse to spend a night here as things are."

Laura had heard enough. She coughed before she entered the room. "Can I show you anything else, Miss Laverty?"

"We should like to see the nursery," Aurelia said. She giggled. "It's a little early to think of such things, but one must be prepared."

Laura continued the inspection, taking them from room to room while trying to answer their questions helpfully. She could not view her home as critically as they did, and their comments made her exhausted by the time Robert appeared to escort them out into the gardens. It left her feeling fragile at the stark realization that she would soon leave her home.

"You seemed to get on well with Aurelia," Robert said when he returned after seeing his betrothed and her mother leave in their carriage. "She is lovely, isn't she?"

"Indeed, she is, Robert. And I see she thinks the world of you."

Robert grinned. "She's a very affectionate girl."

He went about the house in remarkably good humor. But he neither made mention of their earlier conversation about Laura's future, nor offered to rent suitable lodgings for her in London after he married. She tried not to fret, believing he would when the time came. She had no intention of remaining at Longworth. The very thought of it horrified her. At least living with Aunt Gertrude, she might have more freedom and subsequently make herself useful to her.

The morning post finally brought Debnam's reply to her letter. Laura stared at the earl's stamp, her heart beating wildly, and ran upstairs to her bedchamber to read it.

She broke the earl's seal and unfolded the letter.

Dearest Laura, he wrote:

I trust this finds you and your brother in good health. I'm sorry I've taken so long to reply. Having returned from London, I've only just read your letter. What you learned from Mr. Wagstaff astonished me. And certainly gave me pause to think. After all this time, I don't hold out much hope of discovering anything new, but I am determined to investigate further. Hearing from you warmed my heart, Laura. I remember every detail of your brief stay here, which I will never forget.

Fondest regards,
Debnam

Tears filled her eyes. *Fondest regards!* It was a carefully constructed missive which gave little away. Did he suspect she had a suitor? Laura read it again, thirsting for a sign that he still felt the same as he had when she'd left. Might he have found someone else? She searched for a message beneath his words. He remembered every detail of her stay at Beechley Park. She put a hand on her breast, feeling her heart pound. Her breath shortened as she vividly recalled the night in the billiard room, when Debnam's kisses and experienced fingers had brought her such exquisite pleasure. And how he'd refused to take her completely, although she'd wished he would. She still wished it. What they'd shared had touched her soul and tied her to him forever. It was the reason she could not marry Edward or any other man.

Try as she might, Laura couldn't rid herself of the belief that she and Debnam were meant to be together. It was unlikely they would meet again. He still seemed determined never to consider marriage. That would not change unless... Unless Wagstaff's revelation led Debnam to a discovery which changed everything. She prayed for Debnam's sake that happened. It was foolish to hope that he would one day come to her. But she was foolish where Debnam was concerned. Love made people so.

DURING THE LAST two weeks, Laura had kept busy readying the house for the guests. As she and the housekeeper dealt with the servants, her mind remained on Debnam. Was he still at Beechley Park? Had he gone away somewhere again? She pushed the idea away, preferring to imagine him at home, riding Bruno with Hunter at his heels.

Edward and his mother had been invited, but they chose not to attend. Aunt Gertrude had remained in bed on the advice of a doctor, after contracting a cold.

At the successful house party, the rain held off, and the guests gathered on the lawns to play quoits. A good deal older than his wife, Mr. Laverty didn't take part in the popular archery contest, preferring to remain at the card tables set up in the drawing room. He looked unwell and relied heavily on a walking stick. Mrs. Laverty, in a fuchsia-colored gown, fussed around him.

That evening, after dinner, dancing began in the great hall, but Laura was too busy to dance. Aurelia and Robert waltzed. They made a handsome couple, she petite and dark-haired and he tall and fair, and Laura was thrilled for him.

Robert announced his engagement to Aurelia. The guests clapped and toasted them with champagne, but no one seemed surprised. The musicians struck up, and the guests converged onto the floor for a country dance.

In the morning, when the overnight guests departed after breakfast for the journey home, the house was quiet again.

As Laura sat wearily in the morning room with a cup of tea, Robert joined her. "You did wonderfully well. All the guests said so, Laura. The Lavertys seemed impressed. I am grateful and proud of you."

She smiled, surprised at his warmth and loquacity. "Thank you, Robert. I am pleased. Did you give any thought to leasing a house for me?"

He frowned. "No, Laura. You are much too young to live alone. I would always be worried about you."

Outraged by how untrue this was, when during their time spent in London, out of sight seemed out of mind, Laura clamped her lips. Deeply disappointed, she barely heard his next sentence.

"You can remain here. This is your home. You will be an agreeable companion for Aurelia. Especially when the children come."

"I won't stay here, Robert. It is Mrs. Laverty's intention to move in some time in the future." Laura wondered if he knew.

"Eh?" Robert's mouth pulled down. "The devil she will." He cast a calculated glance at Laura. "Well, you must live with Aunt Gertrude. If she will forgive you for not marrying Edward."

Laura sighed. "Very well, Robert. I shall go to Aunt Gertrude, but I'd much prefer my own establishment."

"You may have it one day, when Aunt Gertrude is no longer with us."

Laura choked. "I would not wish that on her, Robert. She has only suffered a cold, and she writes that she feels better."

"I shall write to her. I imagine she is in London?"

"No, she dislikes the city in summer."

"Then she will be at her country residence in Richmond. Even better, I will drive there to see her tomorrow."

Laura sagged in her chair. "If you wish."

"Aunt Gertrude might decide to return to London when the weather cools. You can enjoy more society."

"I expect I shall be at her beck and call."

He looked up from his desk. "Laura, don't start. It is the best I can offer." He tapped his pen on the desk. "Aurelia expressed no objection to you continuing to live with us. Nor am I averse to it. But I shall not interfere with your need for independence." He passed a hand over his eyes. "I hoped you and Edward would marry. The family could gather every Sunday for supper after church."

Laura raised her eyebrows. "You really wanted that, Robert?"

"Of course I did. We are a small family, Laura. We should stay together." He frowned. "You have spoiled it, most likely forever, for I doubt you will find a suitable husband with your unreasonable demands. Fellows don't like it. I'm pretty sure Edward didn't."

Tears gathered in her eyes. Was she wrong to want to have some say in how she lived her life?

"I must assist Mrs. Smythe, who is restoring the house after the party," she said as she left him.

Laura went upstairs to her bedchamber. Barely aware of how she'd gotten there, she threw herself onto the bed. Her dream of a happy and free existence had evaporated like mist.

BRENDAN HAD QUESTIONED Beverley, but as he expected, it had been a waste of time. She knew nothing more than what her grandmother had told her. But her granny had been convinced Violet had died from grief and remorse for having failed those she'd served.

He couldn't imagine what that might have entailed. Brendan entered the sitting room he refused to use because of the stark memories. The carpet and sofas had been replaced. He sat, resting his hands on his knees on a wide, tapestry-upholstered chair, and forced his mind back to that terrible time. Something he tried to avoid. Even now, his eyes grew moist, and his throat tightened. What had he heard before he'd entered the room? Two shots, one after the other, had set him running up the stairs. Somewhere a door had banged, which he'd assumed had been servants rushing to investigate. He stood to walk about the room. But which door? If a killer had escaped, it could not have been through his father's suite. His valet had seen no one when he had rushed from the dressing room at the sound of gunshots, and his mother's maid had been in her bedchamber. The other servants had seen nothing untoward as they'd crowded the corridors and the staircase.

He halted. What if Violet had admitted Gaylord into the house? That could certainly cause her anguish. But there would have been no way to bring him up here secretly, or usher him down again without being seen. It was impossible. And again, the reason Gaylord would have done such a vile thing stumped him. Brendan stood before a fine artwork of the landscaped gardens painted in the last century.

While he studied it, his gaze shifted to the gold-and-cream silk panels on the walls, which were original. The gilded timber edge on one panel had come away, lending the panel a slightly skewed appearance.

Brendan fingered the panel, wondering what might have damaged it. Suddenly, the whole panel slid back with a bang, revealing a doorway into cobwebbed darkness.

Heart beating hard, Brendan stood for several minutes, his mind working frantically. He knew what it was. One of the servants' passages to service the kitchens, which his parents had believed to be boarded up years ago, along with the rest.

In those days, Brendan had seldom come into the sitting room, his parents' private domain. But that day he'd had exciting news to tell them. He had taken Hercules over his first jump and impressed the groom employed to be his instructor.

Brendan lit a candle and stepped inside the narrow space. His deep breath dragged in the dank and musty smells as he brushed away the cobwebs floating in the draft. With a hand on the wall to steady himself, he felt his way down the wooden stairs. The feeble candlelight barely penetrated the darkness and was hardly enough to guide him safely to the bottom. He cautiously descended. But when he put his foot where he'd expected the next step to be, he found nothing but air. Righting himself at the last moment, he staggered backward, close to crashing down and most likely breaking his neck. With a curse, he continued on carefully, feeling his way. Rotted wood gave way in places, becoming a dangerous trap for the unwary.

With some relief, Brendan felt level ground beneath his feet and fumbled for a latch to open the door. He found it and tugged on it. The door slid open and, blinking into the light, he found himself in the passage beside the scullery, which was, fortunately, empty of servants.

Brendan shut the panel before someone came to investigate. By God, that was the noise he had heard as a young boy. The hidden door snapping shut. With Violet Walcott's help, Gaylord must have used these steps to burst out into the sitting room and murder his mother and father. Afterward, he'd quickly made his escape. With the uproar, despite the blood on his clothes, it would not have been difficult for him to leave the house undetected, and keeping to the tall hedges, dart away through the gardens to the woods.

Sickened, Brendan walked outside among the vegetable beds, dragging in deep gasps of fresh air. How could Gaylord kill his own sister? Murderous fury tightened his gut. What reason would he have had to do this to them? Brendan's fists tightened at his side. Since then, Gaylord must have enjoyed wandering the estate, considering himself safe. Well, he would not be safe for long. Brendan would discover the reason for his villainy, and he would be delighted to see his uncle thrown into Newgate to rot.

He raked his hands through his hair as the realization hit him. This meant his father hadn't been mad. Neither would he himself ever become so. Brendan laughed shakily. Laura! Until he knew the entire story and had proof, he could not go to her, facing the possibility he could be too late. Fighting the impulse to confront Gaylord with a lack of sound evidence, which would only put him on his guard, Brendan returned to the library. He must think about what to do.

Chapter Twenty

"AUNT GERTRUDE HAS agreed to take you in, Laura," Robert said, having summoned Laura into his study after he'd returned from a visit to Aunt Gertrude's home in Richmond. "It displeased her to learn you refused Edward. She thinks you made a poor decision and will no doubt tell you so."

Laura bit her lip. "Aunt Gertrude is always forthright in her opinions."

"She plans to return to Mayfair when the weather is cooler and intends to accept some invitations." Robert glanced at her. "I am expecting Aurelia and her mother tomorrow with a decorator. He'll take measurements of the baroness's suite and some of the other chambers, with plans to refurbish them. Aurelia wishes her rooms to be completed before we return from our honeymoon."

Laura sighed. Would the changes include her bedchamber? It was the largest and had the best aspect of the gardens. How did Robert feel about it? He gave nothing away. Was she unreasonable to consider the plans of unseemly haste? To be fair, Laura had to admit Aurelia, soon to be the new mistress of Longworth, had a perfect right to make the home her own.

"If you can manage without me, I shall go to Aunt Gertrude next week," she said. "And I'll take Tibby with me."

Robert frowned, but after a moment, nodded his head.

Silly to think Robert would miss the cat more than her. Laura tried not to be hurt. She had brought this on herself. And despite everything, she knew instinctively that it was right for her. Somehow, she would make her future work.

On Friday morning, Laura departed from her childhood home as a resident for the last time. As sounds of banging came from the baroness's suite, where the men had begun their work on her mother's bedchamber, the servants came into the great hall to see her off, including a sorrowful Wagstaff and a red-eyed Mrs. Amery. She placated them with a promise to visit soon.

"Be happy, Lolly." Robert hugged her before assisting her into the coach, along with Tibby in his basket. "I will see you in London at the wedding."

In the afternoon, Laura sat with her aunt in her parlor drinking tea at her manor house overlooking the river in Richmond.

Aunt Gertrude was not about to let her off lightly. "You have been very foolish, Laura. You did not listen to my advice. And you may come to regret it as the years pass and you find yourself alone."

"I am not afraid of that, Aunt."

"You mean to bury yourself in novels, I suppose. Books are all very well. You aren't entirely unlike me, girl. I enjoy a good story myself. But you will come to realize living through books is not enough." Aunt Gertrude stroked the tiny, yappy black-and-white spaniel on her knee while Laura's cat hissed from beneath her chair.

Hoping her aunt would someday tell her why she had never married, Laura bent down and picked up her cat, rigid with indignation. "I'll take Tibby up to my bedchamber. We shall have to introduce these two more slowly." She feared her cat would hurt the dog rather than the other way around.

"Laura?"

Laura turned at the door. "Yes, Aunt Gertrude?"

"I trust we will rub along well together. But I will never accept you settling into a spinster's life. Do you think you will be independent? Even if you plan to take up some cause, your opinion will seldom be considered." She glowered. "And when we return to London, I shall put it about that you are to inherit my entire fortune when I die."

Laura gasped. "Aunt, no! You must not deny Robert his rightful inheritance."

"Your brother inherited everything from your parent—the estate, the lands, the furniture and paintings, the horses and carriages. Even your mother's jewelry." She sighed. "Very well, but when I'm gone, your inheritance will support you in the future if no husband arises. I still hope to see a gentleman court you with a view to marriage before you get any older."

Laura clutched Tibby's warm body to her chest. "I shall try never to be a nuisance, Aunt. Is there is anything you wish me to do for you?" She hated the idea of some gentleman courting her. He would not hold a candle to Debnam, and the thought of having to go through that again after the strain of refusing Edward exhausted her.

"You can bring my embroidery bag down when you come." Aunt Gertrude put on her spectacles and picked up a magazine.

Laura's cheeks were maddeningly wet when she reached her room. She took a handkerchief from the drawer, wiped her eyes, then sank onto the bed with Tibby on her lap. It was too late to change her mind. Not that she would. It wasn't as if any other viable option had presented itself.

She tried to look on the bright side. Aunt Gertrude would permit her to go about London if a maid accompanied her. There were so many places Laura wasn't able to see during the Season. Her time there was always so rushed. Buoyed at the thought of visiting Hatchards bookshop in Piccadilly, the lending library, and the Greek and Egyptian exhibitions at the museum, she put Tibby down on the bed and moved away. The cat mewed a protest. "It's your fault, Tibby. You shouldn't have hissed at Beau. And after he wagged his tail, too." She went to find Aunt Gertrude's embroidery.

BRENDAN SPENT THE next sennight searching through his father's papers and his mother's letters for something which might point to their murders. He found nothing and, tiring of being indoors, drove to Chichester to visit the livestock markets and inspect cattle for the home farm.

A fine, old cathedral graced Chichester, lending it an air of importance the small town might not otherwise have had. The summer sun burned hot overhead, while a blessedly cool breeze whipped through the streets, carrying the salty tang of the sea.

Impressed with the Friesian cows, Brendan bid successfully at auction and afterward stopped for luncheon at the Royal Oak Inn. While eating his bread, ham, and cheese, his thoughts turned to Uncle Simon, Gaylord's older brother. He had lost his life in this town some twenty years ago, stabbed to death in the lane behind the tavern. They'd never found his murderer. Brendan didn't remember Simon well, only a vague image of a fair-haired man who'd seemed big and jolly to the Brendan still in short trousers. But he remembered how distressed his mother had been at his death. She had loved her brother.

Finishing the last of his meal, Brendan walked down the street to the Nag's Head tavern. He went inside the old black-and-white Tudor building, ordered an ale, and asked to speak to the proprietor, although he held little hope of learning anything about Simon's murder after all this time.

Tom Lance, the short, rotund tavern owner, scratched his head. "Naturally, I know all about the murder which took place behind this inn. It has become like folklore. An important personage as he was. Something to do with smuggling, wasn't it? But beyond that, I cannot help you, milord. I purchased the inn six years ago. Didn't live 'round here before then."

"Could any of your servants have worked here twenty years ago?"

Tom shook his head. "Not a one."

Brendan left the tavern to return to his curricle and drive home but changed his mind and walked down beside the inn to the laneway behind.

A horse stood tied to a post awaiting its owner. But the area offered no clue as to Simon's demise. Brendan hadn't expected it to. Across the lane, in a farrier's shop, the sound of a hammer striking lead rang out. Brendan walked over and entered a blast of heat.

An enormous, dark-haired man somewhere in middle age bent over a roaring fire. Looking like the god Prometheus, his muscled arms flexing, he hammered an iron horseshoe over an anvil, bending it as if made of tin. The hot air reeked of sweat.

"Got a minute, sir?" Brendan asked him.

The farrier looked up. His gaze took in Brendan's coat to his top boots. Still holding his heavy hammer, he bowed his head. "Johnson, milord. Need a horse shod? I won't be long. If you'll wait outside." He chuckled. "Hot as hell in here today."

"No. I am after information about the murder which took place in this lane, close to twenty years ago. Would you have been in business back then?

Johnson's dark eyes widened. "Well, yes. My father's business it was then, but I was here, not much more than a lad. Long time ago now."

"Might you have witnessed it?"

"As I locked up for my father, I saw two men fighting over behind the inn," he said. "I remember admiring their horses. Thoroughbreds, they was." He wiped the sweat from his brow with a beefy forearm. "Not unusual for drunks and thieves to get into a fight, as there's gambling in the tavern. So I left them to it. But when I returned at cock's crow, there he was, lying dead as yesterday's mutton. Stabbed through the heart. Both horses were gone. Stolen, more like. One, a fine, young chestnut with unusual markings had three white feet, and a white patch on his head in the shape of a crown." He shook his head. "Pity."

"Indeed." Brendan gestured for him to go on.

"A big fuss erupted once they found out the man was the son of a lord. The constable fetched the magistrate. I couldn't tell 'em anything useful. Came out later at the inquest that Mr. Simon Mather had been friendly with a smuggler from these parts, and they thought it likely he'd got offside with 'im. But that notion didn't sit well with me."

"Why not?"

"Them smugglers are a stealthy lot. Don't like to draw attention to themselves. There's those around here who support 'em too." He took several more giant bashes at the horseshoe. Sparks flew and the deafening noise filled the small building. The racket didn't seem to bother him, but Brendan stepped back a pace, resisting the urge to block his ears.

Johnson examined his handiwork. Satisfied, he turned to Brendan. "And to murder a lord? They'd swing for that sure enough. A smuggler would choose somewhere quiet, if you know what I mean, milord." He winked. "No, this was a furious fight. A lot of passion in it. Didn't see a knife, though, or I might have intervened. Knocked their heads together. I was a big youth even then." He looked rueful. "The young lord might be alive today."

"Anything else you remember from that night, anything which seemed out of the ordinary?"

Johnson scratched his armpit with a hand the size of a shovel. "They was both young, not much older than I was. That's about the sum of it."

"Take a moment to think," Brendan urged him. "Something might come to you."

Johnson raised the hammer again. Then, to Brendan's relief, he paused and lowered it. "One thing, but it might not mean much."

"I'd like to hear it." Brendan ran a finger around his sweaty neck beneath his cravat.

"They was both fair headed. Of a similar build, too."

Brendan gave Johnson a shilling for his help and left. Climbing into his curricle, he drove home. Extraordinary as it was to think it, he believed Ralph had killed his brother, Simon. There might have been other reasons behind such a brutal murder, but the one which stuck in Brendan's mind was that Ralph had badly wanted to be the viscount and once their father died, Simon stood in his way. And he'd been rewarded when the upset caused by Simon's death had carried the old viscount off not long afterward. Had Brendan's mother somehow learned of the truth and threatened to expose her brother? And Gaylord had murdered her and his father to keep them quiet?

Brendan considered the way Gaylord might have gone about it. First using his relationship with the maid to press her into helping him enter the house unseen on some ruse, and carrying out the murders before leaving again, undetected, via the old servants' stairs. And when Violet Walcott had realized what she had done, overcome by guilt, she'd killed herself. It could also be why Gaylord kept his ear to the ground at Beechley Park, ensuring nothing ever arose to condemn him. Wagstaff, turning up again, must have shaken him.

It was believable. But how to find the proof? Brendan would take great pleasure in going to Camelia Grove and forcing Gaylord's confession with his fists. But that wouldn't wash with the magistrate, much as Brendan was burning to beat the villain black and blue. He would have to think of another way.

Laura. He felt a step closer to going to her free of his past. Did she still want him? Or could some fellow have already proposed? With a frustrated groan, he uttered a string of curses as he tried to bury his impatience.

Chapter Twenty-One

LAURA RARELY HAD time for herself during her first week in London. Her aunt whisked her about, visiting a modiste to have her old gowns altered, ordering a new ballgown, then shopping for slippers, a new bonnet in the Burlington Arcade, and a fan and reticule in Piccadilly. Afterward, they had tea at Gunther's then visited Hatchards bookshop, where Laura was thrilled to discover copies of the three volumes of *Pride and Prejudice*, while Aunt Gertrude found one of her favorite Gothic novels.

"Thank you for being so generous," Laura said, when they'd returned to her aunt's house.

"No need to thank me. I haven't enjoyed myself so much for ages," Aunt Gertrude said gruffly.

Laura wore her new pink, silk ballgown with silk roses adorning the hem and sleeves to the Lindseys' ball. A grand affair, held in Lindsey Court, the duke and duchess's Mayfair mansion. The large ballroom featured delicately painted ceilings, fluted columns, and marble statues which stood among lavish displays of scented flowers. People sat chatting on sofas upholstered in cream satin, gilt chairs and tables placed beside them. Liveried footmen roamed among the exquisitely dressed and perfumed guests who gathered around the periphery of the dance floor, laughing and talking while the musicians played Beethoven from their dais.

Ianthe, Her Grace, Duchess of Lindsey, so dainty in her pale-blue and silver gown, graciously greeted Laura and her aunt when the butler had announced them.

She turned to her handsome, dark-haired husband at her side. "My love, I don't believe you've met Miss Gertrude Peyton, and Miss Laura Peyton?"

His Grace greeted her aunt, who sank into a low curtsey, then turned to address Laura. "We haven't met the younger Miss Peyton, but I believe you know a friend of mine, the Earl of Debnam. I've noticed you in his company at several balls."

"Your Grace." Laura flushed as she dipped into a curtsey. When she rose, she looked into the duke's smiling eyes, with the oddest feeling he knew about her. Surely not. "Lord Debnam? Yes, we shared an interest in naming horses. I trust he is well? I haven't seen him for an age."

"Very well indeed, when I saw him last." He raised his dark eyebrows, a sparkle in his green eyes, as if they shared a secret. "As I have seen his horses at Tattersalls auction, I'm sure he would benefit from such advice."

"My love, the orchestra is about to strike up for the cotillion." The duchess put a hand on his arm. "Lady Somersby awaits to partner you to open the ball."

As she and her aunt settled in their seats, Laura wondered at the cause of the duke's interest in her. It appeared he and Debnam were close friends, as he seemed to know much about him. Had Debnam spoken of her? Surely not.

"You danced with Lord Debnam?" Aunt Gertrude asked, reminding Laura of a hound on the scent of a fox.

"Once or twice. As I told His Grace, we share an interest in horses. Lord Debnam breeds them, and I suggested a name for his latest mare."

Aunt Gertrude gave her a penetrating stare. "I wasn't aware of your great interest in horses. I find it intriguing."

A gentleman approached with Mrs. Edgar, his gaze on Laura

warm with approval.

"Miss Gertrude Peyton, Miss Laura Peyton, may I introduce Mr. Upjohn to you?" Mrs. Edgar said.

After the introduction, Mr. Upjohn asked Laura to dance. She rose, and they hurried to join the dancers on the ballroom floor.

"I am delighted to see you back in London, Miss Peyton," Mr. Upjohn said when they came together in the dance.

"How good of you to say so, sir," Laura murmured.

"You don't remember me?" He looked amused, but his hazel eyes revealed disappointment.

Laura hastily sorted through the many partners she had danced with over the years. There was nothing unusual about him. He was about thirty years old, and of medium height, his hair an indistinguishable light brown. Suddenly, the knowledge came to her. "Of course I do. We talked of butterflies and insects, did we not? You are a collector."

He smiled, obviously delighted. "So you remembered. I am flattered. I count myself as one of those fortunate of men to have had the pleasure of a dance with you."

Laura laughed. "Now you flatter me, Mr. Upjohn."

He grinned. "How very easy it is, Miss Peyton."

Their dance passed pleasurably. Laura liked his easy manners, although he failed to make her heart beat faster.

"I hope we may dance again, soon, Miss Peyton," Mr. Upjohn said when he returned her to her chair. "Madam." With a bow to her aunt, he left them.

Aunt Gertrude watched him walk away. "Mr. Upjohn is of excellent stock, Laura, although his family is not titled. His father is Sir Eric Upjohn, a high court judge. They may not be of the upper echelon, but they are certainly more than respectable."

Laura sighed. She had no intention of encouraging him but feared her aunt would urge her to. If she thought Laura's future could lie with Mr. Upjohn, she would persist with it as she had with Edward. Her aunt was nothing if not tenacious. Laura would hate any bad feeling between them to spoil their relationship, now that it had proven to be more amiable than she'd expected. "I can't imagine myself married to him, Aunt. I have no interest in cataloguing insects."

"No, I imagine not," her unpredictable aunt agreed with a moue of distaste.

In the early hours, when Laura had gained her bed, although weary, sleep eluded her. She had danced the supper dance with Mr. Upjohn, and they'd gone into supper together, while he'd told her more about himself. She liked how fair-minded he was. He'd revealed none of the arrogance of most of the lords she'd met, nor the superiority over women they'd often exhibited. Could she come to like him enough to marry him? Laura longed for a baby. And while she found Mr. Upjohn a slightly better prospect than Edward, who had wished to marry her for the wrong reasons, he still had not succeeded in banishing Debnam from her thoughts.

Desperately lonely, she knew only one person in the world could fill this ache. What was Debnam doing tonight? Was he with a lady? Unable to bear the pain of such a possibility, she lit the candle beside her bed and went to draw the curtains aside. Bright moonlight flooded into the chamber. A serene moon sailed across a star-studded sky like indigo velvet. Such peace did not reflect her mood, and she closed the curtains again before returning to bed. She blew out the candle and laid her head on the pillow.

Tiny feet roamed across the bedcover and soft fur touched her cheek. "Tibby." Comforted, Laura gathered the soft, purring body to her and slept.

MOUNTED ON BRUNO, with Hunter loping along behind him, Brendan rode over the fields toward the western boundary. A half hour later, he crossed onto Gaylord's land, well out of sight of his house and stables. He emerged from woodland onto meadows which gave way to several paddocks, where a handful of horses grazed.

Brendan released a breath. Having found what he'd sought, he dismounted before a lush, green paddock. Tossing Bruno's reins over a bush, he walked over to rest his hands on the railing. The inquisitive animals trotted over to him. Among them, one horse stood out. An old chestnut with three white feet and white on his forehead in the shape of a crown.

Gaylord had kept Simon's horse hidden away in a back paddock. He could never ride him, but he didn't want anyone else to have him.

"I knew I'd find you here." Brendan reached out to stroke the horse's head, thrust over the top of the railing. "That greedy, arrogant sod thinks himself untouchable."

What might he do with this discovery? It wasn't enough to involve the magistrate. He must come up with more. A lure to draw Gaylord in and cause him to make a mistake. He remembered how Gaylord had jeered at him when he had one of his headaches, how he'd suggested Brendan was unstable. Brendan loathed him and fought a burning desire to find him and take him apart with his fists. And now there was no doubt of Gaylord's culpability. Despite Brendan's rage, his spirits lifted, and the future filled with heady possibilities. Laura, there with him at Beechley Park as his wife. A long, happy life ahead of them. Children.

A rifle shot echoed through the trees and Brendan fell heavily to the ground. With a fierce growl, Hunter, who had been sniffing around nearby, raced away.

A shriek came from somewhere close by. "Damn dog just bit me. Get back, you miserable animal!"

A howl followed by silence chilled Brendan's blood. Gaining his wits, he gazed around him. When Gaylord didn't appear in his limited vision, he forced himself painfully to roll under a nearby bush. Blood seeped from the gunshot wound in his arm. He would have to use his kerchief to stem the flow before he bled to death. But right now, he had a worse problem to face. He'd left his shotgun in Bruno's saddle scabbard.

The horses in the paddock were spooked, tossing their manes and galloping around the enclosure. Bruno, similarly affected, whinnied and pulled hard at his reins, still tangled in the bushes.

"Where the devil are you, Brendan?" Gaylord called, sounding excited as he closed in on his quarry. "Have I winged you? I'll find you. You can't remain hidden for long." The stomp of his boots over the soggy, leaf-strewn ground grew near. "After Wagstaff turned up, I expected you to doubt what you'd come to believe and search for answers. Your gamekeeper suddenly clammed up and refused to answer my questions. That gave the game away. You forced my hand, Brendan. I should have gotten rid of the horse. Don't know why I didn't. I took pleasure in having it, I suppose. Another small, delicious victory. Where are you hiding, Brendan? You moved just as I fired. Not like me to miss. I hope you're dead. It offends my sensibilities to have to finish you off. But I have a perfect right to shoot a prowler on my land." His voice rose, taunting Brendan. "I'll say I saw you moving through the trees and thought it was someone after the horses. Fired before I realized it was you coming to visit me. A terrible mistake. The loss of my dear nephew shall devastate me."

His boots passed by Brendan, who in his brown coat thankfully blended well into the dense shrubbery. He could hear Gaylord beating the bushes somewhere farther on, then cursing as he reloaded his shotgun.

Brendan drew his kerchief from his pocket and wound it tightly around his arm above the wound, pulling it tightly with his teeth. He gave a low whistle to summon Bruno.

The horse shook his head and tugged hard at his reins. The thin branch came away, and he trotted to where Brendan lay hidden.

Brendan came out of the bushes in a rush and grabbed his shotgun from the saddle, just as Gaylord ran back toward him, his gun aimed at Brendan's heart.

Brendan wasn't about to give him another chance to shoot him. He fired and watched his uncle crumple to the ground as Gaylord's shot burned past Brendan's ear.

Gaylord's face became ghastly white. He clutched his chest where a scarlet stain spread, his wound undoubtedly fatal. Brendan kneeled beside him. "Tell me why, Gaylord. Confess before you go to meet your maker."

Ralph gasped. "You'll never prove it was me."

Brendan shook his head. "I don't have to, Ralph. I know my father wasn't mad. And neither will I ever be. You have set me free."

"No!" Gaylord tried to raise himself up and fell back.

"Tell me why," Brendan repeated.

His uncle's eyes went dark with hatred. "What would you know? You were a beloved son, like my brother. Simon was always the favored one. Neither my mother nor my father made any bones about their preference for him." He coughed, bloody froth touching his lips. "I would not have done it, but I lost money gambling, and a dangerous gang threatened me. Father would not give me the money. He threatened to kick me out. When Simon died that all changed. Suddenly, I was his precious heir. I would have killed Father too, but he died before it became necessary." He choked, blood running down his chin. "Then I was Viscount Gaylord. No one could touch me."

Brendan itched to shake him, to force him to reveal his secrets. "But to kill my parents, Gaylord, why?"

"Long after Simon's death, someone told your mother they'd seen me in Chichester that night. Constance wrote to me, demanded I come and explain." His rasping breath slowed, and his eyelids drooped. "There was no love lost between us. I couldn't risk her keeping silent. I had no alibi. I'd told the magistrate I was in Worthing visiting a lady friend. And your father was such an upright gentleman..." He sneered, then coughed violently, struggling for breath. "The earl wouldn't have let it go. Didn't know how much they knew.

"It all seemed to go against me, and I had…to…"

His gaze turned cunning.

"It pleased me to seduce a maid from your father's house. I fed her a story that I was going to surprise your father and mother. It was just a joke. If she could help me find a way in. She even managed to get your father's dueling pistol for me…" He panted, his words beginning to slur. "Afterward, I thought I was safe, but I kept an eye on Beechley Park whenever I could. But then my butler, Wagstaff, due to some misplaced sense of justice over a foolish maid I'd slapped around a little, accused me of having blood on my clothes the day your parents were shot. Didn't believe I'd killed a fox." His eyes widened, pleading, he reached out a hand to grasp Brendan's coat. "I was afraid."

Was Gaylord seeking forgiveness? He would not get it from Brendan.

Gaylord's hand dropped. He breathed his last and lay still.

Blood dripping from his fingers, Brendan climbed to his feet, shocked to see his uncle dead. Gaylord looked so harmless lying there, pale-skinned and aristocratic. His excuses for savagely destroying so many lives seemed feeble. Brendan still wanted to yell at him and shake him. His uncle had never married. Perhaps the burden he'd carried had prohibited him from sharing his life with a woman. He'd given up a peaceful life to gain a title.

Brendan looked down at him. "You were the mad one, Gaylord."

He turned and ran over to the still body of his dog, crouching down beside him. There was blood on his head. That villain Gaylord had struck him savagely with the butt of his shotgun.

"*Hunter?*"

His heart in his mouth, Brendan stroked the soft fur on the dog's back and was rewarded with a small wag of his tail. Hunter tried to rise. "Still, boy. I'll go for help. I take back everything I said about your hunting abilities."

Brendan picked up both shotguns and secured them on his

saddle. With one arm hanging useless, he struggled to mount Bruno. Fortunately, the patient horse stood still. He swayed dizzily. The reins sliding through his bloody fingers, he nudged Bruno and turned him in the direction of Camelia Grove house. He fought to hang on. *Must have this wound attended to. Get help for Hunter. Send a footman for the magistrate.*

When he emerged on the drive, the sight of the mansion through the trees in the park heartened him. He shook his head to try to rid his eyes of the mist clouding his vision, but a dark veil threatened, and as he neared the house, it blinded him. He slumped forward in the saddle.

"Good heavens! What has happened? My lord?"

Brendan was vaguely aware of the butler issuing sharp orders.

"You'll need the magistrate. Lord Gaylord is dead," he forced out. "Send someone down to the horse paddock to help my dog. He's hurt." Strong hands dragged him from his horse, and then he knew no more.

Chapter Twenty-Two

ROBERT'S WEDDING, AT St. George's in Hanover Square, was an elaborate affair, as was the reception held at the Lavertys' townhome in Westminster. Handsome in a dark-blue coat, Laura's brother stood beside his pretty bride, Aurelia, who wore a white-and-silver gown, inspired by the famous wedding gown worn by Princess Charlotte.

Beaming, Mr. and Mrs. Laverty welcomed Robert into the family and made a fuss of Aunt Gertrude, who was very much the lady in a dark-blue, lace gown made by her French modiste, as well as a wide-brimmed hat adorned with ostrich feathers.

"The Lavertys are not of the *ton*, but Robert is happy, and they are wealthy, so it is a successful union." Aunt Gertrude's observation as she and Laura traveled back to Mayfair, made Laura gasp.

She couldn't help giggling. "They love each other. You are an awful snob, Aunt."

Aunt Gertrude nodded sagely. "It is how society works."

Laura had had enough of society's rules. It was undeniably true that his business made Mr. Laverty wealthy, which, in her mind, was admirable. She liked the sober-minded gentleman, who, although not in the best of health, had had a twinkle in his eye as they'd chatted at the wedding breakfast. And she couldn't be more pleased for her brother, especially as Aurelia so obviously adored him.

"Cherish her, Robert," Laura had told him as they'd said goodbye. "Aurelia loves you and deserves the best of you."

Robert had attempted to frown, but today had found it impossible to wipe the grin from his face. "I plan to be the best of husbands and turn Longworth into something Papa would have been proud of."

Laura's eyes had grown teary as she'd kissed him. "I will miss you and everyone there. Please send my regards to Wagstaff and Mrs. Amery."

"One day, I hope to attend your wedding, Laura. It might have been Edward. I hope you won't come to regret your decision," he'd said pointedly. Then, pleased with his parting shot, he'd left her to return to his bride, who'd been busily describing in some detail the improvements she had made at Longworth to a fascinated gathering.

A week later, Laura attended the last ball of the Season with her aunt before parliament closed and the *ton* escaped to their country estates.

Partnered for every dance, Laura sat wanting to rub her sore toes, while hoping Mr. Upjohn would not ask her to dance again. Her aunt had warmed to him, often mentioning his virtues, which Laura had to admit were considerable. She liked him but had little in common with him and feared she could never truly love him. While her aunt spoke sensibly of compromise, Laura thought more about how it would be when he kissed her, and when he took her to bed. He wasn't Debnam. He lacked Debnam's charm, his wicked humor and passion, inviting her to give in to her desires and be her true self. To laugh with him. But as her aunt had pointed out, marriage was not only about the bedchamber; there was much more to be enjoyed, especially raising children.

"Why didn't you marry, Aunt?" Laura had asked her as they'd sat together in the evening watching Tibby and Beau playing together on the rug, having finally decided to be friends.

"You're going to want me to say I fell in love and only want-ed one man. And when I couldn't have him, I chose never to marry," she'd said, with a shrewd glance over the top of the periodical she'd read. "Because it would fit nicely with what you have decided for yourself."

"Not at all, I…"

Aunt Gertrude had shaken her head. "Hush, child. You can-not fool a wily, old bird like me. As for myself, I did want one particular man, but he was married. I used him to measure the rest of them, which was a mistake. None interested me enough to spend the whole of my life with. And that was the biggest mistake of all. The years quickly passed, and I found myself alone."

"Oh, Aunt."

"Don't cry for me, please, Laura! I have a very good life and many friends."

"You do." Laura had said, but her aunt's words had had the desired effect to make her think.

She searched the milling crowd, as she always did for Debnam. But she hadn't heard from him. *And why would he write?* Her common sense demanded. He had disappeared from her life since she'd left Beechley Park.

"I am surprised to see him here," her aunt said after a mo-ment.

"Who, Aunt?" Laura asked idly as she fiddled with the ivory struts on her fan.

"The Earl of Debnam. He appears to be wounded."

"What?" Laura swung around in the direction her aunt was looking. "Debnam?"

"I must say, niece, I have never seen such a reaction from you before. What does this man mean to you? And how have you kept it from me?"

Laura's heart was pounding. "He means simply everything, Aunt," she said with a deep, indrawn breath.

She leaped to her feet without thinking. Debnam's gaze met hers from across the room. With a distressed gasp, she saw a sling on his left arm. Hurrying to meet him, she immediately noticed the change in him, his smile and easy stride as he walked toward her. He looked different. She realized now what it was. He looked at peace with himself.

To her left, Mr. Upjohn emerged from the crush seeking the next dance.

When their paths threatened to converge, Debnam saw him and stopped. *He mustn't think…* Laura couldn't bear it. She almost ran, ignoring her aunt's disapproval at her unseemly haste and causing Mr. Upjohn to halt and swing his gaze from her to Debnam.

Laura cast Mr. Upjohn a sympathetic glance for a moment, but there before her stood the love of her life, whom she yearned to touch. "You've been hurt."

"Almost healed now." He turned to look toward Mr. Upjohn, who retreated into the crowd. "You and that gentleman, Laura, are you…?"

"No." Laura shook her head. "I waited… I hoped." She had no pride where Debnam was concerned. The special look he had for her in his eyes thrilled her to her toes.

"My love." He kissed her hand. "Come. You must introduce me to your aunt."

They walked over to where her aunt sat watching them, having donned her glasses.

"Aunt Gertrude, may I introduce you to the Earl of Debnam."

Her aunt scrutinized him and nodded.

He bowed. "Miss Peyton. I don't believe we have met." He raised her proffered hand to his lips.

It brought a surprising flush to her aunt's cheeks before she regally bowed her head. "I have not had that pleasure. But I see you and my niece are well acquainted, my lord." She turned her wily gaze on Laura. "My niece and companion, who has not seen fit to mention such an occurrence to me."

"We became better acquainted at the Grosvenors' ball some

months ago," Debnam explained. "If you will allow it, madam, I should like Miss Peyton to take a turn around the dance floor with me."

Aunt Gertrude waved with her fan to encompass most of the guests, some of whom had turned to view them. "Certainly, my lord. The *ton* is in dire need of more entertainment."

Debnam chuckled and held out his arm. Laura rested her hand on his sleeve, and they walked together along the edge of the ballroom. She glanced up at his handsome profile, wanting to pinch herself. Was she dreaming? Guests stopped in their conversations and turned to observe them as they passed. Some hailed Debnam, while others greeted her. Whispers followed them.

He led her through an archway into a corridor. They walked down it. Opening the door, they entered the library. It was unoccupied and bathed in shadows, with faint candlelight from a candelabra on a table at the far end, where sofas and chairs were grouped before the fireplace.

Laura spun around to face him, her gaze roaming his face, taking note with pleasure his lightly tanned skin, his sculptured features, somehow less strained than she'd remembered, his mouth softer. She put a hand on his chest. "Will you please tell me what has happened? How were you hurt?"

"I see you haven't learned patience, Miss Peyton." He chuckled. "Never learn it, sweetheart," he murmured. As his good arm held her in place against him, he kissed her, long and deeply. Too soon, he ended it, took her hand, and led her over to a sofa. "Shall we have a glass of wine? I have much to tell you."

Impatient, she bit her lip while Debnam delayed answering her questions. At the drinks table, he poured himself a brandy and a glass of Madeira for her. Coming to hand her the glass, he returned for his own, then sat beside her.

"Now," Laura demanded.

"Very well," he said, amusement brightening his eyes.

She sipped the wine, delighting in the rich timber of his voice.

What he told her grew more extraordinary as Gaylord's murderous plan and subsequent demise unfolded.

"Gaylord shot you?" She shook her head in horror. "He might have killed you."

"That was his intention. Hunter saved me. Attacked him and gave me more time."

Her eyebrows flew up. "Hunter?"

Debnam nodded. "He attacked Gaylord but was bludgeoned for his pains."

Laura moaned. "Oh, no. Not Hunter. Is he…?"

"He has healed well," Debnam grinned. "And is almost back to his old tricks."

"I'm so relieved. I know Gaylord hated him."

"You knew?"

"The day I met the viscount at the lake, he threatened Hunter. Said he interfered with his hunting. He eyed the dog as if he would like to kill him. It frightened me. I couldn't get Hunter away fast enough."

"My uncle was a monster."

She drew in a sharp breath. "I think I always knew in my heart your father wasn't mad. That there had to be another explanation." She leaned against his shoulder, taking comfort from his familiar scent. "And I knew you would never succumb to madness."

"I inherited my megrims from my father. It gave me cause to worry."

"My mother suffered from them. She found relief with the alternative applications of ice and heat. I shall adopt the practice if you have another."

"It's odd, but since I was shot, I haven't had one. Dare I hope they won't return?"

She reached up and spread her fingers over his chest to reassure herself he was strong and well. "I pray that is so."

He took her hand and kissed it. "I intend to be busy. To continue breeding thoroughbreds."

"What about Honey, Brendan? Do you still have her?"

"I do. I was going to make a gift of her to you when the time was right. It never eventuated. Until now."

She rested her head against his shoulder. "Tell me you no longer fear the future, Debnam."

His gray eyes softened. "I see the future clearly, sweetheart. And I welcome it. If you will share it with me," he said. "I love you dearly, Laura. I don't seem able to live without you. So, will you please marry me?"

"Yes, darling, yes, I will." Her voice hitched and tears came to her eyes. "I love you. I have wanted no one but you."

"It's become clear to me I loved you from the first time we met, which resulted in that shameful bargain I made with your brother," he said huskily. "A way to see more of you. When I believed I could have nothing more, I might have at least had that."

"It was a very good bargain you made, darling," Laura said. "For we got to know each other."

He shook his head. "I was an unmitigated, selfish fool. It could have ended badly."

"But it did not, so please don't be so hard on yourself, and kiss me again."

When he drew away, his eyes brimmed with tenderness and love. "How will your aunt take such news thrust upon her without warning? We've had no courtship. I expect she'll be shocked and wish to know the details of how we met. Naturally, we cannot tell her, my sweet."

"I am very fond of Aunt Gertrude. I'd hate to make up a story." She thought for a moment. "I shall say when we met months ago, we were drawn to each other but could not marry because of financial obligations. I am sure our engagement will delight her."

His lips quirked up. "She won't object to you marrying the Phantom Earl?"

She knew her aunt would be happy for her. But she wouldn't

be so easily put off about how it had come about. Laura would handle that when the time came. Aunt Gertrude appreciated a good romance. She had discovered her aunt's Gothic novels, and the much-thumbed *Pamela, or Virtue Rewarded* by Samuel Richardson, on her bookshelf. "You are no phantom, darling. You are real," she murmured, raising her chin for another kiss.

Debnam groaned against her mouth, his hand firm and warm on her waist. After a moment, he drew away, took a deep sip from his brandy glass, and stood. He offered her his hand. "We must do this properly, Laura. I can weather unwelcome gossip, but I won't have you subjected to it."

"I suspect gossip will always follow us, Brendan. But may it be the right kind."

His big hand holding hers, they walked back. She didn't care about her reputation nearly as much as he did, and she would have liked to stay in the library much longer, but she allowed him to lead her into the bright lights of the smoky, noisy ballroom.

⁕⟫⟫⟫⟪⟪⟪⁕

ONCE LAURA'S AUNT had given them her blessing, the news of their engagement spread throughout the ballroom, and friends and acquaintances rushed to congratulate them. Their response heartened Brendan, and with great pleasure, he introduced Laura to Hart and his lovely wife, Madeline.

While the women talked together, Hart expressed his delight at seeing his one remaining single friend entering the parson's mousetrap. And his hope for an invitation to the wedding. "Tate and Ianthe will wish to come."

"If not a large wedding, then a house party at Beechley Park when we return from our honeymoon." Brendan had waited long enough for Laura, and he would endure an elaborate wedding only if she wished for one.

Hart nodded with a knowing wink. "I foresee this wedding

will be a rushed affair." He glanced at Laura. "And I cannot say I blame you."

As his bride-to-be chatted to friends surrounding her, asking eager questions about weddings and honeymoons, Brendan had time to reflect on the last few weeks, which had changed his life so completely. At Camela Grove, after the doctor had come, removed the ball, stemmed the bleeding, and then stitched him up, Brendan had returned to Beechley Park.

Ordered to bed to avoid infection, he'd restlessly waited for news of Hunter. The dog had taken a nasty blow to the head, which could have crippled him. The veterinarian had advised him to have Hunter shot, but Brendan had flatly refused.

As Brendan had healed, so had Hunter, lying on his bed before the fire in the library, while Brendan had worked with his secretary and the steward. The more he got involved in the estate's maintenance, the more interesting and satisfying he found it.

Then, almost two weeks after Gaylord had struck him down, Hunter had stood and crossed the carpet to Brendan on wobbly legs. Brendan had left his chair and sunk to his knees to praise him. From then on, the dog's recovery had been remarkably swift.

Brendan had discussed the matter of Gaylord's death with the magistrate, Sir Ewen McCorquodale, who'd decided he would take no action against him. Sir Ewen said he would make it public that Gaylord had killed Brendan's parents. Brendan had then visited his parents' graves at the family crypt, savoring the fact that, at last, his father's name was cleared.

Then, all he'd wanted was to see Laura. When his letter to Longworth had remained unanswered, he'd feared she had married, and had written to Netterfield. The baron's secretary had replied. Robert was on his honeymoon, and Laura lived with her aunt in Richmond. He'd furnished Brendan with the address.

Brendan had driven there, only to discover they had gone to London. A day later, he'd arrived in Mayfair, prepared to search the city for her, and miraculously found her at the first ball he'd attended.

Laura turned from talking to her friend Miss Burton, and smiling sweetly, nodded to him.

Brendan approached her. "Please excuse us, Miss Burton." He whisked Laura away to a quiet corner.

Once they could speak without being overheard, Brendan broached the possibility of a special license and a wedding within the following weeks. "But not if you have visions of a grand affair, my love."

She laughed. "I do not. That is perfect. Shall we go in search of my aunt and tell her our plan?"

"Will your aunt be disappointed?"

Laura giggled. "Certainly not, for she told me, while you talked to Lord Pembury, that I should snap you up."

Brendan chuckled. "And that's just what I intend to do, Miss Peyton. Snap you up!"

Chapter Twenty-Three

THREE WEEKS PASSED before the wedding day. They wished to wait for Robert and Aurelia's return from Paris. She knew her brother would appreciate her seeking his permission, although it was hardly necessary since she'd turned twenty-one so long ago. He would want to give her away. It had also given her time to consult with Brendan's secretary about the invitations and arrange the wedding breakfast at his home in Mayfair.

When the newlyweds had returned and come to see Laura and Aunt Gertrude, Robert had looked at peace with the world. Aurelia had danced in, gushing about Paris. "You should visit, Miss Peyton, Laura. The shops. The elegant people and the fashions. It's a wonderful city."

"I have been to Paris." Aunt Gertrude patted the sofa beside her. "But I would like to hear more about it, Aurelia."

Grateful for her aunt's thoughtfulness, Laura had joined Robert in the morning room, where she'd explained what had occurred in his absence.

He'd shown considerable surprise but offered no objection to the marriage, reminding her it had been his fervent hope the earl would marry her when he'd first sent her to Beechley Park. "It was obvious early on that the earl was in love with you. I'm glad there was no truth to Lord Gaylord's extraordinary claims, although it alarmed me greatly at the time." He'd shrugged. "But all's well that ends well, as the saying goes."

Laura had refused to debate the matter with him. She'd been too happy. And, as Robert had indeed expressed the opinion, more out of hope than any firm conviction, that Brendan would marry her, she couldn't see the point of pursuing it.

Weeks of incessant rain finally eased on the day of the wedding, and a watery sun broke through the clouds. Laura wore a white gown trimmed with lace and net at the hem and sleeves and decorated with small bows of pink satin, her bonnet trimmed with pink ribbons and rosebuds.

When she and Robert arrived in the carriage at St. James's Church in Piccadilly, quite a crowd gathered on the pavement outside the small church. The wedding of an earl to a former baron's daughter, as well as the impressive guest list, had become known and drawn journalists from *The Times*, *The Morning Chronicle*, *Morning Post*, and *The Star*, and one or two ladies, Laura suspected, who penned the gossip sheets. She didn't fool herself that they were there merely for the bride. Not when they might glimpse the Earl of Debnam, the Duke and Duchess of Lindsey, the Marquess and Marchioness of Pembury, Baron and Baroness Netterfield, and garner interesting information from their servants.

When the organ music struck up, Laura entered on Robert's arm. She smiled at Wagstaff, Mrs. Amery, and Penny seated at the back of the church. As they progressed slowly down the aisle, Laura's bridesmaid, Emma Burton, wearing pale lemon, followed behind.

Before the altar, Brendan, handsome in a tailcoat of dark blue, waited beside his two groomsmen, the duke and the marquess. Their elegant wives sat in the front pews alongside Aunt Gertrude, Aurelia, and her parents.

The rest of the ceremony passed like a wonderful dream, until Laura signed the book with her new name, then, with the realization that she was now the Countess of Debnam, took her husband's arm to walk back down the aisle to the waiting crowd outside. After saying their goodbyes, she and Brendan climbed into the carriage to travel to Brendan's Mayfair mansion and their wedding breakfast.

Laura danced a heavenly waltz with Brendan. As he skillfully guided her over the floor, what he murmured in her ear made her giggle and try not to blush.

When she could spare a moment from her guests, Laura sat with Aunt Gertrude while she ate a piece of wedding cake.

"I never expected you to marry a handsome rake, Laura," her aunt said, fork in hand. "But you're a sensible girl. You'll tame him."

Laura laughed. "Brendan doesn't need to be tamed, Aunt."

"They all need a little nudge in the right direction, niece." Her eyes softened. "I am pleased to see both you and Robert settled at last. And I wish you both happy."

Laura leaned forward and kissed her aunt's cheek, breathing in the scent of powder. "You will come often to see us, won't you?"

"I'll come, but not too often." Her aunt dug her fork into the cake. "My life is busy, you understand?" She swallowed the piece of cake. "Regrettably, Beau *will* miss Tibby."

"You must bring Beau when you do find time to come to visit." Laura understood. Her aunt knew she and Brendan needed to be alone for a while.

Several hours later, after the last of the guests had departed, Laura went up to her bedchamber to change. The countess's suite was as elegant as the bedchambers at Beechley Park, with every comfort. She washed her face and hands at the washstand and sat before the mirror, removing the pins from her hair, as Penny came in.

"It was such a lovely wedding, milady. What shall you wear to dinner?"

"Take out the sea-green silk, please, Penny," she said, amused by her maid's enthusiasm.

Penny could not contain her composure for long. As she

moved about the room, turning down the bedcover and fluffing the pillows, she talked about the wedding. "And the guests, milady!" Her head appeared from around the dressing room door, Laura's hat in her hands. "It must be the society wedding of the year!"

Laura laughed. "It was hardly that, Penny." She turned back to the mirror and picked up the brush. "But it was the most special."

"We toasted you and his lordship with champagne in the servants' hall," Penny said, reemerging. She put a hand to her mouth, her eyes dancing. "The bubbles tickled. I have never tasted the like."

"I'm glad you all enjoyed yourselves. It was his lordship's wish that the servants hold their own celebration below stairs."

"We did, milady. After the wine, Mr. Swan, his lordship's valet, burst into song. He has a fine baritone, and we all joined in to sing 'Greensleeves,'" she said as she rushed to answer a knock on the door.

Brendan came in, followed by Charles carrying a tray with covered dishes, a bottle of wine, and two glasses. He placed it on the table, bowed, and left.

Penny had dropped into a deep curtsy. Brendan looked amused. "Thank you, Penny. That will be all this evening."

The maid put the gown she held on a chair and scurried out.

Laura drew in a nervous breath. "Are you so sure I shan't have need of her?"

"I can undress you quite as well as Penny." He walked over to her. "Better, in fact."

The flutter in her stomach made her put down the brush with an unsteady hand.

He rested his hands on her shoulders, smiling at her visage in the mirror. "You intend to keep Penny as your lady's maid?"

"Yes." Laura turned to look up at him. Did he want someone more experienced for her than Penny? She would hate an overbearing French maid. And once she'd discovered the little maid had learned to read and write at the Parish school, she hadn't hesitated to engage her. "I will train Penny to be quite competent. You'll see."

"I don't care about the state of your clothes, Laura. It's you who matters to me," he said. "Must I wait until you have changed your gown before I remove it again?"

With a shiver of anticipation, she pushed back her chair and rose to face him. He had recently shaved and smelled of a musky soap. She curled her fingers, wanting to trail them over his smooth cheek. How tall he was. How splendid his red-and-blue silk banyan. Was he naked beneath it? With annoyance, she felt the flush rise up her throat and warm her cheeks. A smile brightened his eyes. No wonder he could read her like a book!

"I thought we might have a small supper here, unless you wish to go down for dinner."

She moved closer to him, breathing him in. "No. That is a lovely idea."

He enveloped her in his arms and rested his smooth cheek against hers. "You never lost faith in me, Laura," he murmured. "That mattered more than I can say."

"Once I saw the man I fell in love with emerge from the elusive demeanor he used to keep people at bay," she said, moving back to look up into his face, "I could want no one else."

"I couldn't tell you. To see fear and horror when I looked into your eyes would undo me."

She gave in to the impulse to stroke a finger over his jaw. "But when I learned of your secret, I felt the opposite, darling."

He frowned. "Nor did I want your sympathy."

"You had my sympathy, but love too, and a need to be with you. To face whatever might come, at your side."

He kissed beneath her ear. "*Sweetheart.*"

Her heart thudded. She wanted him so much, she lost her breath. "Take me to bed, Brendan."

"I am more than happy to oblige, Lady Debnam." Brendan's fingers worked to remove the buttons down the back of her gown. "Why all these infernally small buttons?"

She laughed breathlessly. "The buttons are an indulgence. For years, I required my gowns specially designed to be easily managed because I had no maid to assist me."

"You have *me* now." He eased the gown off one shoulder and stooped to kiss the rise of her breast. Then he removed the gown. "But I would appreciate you keeping up the practice. No more of these tiny, pesky buttons."

"I shall keep it in mind, sir." With a sigh, she placed an arm around his neck, and with an open-mouth kiss, her tongue danced with his. "Your wishes will always be obeyed."

Brendan drew away with a moan. "You lull me into a false sense of security, madam."

"Should the wishes be reasonable," she added mischievously. "Aha!"

Her fingers pushed into his thick, silky hair, and she kissed him again. She could feel his arousal through the silk banyan, and she yearned to see him naked.

Breathlessly tearing his lips from hers, he buried his face in the warmth of her neck. "Laura!" He laughed softly. "We best go to bed. I don't intend our first time to happen on the dressing table."

With a surge of pleasure at her power to arouse him, she untied her petticoat. Dropping it to the floor, she stepped out of the pool of fabric and turned her back to him.

Brendan unlaced her corset and tossed the garment on the chair. He slipped his hands around her to cup her breasts and kissed her shoulder.

Laura turned and stood before him in her shift, aware of how it revealed more than it hid. She reached down to gather it up and pull it over her head.

"Leave it on," he said, his voice tight.

Brendan took her hand and led her across the room. Beside the bed, his mouth sought hers again, a breathlessly demanding kiss, while his hands smoothed over the back of her thighs and squeezed her bottom. His stiff arousal rubbed against her most sensitive part through the thin cloth, his masculine smell making her whimper against his lips.

As they grew breathless, he scooped her up and laid her down on the bed.

Laura saw the raw need in his eyes before he turned away to disrobe. Her stomach throbbed with yearning. She put her hand between her legs, finding warmth and moisture. She had longed for this. To be desired by the man she loved.

She watched the banyan slip from Brendan's shoulders and her breath caught.

He stood naked before her, his member proud, erect, his body as beautiful as any statue. Joining her on the bed, he lay beside her. He tweaked her nipples through the chemise, then bent and caressed the stiff peaks with his tongue, making Laura moan with pleasure.

"Shall we take this off?"

With her assisting, he pulled the chemise over her head and tossed it on to the floor, then lay atop her. He explored her thoroughly with hands and lips, planting kisses on her stomach and down to the tuft of hair at the juncture of her thighs. With the lightest of caresses, he pressed his mouth against her there.

Laura flushed with embarrassment. "Brendan?"

"Hush, sweetheart."

She arched herself against him, moving restlessly, not knowing what she craved, except more. Laura tumbled into a wave of sensation, which sent her spinning. Had she cried out? Laura melted, mindless.

Brendan settled between her thighs and nudged them apart.

She loved the heavy weight of him, his large body and clean, male smell, as he lowered his head to take a nipple in his mouth while tweaking the other one. Laura moaned at the exquisite sensation, clutching his head as he gave his attention to the other breast. She stroked her hands over his back everywhere she could reach, feeling the slide of powerful muscles and strong bones beneath smooth skin.

He rose to kiss her, plundering her mouth. Their panting breaths filled the room. His gaze, potent with intent, locked with hers. "You are so beautiful, Laura."

Laura stilled as the blunt force of his erection nudged her tender flesh. She gasped at the jolt of pleasure, pain, and heat as he pushed inside. Filling her. She murmured incoherently at the extraordinary sensations. Her fingers dug into his shoulders and as the pain eased, she lifted her hips to greet each thrust.

With a groan, he held her by her hips and pushed deeper, faster. Then, with a loud groan, he grew still.

Brendan rolled to the side and lay stroking a hand over her breasts and stomach. "Did I hurt you?"

"A little."

He smiled. "But not for all of it?"

"No." She sighed. "It was lovely."

"Then shall we do it again?"

She giggled.

He kissed her, then pulled the bedcover over them. "It gets better, darling."

"Does it?" Laura said sleepily. She loved lying snug against him, and closed her eyes.

"Sleep, my love. It's been a long day."

"Mm. A perfectly wonderful day," she murmured.

BRENDAN GAZED AT his bride. Even in sleep, she was adorable. He wanted to kiss her awake, but he resisted the impulse. They had awakened an hour later and shared a cold supper. And as the sun rose to send rays of golden light through the break in the curtains, Brendan kissed her. More familiar with each other's bodies, they roused each other to passion, and he lost himself in her fragrant warmth.

He leaned back on the pillow and closed his eyes. Laura had come into his soulless life and changed it beyond imagining.

She stirred beside him, and he reached out to stroke a wisp of hair from her cheek.

Laura opened her eyes and gazed at him with drowsy-eyed love.

"I love you, darling." His voice hitched as he pulled her warm body against his and breathed in her scent, enfolding her in his arms.

Epilogue

Beechley Park, Five months later…

LAURA ENTERED THE gunroom in search of her husband. She found him oiling a gun, the not-unpleasant smell permeating the room. "Here you are," she said, going up to slide her hands around his waist. "Escaping the hubbub going on in the house."

He wiped his hands on a cloth. "Now I know why I never wanted to host a crowd for a house party. Fifty people to be fed and entertained for three days!" He eyed her. "I hope you don't exhaust yourself. You should rest. You are carrying my son."

"Or daughter," she said with a lift of her eyebrows.

A young girl of twelve came to the door. "Lady Debnam, I've arranged the flowers for the drawing room. Mrs. Brandt thinks they will suffice. Will you come look?"

"I'll be there in a moment, Mary."

Mary disappeared.

"You know, my love, your brother warned me about your tendency to nurture every small animal or human in need who came within your purview. I laughed, but by God, he was right." Brendan gathered her to him and whispered against her hair. "It's my hope that your children will fulfill this need."

"Until then, we will try to give Mary a good life," Laura said. "After all, you saved her life in the river.

She drew away and looked at him. "You know, Mary began writing to me when her mother, Mrs. Joyce, died. Her aunt didn't want her and mistreated her. I couldn't in good conscience ignore her." She gestured to the room. "And we have so much space here." She narrowed her eyes. "You know you like Mary. You are teaching her to play chess."

"Out of the need for a partner, madam." He bent his head and kissed her as Hunter scampered in, followed closely by Tibby.

"Come on, boy. Let's escape the madhouse and walk over to the stables."

Laura picked up the cat and hugged him as she watched Brendan walk over the lawn with the gun over his shoulder and the dog following. She put a hand to her stomach as their son stirred and moved his long limbs to poke at her. Laura planned a daughter next, God willing.

About the Author

A USA TODAY bestselling author of Regency romances, with over 35 books published, Maggi's Regency series are International bestsellers. Stay tuned for Maggi's latest Regency series out next year. Her novels include Victorian mysteries, contemporary romantic suspense and young adult. Maggi holds a BA in English and Master of Arts Degree in Creative Writing. She supports the RSPCA and animals often feature in her books.

Like to keep abreast of my latest news? Join my newsletter.
bit.ly/1m70lJJ

Blog: maggiandersen.blogspot.com
Find excerpts and reviews on my website: bit.ly/1m70lJJ
Twitter: @maggiandersen: bit.ly/1Aq8eHg
Facebook: Maggi Andersen Author: on.fb.me/1KiyP9g
Goodreads: bit.ly/1TApe0A
Pinterest: pinterest.com.au/maggiandersen

Maggi's Amazon page for her books with Dragonblade Publishing.
tinyurl.com/y34dmquj

9 781961 275874